A Conspiracy of Patriots

A Novel

Thomas Hofstedt

Each must for himself alone decide what is right and what is wrong, and which course is patriotic and which isn't. You cannot shirk this and be a man. To decide against your convictions is to be an unqualified and inexcusable traitor, both to yourself and to your country, let man label you as they may.

(Mark Twain)

Table of Contents

Prologue

If I believed in a God, I would ask for a less ambiguous sign!

The man in San Francisco put the phone receiver down very gently and walked to the window, as was his habit when he needed to think. There was a strong breeze propelling sunlit whitecaps on San Francisco Bay and a lone sailboat on a long traverse around Alcatraz, moving against both tide and wind.

He felt an affinity for the boat.

His next thought was of all the "good news, bad news" jokes that he had heard over his lifetime. But the only one that he could recall was the airline pilot's announcement, "We're lost, but we're making good time!" The phone call – if not a sign from the god that he no longer believed in -- surely fell within that genre, although it would require a highly sardonic sense of humor.

The unequivocally bad news? "The disease is incurable."

The more nuanced good news? "You have approximately twelve months left to live."

OK. I've been given a gift. Twelve months is a long time in many ways. Enough time to do much of what I want to do. But a number of things have to be accelerated, some short cuts taken. On the other hand, it simplifies the choices. So many complications are no longer important. None of the old inhibitors hold any longer – fear of failure, risk of exposure, loss of reputation, going too far too fast – all of them out the window. It's liberating.

Like a kamikaze pilot with a nagging wife and a lot of overdue bills.

But what about 'legacy,' supposedly the final motivator for honorable behavior when the ordinary incentives become meaningless?

That one bothered him. It is, after all, one thing to be reconciled to dying, but entirely a different thing to become comfortable with the idea of being despised for how one lived his life.

He thought about that.

The people whose opinion I value are very few and mostly gone. And if I choose to go quietly, I will be merely one of thousands of deceased tycoons and politicians who are remembered – briefly -- as high achievers. They all have their foundations doling out their wealth, their public monuments and earnest biographers deconstructing their lives for posterity. But so much more is possible if one is clearheaded enough. And ruthless enough.

The hell with legacy!

Death of a Bookkeeper

Marie Lynne Broder had never heard of Jainism, the Indian religion whose central tenet is non-violence toward all living creatures, even the insects that cross one's path. She would have scoffed at the idea that she subscribed to any particular philosophy of life, let alone one so far out of the mainstream of American culture. Despite her ignorance, however, it is the case that she behaved as if she was the most fanatical member of the sect. She carried spiders outside rather than squashing them in place. She swerved to avoid frogs in the road. She was, of course, a vegetarian.

It went far beyond non-violence. She lived her life so as to never be an inconvenience to others; apologizing for imaginary slights, nodding constantly at whatever was said no matter how nonsensical, always giving way both physically and emotionally. She over-tipped, stopped for pedestrians whether or not in crosswalks, and smiled continuously.

Many would see her timidity as a commendable flaw, others as a diagnosable neurosis. Perhaps it was innate, a missing "aggression gene" or an excess of estrogen. Perhaps it could be blamed on her evangelical parents with their Old Testament views about raising god-fearing children. Perhaps she really believed what she was taught in Sunday School – how you should turn the other cheek, that the meek shall inherit the earth. Maybe a different name, something more than two first names strung together, would have altered the course of her life. When she gave her name – "Marie Lynne"

– people either called her "Ms. Lynne" or stereotyped her as someone they did not have to take seriously.

The intensity of her meekness robbed her of a specific identity. A therapist would quickly note that even her job was one that minimized social risk and rarely involved confrontation. As supervisor of the Accounts Payable department for a major company, her main relationship was with a flow of paper. She oversaw the payment of bills, distributing millions of dollars a day according to strict rules. She loved the rigorous neutrality of accounting: the equal and offsetting debits and credits, the balancing of statements, the reconciliation of accounts and their contents arranged in tabular arrays, the indisputable *facts* that became columns of numbers aligned so neatly on a white page with just-so borders.

The totality of what she was made her a natural victim. Ironically however, her present dire situation had absolutely nothing to do with the aura of victimhood that she wore like a suit of clothes.

Her stalker targeted her for reasons that had nothing to do with her history or neuroses. But, even then, he could not and did not fail to sense the vulnerability that she transmitted, in the way that sharks readily distinguish the motions of distress in the water. It was a continuous pulsating *"please don't hurt me too badly"* signal that attracted rather than repelled urban predators. The woman he had been watching for the past two days oozed insecurity – in her voice, her body language, her little girl outfits and hairstyle. Even the message on her answering machine apologized at length for the inconvenience caused for the caller by her present absence.

Not for the first time in his profession, he was struck by the sheer unfairness of what he was about to do. The thought did not lead to hesitation or remorse. He simply wondered how such a person could be threatening to anyone.

Five minutes ago, Marie Lynne walked into her kitchen carrying some apples and oranges in a recyclable cloth bag with a Greenpeace logo on it. She remembers now, with wonder, the normalcy of her kitchen; everything in place, the family photos on the refrigerator door, the aroma of overripe bananas …

Then the horror. The sudden noose tightening around her neck, cutting off speech and breath, driving her to her knees. The voice. So reasonable sounding, saying such horrible things …

"Don't struggle. I'll just pull it tighter and it will hurt worse. Do as I say and I'll be gone that much sooner."

She fought at first, instinctively clawing at the rope cutting into her neck, twisting to see the figure behind her. But he pulled the rope tighter, hurting her terribly and making her vision blurry. There were intervals where she lost consciousness. Then he would loosen the pressure and wait patiently for her to be aware again of what he needed her to do.

Why does this man hate me? What does he want? Who is he?

She tried to do what he told her, to please him and make it stop hurting. She began to welcome the slipping into unconsciousness, the stopping of both pain and time, only to return to new demands. It was very confusing. This last time, she returned to full consciousness to find herself at eye level with the top shelf of the bamboo bookshelves she was so proud of, with the long row of hand-painted Delft figurines she had bought in Amsterdam and so carefully anchored in case of earthquakes. She realized that she was standing unsteadily near the top of a ladder, the backs of her calves braced against the oaken beam that traversed her vaulted ceiling. She recognized the familiar paint stain on the stepladder; it was from her garage. The hateful cord around her neck was finally slack, no longer hurting, curling behind her to the beam. She could almost breathe normally. The dark figure with the reasonable voice was still there, standing behind her with one gloved hand on her leg, steadying her. Finally, she could turn her head and see him, and – in a voice roughened by the choking rope – finally ask the question that was so important.

"Why are you hurting me? What have I done to you?"

Later, he would wonder why he answered at all or why he said what he did.

"You have done nothing to me. I'm sorry that I had to hurt you. It's not your fault. You're in the wrong place at the wrong time."

She felt and heard him step off the ladder and, for the first time, she realized that she was going to die, now, in her living room, for reasons she did not understand. The ladder suddenly fell away from beneath her feet, leaving her in free fall, leaning forward toward the upcoming floor. She instinctively put her arms out and braced herself to break her fall. Then the rope snapped her viciously upright, cutting cruelly into the softness of her neck and leaving all her questions unanswered in the sudden darkness.

The Consultant

Robert Harris Owens III – known as 'Rho' to his friends -- was bored.

Maybe it's the dreaded midlife crisis? He thought about it and promptly rejected the idea, in part because it was such a cliché and he could not stomach the idea that he was subject to easy classifications. *Why not? You're forty-two and have done more stuff and gone more places than most men of your age. You'd be a poster boy for the Over-Achiever's Club. What makes you exempt?*

He paused in his internal monologue, looked around him and laughed out loud. It was if a Hollywood director – someone with Woody Allen's ironic sensibilities – had staged a movie scene that would visually set up a debate about midlife crisis. He was sitting on a wooden bench at the Marina, sipping a latte from Starbucks and looking out at a wind-roughened San Francisco Bay, with unobstructed views of Alcatraz and the Golden Gate Bridge. About the only prop lacking was a bright red Ferrari in the background to suggest material wealth.

He ran through a checklist in his head. The hallmark of the classic midlife crisis was dissatisfaction, a restlessness that manifested itself in clichés; to be treated with new cars, cosmetic surgery, trysts with younger women. None of these pertained to his present case. If there was an element of dissatisfaction, it surely would stem from having too much rather than too little. He had two graduate degrees – law and business – from first-rate schools. He owned his own business, which generated enough money to retire now if he wanted to. He had a home in the high-rent district of one of the world's greatest cities, and ample friends. He was good looking, athletic, popular among his peers, self-confident and had a slightly dark but eclectic sense of humor.

The major missing element was a woman. *That's not quite right. It should be the woman, not a woman.*

He did not lack opportunity: there were many women available to him. He would be near the top of any gossip columnist's "most eligible" list, especially in San Francisco with its record level concentration of gay men removed from competition. His obvious attractiveness was part of the problem. His friends were constantly matching him up with "just the right person for you," creating an audition-like atmosphere around what should be a simple dinner or walk on the beach. It strengthened a growing wariness in him -- a feeling that he was being stalked by well-meaning predators – and he worried that he had lost the capacity to take a woman at face value.

This was especially painful for him because he was a classic romantic, an idealistic believer in the existence and power of love between two people. The kind of feeling where "Whither thou goest, I will go" and "Thy people shall be my people" were real promises and not just wedding poetry.

The painfulness was compounded by his divorce four years ago. He'd been married for ten years to Angela and had assumed that it was for life. The fault lines in their marriage appeared incrementally – usually around managing two meteoric careers -- but seemed reconcilable. When she became involuntarily pregnant, he looked forward to raising their child together in San Francisco. She, however, had an abortion and moved to London. She was now well on her way to being CEO of a major British investment bank.

This flaw, his romanticism, was turning out to be a major impediment in his sex life. He liked sex for its combination of playfulness and passion, for its incredible closeness with another person. But he feared its very availability. The women he dated seemed to see sex as an essential part of their "audition," like an Olympic gymnast or diver required to demonstrate certain mandatory skills early in their competitive routine. In his view, that of the closet romantic, it should be a natural extension of a proven compatibility; an act of more significance than a handshake with full frontal nudity. At best, he seemed to be becoming a sort of emotional celibate. At worst, a prudish throwback to a past era.

This was one of the reasons he came to this same Marina bench on most mornings with his double latte. The promenade passing in front of him was a popular place for San Francisco joggers, particularly the class of young and shapely career women that seemed so plentiful in the city. He could watch the women for about a hundred-yard stretch as they approached along the promenade with their flashing legs, spandexed breasts and – as they receded – firm and suggestive butts. He thought of it as harmless voyeurism, but every now and then pictured himself as an old man doing the same thing, decades from now.

I need a woman, he thought, but promptly corrected himself. *No. I need the woman.*

His cell phone rang, the caller ID indicating his office.

"Hi, Celia. What's up?"

"I apologize for interrupting your girl watching, boss. But an actual client called and I thought you should know."

Celia Gonzalez was his administrative assistant, the first employee he had hired and a longtime close friend. She was sixty-five years old and as canny about people as anybody he had ever come across. She probably knew him better than anyone except his ex-wife. He usually took her advice and regretted not doing so the few times he substituted his own instincts.

"Actually, I'm admiring the boats on the Bay. The damn women just obstruct my view. They're really annoying!"

"Right! If you say so. In any case, I've got you a date, if you're willing."

"Not you too! Tell me about her."

"Her name is Marcia Littleton, and she's very secretive."

"That will be hard. She's one of the more well-known women in our city. Why the secrecy? Is she ashamed to be seen with me?"

"She won't tell me why she wants to meet with you, which is slightly unusual. And she doesn't want to meet at her office or yours. It's all very mysterious."

"I was feeling a little bored, so mystery is good. Where and when?"

"Six this evening. At the Top of the Mark. She'll have a table reserved in your name. I told her you'd be there."

"All right. I suppose I can still watch the boats on the Bay from up there while I listen to her mystery unfold."

"I've seen pictures of Ms. Littleton in our local paper and I suspect the boats will not be serious competition for your attention. Anyway, you'd need a telescope to watch the girls from there."

Then her tone changed, becoming quite businesslike. "I'm putting together the usual dossier on her and her company and I'll have it for you by noon. I've already seen enough to confirm the appointment for you. I think you'll find it to be an interesting meeting."

He ended the call and thought about what he knew about Marcia Littleton. *Celia's right: it should be an interesting meeting.* He looked down the promenade, but saw only a group of about seven or eight seniors shuffling toward him very slowly with canes or walkers.

Time to go.

The Inventor

So very American! This inventing of things in garages!

The garage was near the crest of Skyline Drive, on the western slope of the coastal range and approximately midway between San Jose and San Francisco. The man had rented the property for its splendid isolation from its neighbors. The house and garage were almost invisible, both physically and legally. The buildings were three hundred yards from the highway, with a dense barrier of redwoods and a locked gate to shield them from view. The nominal owner was a French bank that was acting as a trustee for an estate mired in litigation.

The view of the Pacific through a gap in the redwoods and the surprising serenity of morning fog were not necessary for Ahmed's purposes, but he had come to value both qualities. Perhaps it was the irony, as though such a tranquil setting facilitated the creation of destructive devices.

He did not think of himself as an inventor. And they were not his inventions, technically speaking. In fact, the underlying ideas were stolen. But over the past few months, as his ideas and devices took shape in the nondescript garage, he began to take a pride of ownership in the features that he had added; features that enabled entirely new applications that the original inventors – many of them long dead – would have appreciated. For their elegance; not for their intended use.

His last graduate training was as a theoretical chemist in Germany, but his avocation was engineering. Once, when he was younger and much more naïve, he had designed and built great curving blades for the giant wind turbines that dotted windswept landscapes of Europe and North America, using composite materials that married strength with incredible lightness. Ahmed loved the creation of the huge blades with their exquisitely engineered shapes that were so sensitive to the touch of the wind, turning in such deliberate stately circles. He thought of them as scimitars, the swords that his ninth-century Muslim ancestors carried into battle.

He was still young, in his thirties, but the naiveté was long gone, replaced by an emotion that he could not name; something less than vengeful but still greater than the sense of injustice that seemed to permeate so many of his more passive colleagues. *But not enough to stir them to action. They write blogs, letters to the editor, go to meetings, complain about the West. But they go home at night to their wife, two children and big-screen TV.* Whatever the emotion was, that and his interest in nanotechnology were sufficient to bring him to this Northern California hilltop overlooking the Pacific.

And father, of course. With his visions of what could be, looking far beyond today. My father, with his interesting friends with so much money and so many questions.

At first, Ahmed disdained his work in the hillside barn in Northern California. It required pouring chemicals into test tubes and beakers and mixing the resulting liquids, always in small test amounts. The work lacked drama, and he came to detest the word "scalable" with its implication that bigger was inevitably better

He smiled when he thought of the first approach from the fanatics. *They wanted me to build them a better bomb – an 'improvised explosive device' to be delivered by camels and detonated by ignorant boys with cell phones! Exploding underwear with fuses to be lit with matches!*

In contrast to them, the American and the Israeli – his father's interesting friends -- knew little of explosives. But they had vivid imaginations and no egos, so they could ask the kind of "dumb" questions that stimulated invention.

How could you detonate a bomb that is buried under ten feet of concrete? How small can you make a bomb? Can you "chain" a series of very small bombs so as to make a very large explosion? Can you detonate a bomb with a laser beam? How would you hide a bomb in plain sight? Can a liquefied explosive be frozen for later use? Can you formulate a concrete mix that will burn?

And they had money, a seemingly inexhaustible supply. He looked around the garage and smiled, admiring the elegance of his devices. He liked to think of them as scimitars of a modern tribe, but still with the same ancient purpose – the destruction of infidels.

The CFO

Marcia Littleton was unsure of herself, something that had rarely happened to her during her thirty-eight years. It was a strange sensation and she didn't like it.

It was not self-doubt; that form of corrosive uncertainty simply did not exist for her. And it wasn't the difficulty of making a hard choice in the face of incomplete information. She did that ten times a day in her job and had long ago learned to accept losses, as long as the original decision was sound. It helped, of course, that most of the time she was right. And when she wasn't, the losses were well within known tolerances.

This was different, coming from that category of *things that you don't know you don't know* that had proven so deadly to countless others, usually high-achievement types on a momentary pinnacle; folks who probably had multiple, branching contingency plans for the *unknowns* and the *things that they knew they didn't know*. And then were blindsided.

The reality that it wasn't really their fault may have comforted those others even as they saw disgrace looming. *After all, how can you be held accountable for something that you didn't know you didn't know?* Marcia, however, did not like surprises and did her best – which was very good indeed – to avoid them.

Which is why she found herself in a dimly lit cocktail lounge at six in the evening, amid coveys of over-loud tourists. The bar at the top of the Mark Hopkins Hotel was a strange choice of venues for a business meeting, but she wanted a place where she would not run into any locals. She had pulled some strings with the restaurant manager to make sure that she was seated at a corner table. The location had two advantages. First, it provided one of the best views in the world, a two-hundred-seventy degree panorama of San Francisco and the Bay. Second, it gave the two of them as much privacy as possible. But the real privacy came from the ambient noise – din, really – of a bar overrun by boisterous tourists.

She was sitting opposite a person with the pretentious name of Robert Harris Owens III. She already knew a great deal about him, the sort of biographical data that is easily obtained unless the subject is making a deliberate effort to remain private. Her present goal was to assess those dimensions that are resistant to electronic media – appearance, personality, integrity. *Like on-line dating, the really important stuff doesn't show up on-screen.*

Her first reaction when he came to the table was that he didn't look like someone with a Roman numeral after his surname. She had expected more visible self-importance. He was good-looking and obviously fit. *A runner, I think.* He was dressed casually and clearly quite relaxed. Unlike her.

They each ordered a glass of wine, and then she began talking without any preamble. Even to herself, her tone sounded harsh and condescending.

"I want to hire you to conduct a very discreet investigation."

He looked at her with a cold stare for about ten seconds without responding, his expression making it quite clear that he did not like her peremptory manner.

Not a good start, Marcia!

When he spoke, his tone was dismissive. "We're a management consulting firm. It sounds like you want a detective agency. Shall I recommend someone?" He shifted in his chair as if preparing to stand up.

"Mr. Owens, I know about your firm. It's a boutique consulting operation with a who's who list of clients, very up and coming. However, I also know that you personally have -- occasionally and without any fanfare -- taken on some very sensitive inquiries on behalf of corporate clients; inquiries that seem to blur the line between consulting – giving advice – and detective work – solving puzzles. Like what you did for Meridale ..."

Rho wondered how she had discovered that little bit of information. He had set up an undercover team posing as mid-level project managers to find the engineer that was selling Meridale's new product specs to a Chinese competitor. And she was right, his firm's access to the insides of their clients did put them in position to both detect and solve puzzles.

He sat back. "OK. I'll listen, but that's all I can promise."

"Before we go too far, I have two non-negotiable conditions."

His retort was instantaneous. "You can have as many as you like. When you're done listing them, I'll decide whether to accept them or not."

This is not going well. Let's try a different line ... See if the man has a sense of humor.

"Are you always this abrasive? Are you trying to live up to – or down – to some macho behavioral code? Something that requires you to alienate potential customers? You know, like a waiter with sore feet in a Manhattan deli.

Or, since we're talking about detectives, are you just channeling Sam Spade or Lew Archer?"

He leaned back, clearly amused by the question. "Actually, Lew Archer was a liberal humanist with a high degree of tolerance for moral ambiguities. A person who identified with his client's pathologies. A much more complex detective than Spade, by the way, whose first response to ambiguity was usually violence."

What the hell? I know he has a law degree and an MBA. Must be an English major in there somewhere as well.

She picked up and waved her white linen napkin in mock surrender. "I give up," she said. "No more literary references! About all I get to read any more is Excel spreadsheets. No dialogue, lousy plots."

He let the silence persist, then spoke in a carefully neutral tone. "Look, Ms. Littleton, let's call a truce. We both know this meeting is an audition, but we seem to disagree as to which one of us is the auditionee. Why don't you just tell me your two non-negotiables?"

She smiled to acknowledge the overture. "First, I don't want anyone to know you're working for me. If possible, I don't even want them to know that you're conducting an investigation."

Rho took a sip of wine before he answered. "The first part is easy. I don't tell anyone who my clients are unless the person doing the asking has a badge or a subpoena. And even then, I'll resist as long as I can. Your second point might be tough. After all, if an outsider barges into a private company and starts asking a lot of pointed questions, most intelligent people would construe that as an investigation."

"Yes, I know. But I think there's a way to mislead them as to what exactly you are investigating … sort of an old hidden ball trick, to use a sports metaphor!"

"We'll get to that. What's your second demand?"

"I know that you are the head of a fairly sophisticated agency; that you employ a lot of smart MBAs and specialists to do the legwork.   Most of your own time is spent supervising them and being a rainmaker."

"So?"

"I want you to do this job yourself … Minimum involvement of other people."

His first reaction was a gruff, "*If* I do it, which is still unsettled."

Then he thought for about ten seconds. "OK, I think I can live with that. I'll take the lead, but I get to interpret what 'minimum involvement of other people' means. And I'll let you know who else needs to be involved."

"I need to know – "

He waved his hand impatiently.   "Whoa! You said *two* non-negotiables.   Look, Ms. Littleton, you either trust me or you don't. It's pretty binary. If you don't, then you should run like hell the other way. It sounds to me like you're trying to talk yourself into this arrangement. I'm just a convenient sounding board."

She knew he was right, but she didn't like it.

Rho tried again for a reasonable tone. "What don't we start back at Square One? Why don't you tell me how you think my firm can help you?"

Marcia took a deep breath, clearly nervous. "Why do I feel like I did when I said "I do" at my wedding?"

"You'll have to ask your therapist. Or better yet, consult a creative writing instructor about your use of tortured metaphors! We're not getting married, just engaging in a bit of commercial foreplay."

She sat up straighter and frowned slightly, as though in disapproval of the way their dialogue had slipped into sexual innuendo. Actually, she was thinking of the best way to begin to describe her concerns without seeming to be an overwrought twit.

"I'm the CFO of the Morrison Group. I'm responsible for – "

"Ms. Littleton. Look, I can save you some time. I know who you are, what you do, what the Morrison Group does. I know the organization structure of the Group and of the finance function that you head. I know where you went to school, what jobs you've had, who your first husband is and how much support you're paying to him. I know that you're spending most of your time and emotional energy right now on getting ready for an IPO and negotiating the acquisition of DaVinci Associates. You should assume that I'm the head of a major and sophisticated agency with access to vast data bases, both public and private. Also assume that I am highly discriminating about which clients I agree to work with. About the only thing I *don't* know is why you want to hire me. Why don't we save a lot of time and start there?"

Marcia sat quietly through his faintly angry monologue. *This is not going well. All we've done is irritate each other from the second we said hello.*

Thinking to change the level of contentiousness, she asked, "Do you believe in hunches?"

"If you're asking whether I occasionally draw conclusions without having any apparent reason, I absolutely do. Do you have a hunch?"

"Sort of. I feel like something is wrong and about to blow up. But I don't know what it is or why I feel that way."

Rho grimaced. "Sounds like the latter days of my marriage. Tell me more."

"There are two things. First, the head of my Accounts Payable unit just killed herself. She was found – "

"A woman named Broder. I read about it in the Chronicle. Sounded like a sad end to a sad life ... "

"By some standards, yes. But she was not unhappy. She loved her job. I had to chase her out of the office sometimes. I know this sounds like a cliché, but she was not the type to commit suicide."

"It is a cliché. Most of us have a hard time accepting a friend's suicide. Was there anything unusual about what she was working on? Shortages in accounts? Sexual harassment at the office? It's pretty sick, but I'm recalling an old joke about the accountant who absconded with Accounts Payable!"

Marcia smiled politely. "Everything was fine. Her work is ... was ... impeccable. The first surprise was that she asked to be assigned to the due diligence team on the DaVinci deal. It was fine with me, and I approved it. But it wasn't her usual style. Then three days ago – the day before she died -- she scheduled an appointment to talk to me. She wouldn't tell me why, but she was the sort of woman that hated to be a bother to anybody, so I think that it was something that was important to her."

She paused, clearly visualizing her last interactions with Broder. Rho took the opportunity to say, "It always starts a lot of rumors when a key finance officer kills themself. Everybody from their boss to shareholders to the SEC wonders about the motive."

"Especially when you're trying to go public and acquire another company, all at the same time." Again, she paused and looked worried. "I guess what I really want is for you to tell me that I shouldn't worry."

Rho grimaced. "I can say the words, but you and I both know it won't work."

She smiled sadly and – for the first time – Rho felt the stirring of an urge to help. Both the smile and the sadness were real, probably the first unrehearsed features of her sales pitch.

He said, "This is pretty straightforward. We have a couple of experts in fraud investigations. They'll need to rummage around in her files and the Payables department."

Littleton squirmed slightly and looked decidedly uncomfortable. "There are some complications. I don't want to look like I'm following up on Marie Lynne's suicide."

Rho didn't say anything, but his expression was equivalent to a very large question mark.

She waved her hand. "In this case, it's easy to disguise the purpose. I intend to initiate a major reengineering initiative for the entire General Accounting area. You can be one of many consultants involved in the initial data gathering."

"I can do that. I once worked – "

"As an Internal Auditor at GE's Medical Division. I know. You were twenty-four years old at the time. Mr. Owens, I know who you are, what you do and how your firm is organized. I know where you went to school, what jobs you've had, who your first wife is and how much support you're paying. Assume that I am obsessively curious and have access to the same data bases that you do. You should also assume that I too am highly discriminating about who I choose to work with."

To her surprise, Owens smiled. As though he was pleased with her.

"You said there were two things that were nagging at you? The recently deceased Marie Lynne is one. What's the other?"

"Again, this has to be just between you and I."

"Ms. Littleton, please. You're insulting me. Did you learn nothing about me when you doing all that salacious research?"

"I'm sorry. That was stupid of me. But I'm risking my career on this ... this vague intuition."

"Based on what I've seen of your track record, I'd guess that your instincts are pretty good."

"Since you seem to like allusions to great detectives, let's just say that this is a variant of one of the Sherlock Holmes stories – I forget which one – but it was about the dog that didn't bark... where it is the *absence* of something that doesn't make any sense."

"So what is it that's not happening that's bothering you? The story was called 'Silver Blaze,' by the way."

She paused and gazed out the window at the fog creeping into the Bay and enveloping the city. It came – quite quickly -- from the ground up, until she was looking down at a vast all-white landscape studded with the tops of the taller buildings, backlit by a setting sun. It was quite beautiful. *An urban Stonehenge. I wish I had a camera.* She felt momentarily sorry for the tourists surrounding them, dressed in their T-shirts and about to reenter an environment where the temperature had just fallen about twenty degrees.

"Ms. Littleton?"

Marcia snapped back to the present, recalling his question before she had gotten involved with the fog.

"I want you to find out what my boss is keeping from me."

"That would be Mr. Daniel Carlton, your Chief Executive Officer. The one recently named as one of the ten best CEO's in America in the Wall Street Journal?"

"Yes."

"I can see why you might be a little nervous about a leak. You're being disloyal in the extreme, aren't you?"

"I've never done anything like this before ... And I don't like doing it!"

"So why are you?"

"I don't want to tell you."

Rho leaned back, crossed his arms over his chest and glared at her. "Right. So what I need to do is to discover everything Carlton knows, and then subtract everything that he's told you. Obviously, everything left over will be – by definition – something that your boss is keeping from you ... Piece of cake!"

She grinned, looking like she'd been exposed playing a bad practical joke. "OK. You're right: I can't have it both ways. I've got three things that are bothering me. First, the DaVinci acquisition is going to be a billion dollar deal. It has the potential to make or break this company. And Carlton's treating it like it's a done deal! The due diligence is a joke. The economic analysis is a bunch of simpleminded assumptions driving an Excel spreadsheet. The pricing is either absurdly high or absurdly low, but he doesn't seem to care. And, worst of all, he's doing everything he can to keep me from getting involved."

"Maybe it's a management style kind of thing. Likes to do it himself. Man on a white horse. Bold decision maker."

She was shaking her head before he finished. "At least a couple of problems with that. First, it's not his style. He's famous for seeing the so-called big picture and delegating the details to others. We've made a bunch of acquisitions in the short time that I've been here, and they've been team deals, carefully done on both sides but with me in charge. And I'm the CFO. He's not a finance guy; he's sales and marketing. He needs me! It's almost seems that he's afraid I'll find out something and kill the deal. He's even tried to keep me from the Board discussions pertaining to the acquisition."

"And the Board let him? Keep the CFO out?"

"Walter Morrison – the founder of the Group -- is the Chair, and he and Carlton are very tight. There are five other members, and they're all cronies of Morrison's.

"And it's more than the DaVinci deal. In the last month or so, Carlton has gotten very interested in specific projects, even to the point of overriding the field people. He's jumping down a couple of managerial levels to push for decisions that he really doesn't know much about. That's new behavior for him. And it's inappropriate."

"What about Morrison? He's the one responsible for Carlton."

"As far as I can tell, he's perfectly content with what Carlton is doing."

"So we've got Broder's suicide and Carlton's recent odd behavior. Anything else?"

She grinned in a very sheepish way. "It's pretty personal, and I think I know what you'll say when I tell you. But it was a major shock to me, and it's another thing that makes no sense."

"I overheard Carlton and Morrison talking after last week's board meeting. They were standing and waiting for their cars to be brought out from valet parking. I was sitting in a limo parked at the curb with the window down. I was reading a report about the acquisition and was only vaguely aware of them talking in the background. Then I heard my name. I'm embarrassed about it, but I listened as hard as I could. And I definitely heard Carlton say to Morrison, 'Maybe it's time to get rid of Littleton.'"

Rho thought about how to say what needed to be said. He finally decided on the direct approach.

"Maybe they think you're under-performing? That they can do better? You're in the big leagues now, with the big egos and sharp knives. CFO's get fired all the time."

"Not the good ones. And I'm one of the best."

She said this without any visible self-consciousness, a very matter-of-fact statement.

She went on. "Morrison brought me here to position the Group for an IPO within twelve months, less if possible. And I've done that. There have been absolutely no performance issues – zero, nada, none. If you have been paying attention while Googling me, you know that. And you also know the negative press they'd get if they tried to fire me at this point in time. The IPO price would crater. It doesn't make any sense."

Rho knew that she was right. Littleton had an impeccable record before showing up at the Morrison Group. And during her brief tenure as CFO, she was credited with significantly upgrading the administrative infrastructure, setting what the business press labeled "a bold new strategic course" and engineering half-a-dozen medium-sized acquisitions to make the Group into one of the top five engineering & construction firms in the world, and the only privately-owned one of its size. The market was eagerly anticipating the initial public offering sometime within the next few weeks. She was probably one of the most closely watched and admired women executives in the U.S.

Rho nodded, wondering how to say what he was thinking. "There is no way I can ask this question without insulting your integrity or your intelligence. Maybe both. Have you –"

She interrupted him. And this time, her grin was anything but sheepish. "I am not sleeping with, have not slept with, and have no intention of sleeping with anybody that I work with. That includes Carlton, Morrison and everybody else in the office."

Both the grin and her lack of self-consciousness about her vow of abstinence jolted Rho – for the first time since he had sat down at the table – into the sudden realization that this woman was a sexual being. *And, I think, a woman that would be fun to be in bed with.*

He did his best to keep his tone as impersonal as possible. "Maybe that's the problem. Such an emphatic lack of interest might be perceived as an insult. These are men used to getting their way and unrequited love is a fairly powerful emotion. Has either of them ever indicated some desires along those lines? Any invitations to late night 'business' dinners … stuff like that?"

She was not surprised by the question and Rho suspected that she had already considered it within her own mind. She was an intelligent and attractive woman set in the midst of some of the most testosterone-soaked turfs in the modern world – Wall Street, high finance, corporate boardrooms. She must have experienced – and apparently rejected – countless propositions.

"Not a one. Frankly and just between the two of us, their lack of interest surprised me. Morrison is a widower and Carlton divorced. But they're both considered highly eligible and frequently are seen around town escorting beautiful women, usually at big society dos. Originally, when I first took the job, I thought it might be a problem. But it hasn't been. As far as I can tell, neither of them has any interest in me whatsoever as a sex object."

He could not detect the slightest trace of disappointment or resentment in her voice. *This woman has enough self-esteem for the both of us.*

"OK. Same question as before. I need to poke around and ask a lot of questions. What's my cover? How do I insinuate myself into senior management affairs ... get them to talk to me ... and keep you out of the picture?"

"You know the acronym 'KISS'?"

"Keep it simple, stupid! I view it as a philosophy of life, right up there with the four great religions of the world! "

"We don't need an elaborate conspiracy. You run a significant consulting firm with a very strong client list. I'm going to hire your firm to conduct a feasibility study and help us execute two major initiatives: reengineering of the finance function and revising the Group's strategic planning process. Those two projects will require you to have top-to-bottom access throughout the company and to ask highly detailed questions."

"That's a major consulting project, probably priced at a couple of million dollars for a firm like the Morrison Group if it was real."

"It is real. I want the studies done in a highly professional manner, with all the bells and whistles. Those two projects have been on my 'to-do' list since the day I arrived. And both Morrison and Carlton have already signed off on the expenditure, so they'll view your snooping as just standard consulting practice. You can use your MBA's and systems experts, but I want you to spend your own time on our little project."

"It will take at least a few days to –"

"I don't think so. Here's your contract."

Littleton pulled a two-inch-thick document in a black cover from her briefcase and handed it to Rho. He took about thirty seconds to scan random pages.

"You're really quite sure of yourself, aren't you?"

She shook her head. "To the contrary, this is the first time in my professional life that I have felt at all unsure about what I'm doing."

"What's bothering me – and I don't think I like it very much – is that you also seem very sure about me." He held the contract up and then let it fall flat onto the table. It made a very loud "Whap!" and she jumped slightly.

She visibly gathered herself, sitting up straighter and thinking about what to say next. As Rho watched, he thought he knew what was coming. He had watched a video of her being interviewed by a relatively hostile MSNBC reporter and admired the way that she had coolly shredded his arguments one-by-one, leaving him groping for an exit line. It was one of the few times Rho had felt any sympathy for a TV journalist.

She laid her palm on the bound document and spoke in a calm, reasonable voice, as though explaining to a graduate student with poor English skills that he'd failed the exam.

"We both know that this is a sweetheart contract. Bain, BCG, McKinsey or any of your other competitors – and those MBA's you pay so well -- would leap at the opportunity. Why would you turn down a multi-million dollar, high prestige job? It's what you do."

She leaned back in her chair, waiting for his response. Rho simply looked at her, saying nothing. She was right of course, but she was deliberately missing the point, and they both knew it.

The silence went on long enough that it was beginning to feel competitive. Then Littleton made a series of small adjustments, each one not very significant, but collectively transforming her from a stern and hostile debater into a beautiful woman hinting at more ancient negotiations.

She smiled, a sudden warm and complex smile that somehow signaled self-amusement at her own playacting and simultaneously acknowledged him for seeing through it. The smile added wrinkles to the corners of her eyes and emphasized her red lipstick against white teeth. At the same time, she leaned forward very slightly and the motion caused her long hair to shadow the left side of her face, adding some slight mystery to whatever she was about to say. Rho became aware of the reduced distance between them and for the first time noticed the small diamond pendant that now stood out against the triangle of tanned skin at the neckline of her blue silk blouse. The quality of air surrounding them seemed to shift, partly because of the scent she gave off. Somehow, the ambient noise seemed to fade and took on an expectant air. When she started speaking, her voice was softer, more tentative.

"Rho … May I call you that? I've done my research. You're absolutely the right person to take this on. You're the only one who has the mix of experience and smarts to move in these circles. The people I asked about you? The word 'integrity' came up over and over, along with others like 'independent' and 'hard to control.' I need you. I really do."

He found himself actually leaning slightly toward her, as though her words and posture had activated a magnetic force. *Does she practice that? Or is it built into the female DNA, some sort of vestigial adaptive mechanism for dealing with alpha males? Is she even aware of the almost-promises – the hinted-at quid pro quos -- that are implied in what she has just done?*

He leaned back, as though to acknowledge the changed atmosphere. "OK. We'll take the job. You're right, of course. I can't turn down a project of that scope with your quality of customer. And the Morrison Group will get its money's worth. We both know that. But I want one adjustment to the contract."

She nodded and waited.

"It's overpriced, presumably because you've included a sweetener for our little bolted-on clandestine snooping project. I want the price cut by fifteen percent."

She smiled, nodded, and again said nothing.

"We'll get started on the consulting stuff immediately. And I'll make some discreet and highly preliminary inquiries along the lines you've suggested – Broder's suicide and Carlton's reticence. Depending on what turns up, I'll decide whether to take our little side-project further or not. And, if I do, I'll send you a separate bill for my time and expenses."

"That's fair."

She raised her wine glass to his, the "clink" sealing their tentative bargain. As he watched, she again used imperceptible changes of posture and expression to somehow transform herself back into a relatively sexless and impatient executive with contracts to negotiate. He marveled at it, while regretting the switch and wondering which of the two manifestations was the real one.

Project Planning

Rho started on the Morrison project the morning after his meeting with Littleton at the Mark Hopkins. He skipped his usual morning latte on the Marina and was in the office at eight. His first stop was at the office of Robert Huggins.

Huggins was Rho's chief operating officer, the key organizing force for the half-dozen or so major consulting projects that would be running at any particular time. Huggins was also a close friend that he had first met in graduate school. They were both married and older than the other MBAs and discovered that they shared an impatience with bureaucracy. Among other things, Huggins had commanded a Ranger company in the first Iraq War and had spent time with Bain Consulting before joining Rho. Rho had been the best man at his wedding and was the godfather of his just-born daughter.

Rho briefed him on the Morrison contract and was not surprised when Huggins was skeptical.

"Let me see if I understand this. A client you've never seen before, for whom we have done zero due diligence, gave you a sweetheart contract for – what? – a couple of million dollars. And he – she? -- wants us to move it to the head of the queue under your personal guidance. Kinda makes me wonder why we spend so much time and money developing long term relationships with prospective clients."

He was not surprised that Huggins was slightly ruffled that such a significant contract was developed without his knowledge or input, but apparently satisfied when Rho emphasized the client's passion for secrecy and swift action. Rho had debated whether or not to share Littleton's real agenda – their secret little side deal – but had decided against it for the time being. *That part may not even happen.*

"I want to get started as soon as we can. You and I will do a 'show and tell' bit with their Board as soon as the CFO gets all her ducks lined up. But I do want to make this a priority project, with you running it personally. Put all available resources on it and keep me informed every couple of days on how it's going. And tell our people to watch for anything that seems out-of-line. The Group's about to come out as an IPO and I think we can really help them sort out what needs to be fixed before they go public."

"This is probably a three month project. What do you want to do first?"

"I have a couple of priorities. Between you and me, the CFO isn't all that comfortable with their internal controls, so I want you to personally make a judgment as to how sophisticated they are in Receivables and Payables as a starting point. Take a look at their General Accounting department in as much detail as you can. If we can identify the savings potential from reengineering that particular area, that will give us a feel for how to spend our time elsewhere."

Huggins was taking notes. "OK. That's pretty standard. It will also give us a quick insight into their overall network of customers and vendors. From there, we can decide how to allocate time and people. What's your other priority?"

"Spend some serious time with Daniel Carlton, their COO. Find out how committed he is to these projects. I'm worried that we're going to run into some palace politics that will complicate things. Like why isn't the CFO more involved? She's the one with most of the info."

"Palace politics, huh? So what's new about that? But as my favorite management philosopher advises, "Follow the money!"

"Peter Drucker? Warren Buffett?"

"Nope, John LeCarre!"

Well that's appropriate! Who better than an author of spy stories to kick off this curious project?

Opposing Interests

Marcia Littleton called Rho on his private line. He was not surprised that she had the number.

"I've set up a meeting for you with the Executive Committee of the Board. That's Morrison, Carlton and Mervin Cannell. The agenda will be one item – a ninety minute presentation on the two projects the Owens firm has taken on, reengineering and strategic planning process. That's pretty standard protocol for projects like this."

"Will you be in the room?"

"Yes, but mostly as an observer. I'll introduce you and then sit quietly."

"Can I provoke them? Professionally, of course."

"As long as it fits within the context of the meeting. I've told them that you're a bit of a maverick. But I suggest you view this as a chance to set up further conversations down the road."

Celia and the Board Secretary for the Morrison Group worked out all of the logistical details and Rho showed up at Littleton's office with Huggins at a quarter-to-ten two mornings later with five copies of the traditional black three-ring binder with a Powerpoint presentation inserted. As usual, the binder was the end product of approximately a hundred hours of intensive analysis done by a group of MBAs sifting through the considerable amount of public information about the Morrison Group. Rho was continually amazed at how three or four really smart kids – that's how he thought of the analysts – could not only understand a complex organization, but also identify its probable disorders by simply sitting in front of a computer screen for two or three days. The irony was that all of that considerable knowledge was then recompressed into the cryptic bullet points and flying icons of a Powerpoint presentation.

He introduced Huggins to Littleton, noting that Chip would be the project leader and make the actual presentation. They walked about thirty feet from Littleton's office on the top floor to a conference room where the three men were seated and waiting. Littleton introduced Rho and Huggins, and then took about two minutes to describe the project and Rho's firm in a straightforward way. Huggins used the time to hook up his laptop to the built-in presentation hardware and bring the first page of the presentation onto the screen at one end of the room.

All three men were in standard executive form – custom-tailored dark suits with faint stripes, white shirts with cuff links showing, expensive haircuts and slightly skeptical expressions, as though irretrievably doubtful about whatever was about to be said.

The predictability depressed Rho, reminding him of his worries about slipping into midlife crisis. He had seen expressions and tableaus like this in dozens of executive boardrooms around the world. *There's your catalyst for your classic midlife crisis: finding yourself about to do something you've done a hundred times before.* As Huggins began talking, Rho devoted himself to studying the three men, each of whom seemed intent on the presentation.

Mervin Cannell was an ex-Marine Corps general and looked the part. He sat ramrod straight and was the only one of the three to make notes on the pad in front of him as

Huggins advanced the slide deck. Cannell had the reputation of being smart and politically connected to a vast network of his cronies still in the Pentagon. Rho knew that he was one of three ex-generals on the Group Board of Directors, reflecting the Group's concentration on either defense projects or on infrastructure projects in contested parts of the world. The firm's web site noted their extensive involvement in the Middle East and Africa.

He could be the poster child for the military/industrial complex that Eisenhower fretted about.

Carlton was the youngest of the three and looked exactly like the super salesman he was reputed to be. *He looks like a TV evangelist gone corporate.* He was short, well under six feet tall, with thick wavy hair and designer glasses. Somehow, his facial expressions and body language seemed to radiate sincerity and trustworthiness. Rho knew that this was a deceptive facade. Carlton had begun his business career with the Morrison Group and had risen rapidly to his present role as President of the Group, mainly because of his ability to schmooze with both customers and congressmen. Along the way, he used tactics that left questions about both legality and ethics. Rumors abounded of bribes to foreign government officials, hardball maneuvers with vendors, lavish parties for congressmen – a "how-to-do-business-in-the-military/industrial-complex" tale that couldn't be told due to libel and slander laws.

Walter Morrison looked like the diplomat he had become. He was probably one of the best-known corporate executives in the Western world. He started fifty years ago by drilling a single wildcat well in Eastern Texas and went on from there to build one of the largest privately-owned engineering design firms in the world, worth an estimated five billion dollars. When he began, the industry was composed of small entrepreneurial firms, each operating within a well-defined geographic area and industry. He built the company by "rolling up" these firms, first in the U.S. and then around the world. His pitch was the same to all entrepreneurs – "Join us and get access to a global market, centralized services and continued autonomy within the corporate family." It worked because of Morrison's personal charisma and the growing global demand for sophisticated engineering design and construction support services around the world.

Today, Morrison spent most of his time cultivating the politicians and defense executives that were his customers. Large infrastructure projects such as pipelines, airports and nuclear generating plants required long lead times and involved a decision process that was at least as political as it was analytical. Outside the U.S., projects almost always required working with a foreign partner. Inevitably, the same political power brokers that he cultivated on the business side found him useful as a "back channel" for sensitive non-commercial negotiations.

Five minutes into the presentation, Huggins flashed an organization chart of the Morrison Group on the screen. It looked like the wiring diagram for a spaceship, reflecting the way the Group had been assembled as a loosely knit confederation of independent companies rather than with a textbook emphasis on tree-like structures and span of control. There were probably a hundred or more organizational units represented. Huggins had used color-coding on the Powerpoint slide to indicate various groupings.

Cannell sat up even straighter and interrupted. It was the first break in the presentation flow.

"Those units in red? What's your rationale for grouping them together?"

Huggins answered promptly, "Most of their revenues come from defense contracts, either directly or indirectly."

"You do know that some of those contracts are highly classified, don't you?"

"We assumed that to be the case. But for purposes of evaluating your strategic planning processes and recommending changes, we can work around the classification restrictions. We've done lots of projects for – "

Cannell's voice changed and Rho was amused to see how quickly he reverted to his Marine Corps persona. "Don't tell me what you've done for somebody else. I don't want to see any young twerps with MBA's rummaging around in those contract files!" From his tone, it was clear that he viewed Huggins as one of the twerps.

An awkward silence set in. Rho quickly realized that both Huggins and Littleton were looking at him with the same air of expectancy. *That didn't take long.* In Rho's experience, most "audition" presentations had a critical moment, a time where the conflicting interests were in stark relief, where the next comment would make or break the deal. He was in the room precisely to deal with this kind of awkwardness. Before he spoke, he glanced at Morrison and noted that he was pointedly gazing out the window, clearly waiting to see how the underlings worked through the momentary snag. Rho decided on a frontal attack.

"General Cannell. Bear with me for a moment. As an ex-military commander, you know the importance of strategy, and based on your past testimony before the Armed Services Committee in the U.S. Congress, you're well aware of what happens when you're forced to operate without it."

Cannell nodded tentatively, suspecting a trap, but Rho's references to his military background and Congressional appearances – with the very faint hint of some failure on his part -- had put him in a temporary corner. As Rho had intended.

Rho waved his hand at the dense array of interwoven lines on the screen. "Look at that diagram and then tell me what the overarching strategy is."

He waited just long enough for the silence to make the point for him. Then he said, "The Group does not have a way to answer that question. That's why we're here."

Cannell bristled and snapped back, "The Group has done all right –"

Rho interrupted, "By acquiring other companies and bolting them on. You're not managing; you're herding a bunch of cats. Now it's time to find a way to make them work together. You have enormous slack in your organization. That's an inefficiency that won't be tolerated in a public company, which you aspire to be. Our *twerps* – he emphasized the word very slightly -- have estimated that you can add a billion dollars to your market cap if you just rationalize what you've got, without acquiring another company or major contract."

It was obvious that Cannell was searching for a response, and that it would be delivered in an outraged tone. Before he could speak, Rho continued. "And, by the way, some of the so-called twerps in our firm were decorated Marine Corps officers in Iraq and Afghanistan. That includes Mr. Huggins here. And we also have other twerps with top-secret classifications."

Rho glanced at Littleton when he finished. He was pleased to see that she was exhibiting more amusement than alarm at his putdown of a board member.

Cannell's face reddened and he put his hands on the table as though he was about to stand up. *He may be retired, but he thinks he's still in the Corps.* Rho wondered if he'd triggered the drill sergeant that apparently was just beneath the corporate veneer. But he didn't get the chance to find out.

"Merv ...," said Morrison very softly.

"But that DARPA contract in –"

"Merv ...," this time in a steely tone. "Mr. Owens is right. And he's telling us the same thing we've been hearing from Ms. Littleton for the last year. Although she put it more diplomatically than Mr. Ormsby just did. We need to learn to manage – really manage – what we've got. Think of how much of that billion dollars will wind up in your pocket as a Director of the Group."

Cannell sat back in his chair with a glare, an expression that had been a fixture during the Congressional hearings that Rho had referred to. The expression probably worked well on colonels and majors on his Marine Corps staff, but looked merely petulant in Congress and the boardroom. *The Pentagon should provide a finishing school for generals reentering the civilian world,* was the thought that Rho had at the time of the hearings.

Huggins – who had moved to the side of the room during the interchange – started back toward the front, but stopped when Morrison held up a hand and looked directly at Rho with an amused expression.

"Herding cats? Isn't that a little harsh? Especially for a consultant talking to a prospective client?" He emphasized the word "prospective" quite noticeably.

Rho spoke directly to Morrison. "Cats are fiercely independent creatures. And so are a goodly number of the entrepreneurs you've added to the Group. It's been a great strategy for growing but it has run its course. You're too big and complex to continue without – if you will – domesticating some of the cats. You're in 110 countries with 30,000 employees working on a hundred or so major projects. You're operating across every industrial or geographic sector that has large-scale engineering or construction projects. And your "gobbling up" strategy is running out of steam; there's only a handful of possible acquirees left after DaVinci Associates. And global infrastructure spending is going to be a difficult sell in a world where fiscal austerity has become the fad-of-the-month."

Morrison's look of amusement gradually shifted to a more focused look, as though comparing Rho's litany against his own private checklist.

Rho added one more point, looking directly at Morrison.

"You know that we've worked with several of your major customers on major consulting projects – both governments and corporates. If I weren't bound by professional ethics and confidentiality agreements – which I am – I could cite several recent instances where some of your far-flung and decentralized units" – Rho waved at the organization chart still on the screen – "had serious and costly breakdowns in communication and internal controls. You left both money and reputation on the table."

Carlton spoke for the first time. "Our investment bankers –"

"Are overpaid shills. They're telling you what you want to hear, not what you need to know."

Morrison again held up his hand to keep Cannell or Carlton from retaliating. Both men were leaning forward with outraged expressions, their elbows on the table and ready to attack. Morrison sat for ten seconds, watching Rho with a cryptic half-smile. Then he addressed Littleton.

"Marcia. Didn't we just undergo something similar to this? The DOD compliance study by what's-his-name … Donley, Dooley, …? Something like that?"

The simple question changed the atmosphere of the room. Cannell and Carlton became visibly tense, as though the family black sheep had just showed up at the Thanksgiving dinner. Morrison was looking at Littleton with an amiable sort of curiosity, but Rho detected a new intensity in both the question and the look he had fixed on Littleton.

She responded, looking directly at Morrison and obviously choosing her words carefully. "His name is Donnelly. He's a DOD compliance officer looking at supply chain issues between our units with defense contracts and their vendors, not a strategic assessment at all. And he's got a long way to go on the project in any case. This is a totally different sort of undertaking."

Morrison sat back, steepling his fingers and looking through them at Cannell and Carlton. "I think we can forego the rest of Mr. Huggin's presentation. I for one would like to hear what the Owens Group has to say about our operations after they've done their studies. They certainly bring a refreshing degree of candor – irreverence, maybe – to the project. Cats and shills, indeed!"

Rho was not surprised when Cannell and Carlton sat back, visibly displeased and wanting to object, but silent. *So much for consensus decision-making*, he thought. He glanced at Littleton, who almost but not quite winked at him.

Morrison went on. "A couple of conditions. First, I want the project head – I presume that's you, Mr. Huggins -- to report directly and frequently to Mr. Carlton. The focus is more on strategy than it is on finance, so I think that's the proper channel. Is that OK? Marcia? Daniel? Mr. Owens?"

Carlton and Littleton looked at one another as though conferring, a charade that took about five seconds. Littleton said, "Fine with me. I've got lots to do around the IPO stuff." Cannell just nodded.

"The second condition, more of a reminder really, is that any and all findings are to be shared only with this Executive Committee. You'll find that we're more than slightly paranoid about secrecy around here. There can't be any leaks, inside or outside the Company."

Rho responded immediately. "We don't do leaks. Everybody on our team executes confidentiality agreements, and we enforce them. But ..."

He hesitated long enough that Morrison looked inquiringly at him. "Let me suggest one change, however. A minor one. "

Morrison nodded and Rho went on. "We'll report to Mr. Carlton and make sure he signs off on project scope and major initiatives. He's the client. But I want to use the CFO's office for the detailed day-to-day scheduling and access that we'll need – the project coordination and procedural stuff. Her staff can run interference for us better than anyone in the Group, and get us the kind of information that we need."

Morrison thought about it far longer than he should have. This was a common sense and routine procedure. Finally, he sighed, as though committing to something much more significant. "OK. And Marcia, you'll be sure to let

Daniel know if any of what Mr. Owens calls 'procedural stuff' seems to warrant his attention?"

"Of course."

Morrison stood up, which brought everybody in the room to their feet. He shook hands with Rho and Huggins, a firm handshake with his other hand on their shoulder and a warm smile. Rho was reminded that this man was a world-class negotiator and diplomat, among other things. It was those 'other things' that Rho was curious about at the moment, a curiosity that had been growing as he watched and interacted with Morrison during the brief meeting. *He has an agenda, and we've all just been put through our paces. I think Littleton may be worried about the wrong actor!*

Morrison guided them to the door. "Marcia, why don't you settle those details with Mr. Owens and Mr. Huggins right now? I'd like to get started as soon as possible. Daniel and Merv, can you stay for a moment?"

As Rho left the conference room with Littleton, the three Group executives sat back down. To Rho, they were an interesting contrast: Cannell tight-lipped and imperious; Carlton distracted and seeming puzzled; Morrison genial and imposing. *I would really like to be that proverbial fly on the wall for the next few minutes.*

First Impressions

As they left the meeting of the Executive Committee for the Morrison Group, Huggins said, "That was interesting. Remind me not to buy shares when the IPO hits the street."

"What did you think of the cast of characters?" Rho had learned long ago to respect the snap judgments that Huggins made about people. His characterizations often seemed overly harsh because of their objectivity and clarity, but Rho knew that he evaluated people against a standard that included a deep appreciation for human foibles.

"Cannell's a joke; he thinks he's still in the Corps. Carlton's an empty suit, there to impress customers. He'll do whatever he thinks Morrison wants him to do. Morrison, on the other hand, is impressive. The word 'charisma' comes to mind quite readily. But I don't trust him. Not sure why, but I think he reminds me of a general who would squander his troops on what he deemed to be a higher mission. I'd worry about the body count."

"You left out one person."

"Yeah, Littleton." He thought for a bit. "She's a puzzle. I had high expectations from what I already knew about her. The only real takeaway today is that she doesn't fit in very well with the other three. You get the sense that it's three against one. I had the feeling that she was as intrigued by them as we were."

Rho turned to leave, but Huggins stopped him. "One more thing ... a little wacky ..."

Rho was intrigued by Huggins' hesitation. He seemed embarrassed.

"Littleton seemed more interested in you than what happened or didn't happen in the meeting."

He went on before Rho could object. "I was sidelined once you and Morrison started talking to one another, and I watched her. She looked at you the whole time, and it wasn't like she was worried about what you were going to say to screw up the deal. If I didn't know you better, I'd suspect the two of you had something extra-curricular going on. Not my business in any event."

He's right, but for the wrong reasons. We do have something extra-curricular going on, but it's not what he thinks.

"I can promise you that there's nothing going on. We fought most of our first and only meeting. Maybe she's just trying to decide if she's bet on the right horse?"

"Maybe." But Huggins didn't sound as if he meant it. And, in any case, Rho didn't hear it. He was on a new line of thought.

I think I wouldn't mind if we had something going on.

Inside Executive Row

Morrison watched Littleton and the two men leave the room. He stood up, closed the door and returned to his seat. He spoke softly, more to himself than the others, "Our problem is that Ms. Littleton really is very good at her job."

Carlton muttered, "A walking testimonial to affirmative action, if you ask me."

Morrison laughed, quite genuinely. "Daniel, Daniel! You're stuck in a time warp, one that's populated entirely by engineers, all of them old white males. If I made her CEO in your place, the Morrison Group would be worth twice as much. The stock market doesn't have any gender preferences that I know of."

Carlton momentarily looked like a little boy told that he was too small to go on an amusement park ride.

"Can't we just tell her to stay away from the damn defense contracts? Or at least to stop bringing in outsiders with a mandate to ask hard questions?" This from Cannell, who was paging through his copy of Huggins' Powerpoint presentation. He held it up and said, "If they do what they say they want to do, they're going to be hanging out in some neighborhoods that we may not want them in."

Morrison shook his head. "She's going by the book, and so are they. If we start to put part of the company off limits, it would be like setting off a big, bright red flare. She's too smart. It would be like telling your doctor that you really don't need all of those fancy tests in spite of the alarming symptoms. And we can't threaten her ... same result."

Carlton asked, "So, what do we do?" Both he and Cannell looked at Morrison.

"Fight fires, but only if and when they flare up. The hot spot at the moment is the GSI linkage to DaVinci Associates."

Cannell asked, "That's been taken care of, hasn't it?"

"It's true that our overly-inquisitive accountant is no longer with us. And we've gotten control over her files, so there's no paper trail to pick up on."

Carlton went on. "But this compliance officer – Donnelly? – is picking particular vendors at random for audit purposes. If he was to focus on DaVinci's relationship to GSI, or even start to look at the GPR contract … And what if the Owens team picks up something?"

"We watch, Daniel. We watch. You'll know what the Owens people are doing because they'll be reporting to you. And for God's sake, don't try to tell them what to do. If anything, encourage them to dig really deep. That should slow them down some. And tell DaVinci Associates to lay low for the next few weeks. If either Donnelly or Owens gets too close, we'll do some firefighting."

Morrison turned to Cannell. "What do we know about DOD's compliance procedures? What's this guy Donnelly likely to ask for?"

Cannell straightened even more. "A classic good-news, bad-news story. The bad news? If they see a glimmer of a problem, they'll be all over it. Uncovering something like what's going on at GSI or Special Services could make this guy Donnelly's career. The good news? We have a source in their camp. We'll know which vendors they intend to audit a few days before they start. So far, DaVinci hasn't been on his list. Donnelly should be done next week, so we may dodge that bullet entirely. So far, so good."

Morrison nodded. "Let me know if he even mentions DaVinci Associates or the GPR contract. We need to be able to move very quickly if he gets close."

Carlton's uneasiness had ratcheted up appreciably while he was listening to the exchange between the other two men. He spoke up. "We could be fighting lots of fires on short notice. And fire engines attract a lot of attention, even if they put out the fires."

Morrison nodded. "I know. But we only need to stay clear for the next couple of weeks. By then, all the hatches should be battened down."

"I don't like it. And what about our extra smart CFO? She's all over the place and could stumble across any number of our extra-curricular doings?"

"Yes. She does worry me. She may require a more extreme touch."

A Suicide, But …

Rho thought about Littleton's plaintive request: *I want you to tell me that I shouldn't worry.* He figured that would be a good starting point for his own inquiries. And it required nothing more than a phone call.

Two years ago, the Owens firm led a comprehensive management analysis and reorganization of the San Francisco County court system. It was a $500,000 project, but the County cut off the funding halfway through the project without warning when a prima donna city councilman got upset about racial bias in sentencing. Rho's firm completed the project on a *pro bono* basis. As a result, Rho was fast friends with Arnie Rossoti, an ex-cop, ex-ADA and ex-consultant who effectively acted as the chief operating officer for the sprawling system of courts in the County.

Rho acted as an informal mentor to Arnie, in return for Arnie's promise – so far not taken up – of the usual vague sort, *If there's anything I can ever do …* Every time Rho got a parking ticket – which was a frequent occurrence in San Francisco's neighborhoods -- he thought wistfully about calling Arnie, but refrained from doing so. *I'm probably the only guy in the city that actually pays the damn tickets!*

He figured he could finally give Arnie a chance to make good on his offer. He called his cell, a phone that Arnie somehow always managed to answer within five seconds.

"Rho. What's up?"

"The usual flim-flam, me trying to pretend that I know slightly more than the client. How about you?"

"My so-called clients are either judges in black robes or politicians in designer suits. There's not a chance in hell that they could accept the notion that I – or anyone else – knows more than they do. I just try to stay out of their way."

"Sounds bleak. Especially for an Italian ex-homicide cop with alleged gang connections."

"Look who's talking! My so-called connections are merely alleged. Your uncle Sal is a fact, nothing alleged about him!"

"If we're going to insult each other, let's do it over a beer in a semi-dark barroom. And soon. But I'm hoping you can help me with a puzzle."

"I do owe you. I'll do whatever I can as long as I don't have to break a law or buy the beer when we get together. Whatcha need?"

"Information, mostly. About the death of a woman named Marie Lynne Broder, about a week ago."

"Doesn't ring a bell. And I thought I was up on all the recent homicides. Don't tell anyone, but I still have this morbid interest in murder cases. You'd think I would have gotten over that."

"A psychiatrist could probably help you overcome that. But Broder was probably rated as a suicide. Does Homicide get called in when there's an apparent suicide that's at all questionable?"

"Absolutely. You'd be surprised at how many murderers will try their pathetic best to make it look like suicide. We had one where the alleged suicide victim shot himself in the head – six times!"

"Would you see what you can find out about this one?"

"Sure. But, Rho, I've got to ask. Do you know something about this particular death that the cops would like to know about? What's your interest?"

"All I know is that she was stressed at work. And the only reason I'm curious is that we're consulting for her ex-employer who wants me to reassure her that the death had nothing to do with her work."

"OK. But if being stressed at work is a cause for suicide, you need to watch out for falling bodies when you walk down Montgomery Street. Hell, I'm eligible! But it's easy for me to make some calls and find out who was involved and what they concluded. Marie Lynne, right?"

"Thanks Arnie. And it's Marie Lynne, last name Broder. Give me a call and we'll meet over that beer. We'll do a toast to the memory of Ms. Broder."

Arnie called back the following day.

"I found the officer who drew the Broder case. Someone I used to work with, so I got the full story, I think."

"What did he say?"

"She, actually. Lieutenant Abigail Dishman. She called it a 'suicide but' kind of case."

"Homicide cops named Abigail, huh. We've come a long way. What does the 'but' signify?"

"A rough translation would be 'We're calling it suicide, but if the goddam city fathers would give us enough goddam cops to do the goddam job right, we'd look a goddam lot harder.' And that's the cleaned up version."

"What was it that bothered her?"

"Abbie said that the physical evidence was all consistent with suicide. Broder hung herself with a rope that she apparently picked up from a pile of construction stuff in her courtyard. Not very creative, she did it by jumping off her own stepladder. The knots – one where the rope was tied to the beam and the one around her neck – were simple overhand knots, the kind any amateur would come up with. Effective enough.   There were no bruises or evidence of restraints being used. The preliminary toxicology screen was clear; no booze, no mind altering chemicals were at work."

"Witnesses? A note?"

"No witnesses. She was a loner. She'd still be hanging there except the cleaning lady came the next morning. And no note. But most suicides – three out of four, I think -- don't leave one."

"I'm still waiting for the 'but' part …"

"It's all soft, circumstantial stuff. The kind of stuff that cops don't like and that defense attorneys can twist until it sounds like pixie dust.

"First, the psychological profile is all wrong. She wasn't depressed, worried, suffering incurable diseases or displaying any outward signs of a person contemplating suicide. Most of that comes from her associates at the office. They saw her every day and were stunned by the suicide. She was busy and looking forward to some time off.   Her personal calendar had a number of events penciled in for the next couple of weeks."

"As far as they can tell, she had a normal day at the office. Stopped at the corner grocery, bought some fresh fruit – the bag was still sitting on the counter. Went home and hung herself. What kind of person buys five pounds of organic apples and oranges a few minutes before she commits suicide?"

"Then there's the method she used."

"Hanging? Is that an unusual choice for a woman?"

"For women, firearms or poisoning are the preferred choice for about 80% of suicides -- there's a marketing spin for you -- Hanging about 20%. It's not uncommon. But there are two types of 'hangings'..."

"The slow strangulation or the quick drop leading to a broken neck ..."

"Yep. And Broder chose the latter. It takes some planning and calculation to get it right, not to mention high ceilings. And it's relatively rare for a woman to go that route."

"I see what you mean about the soft, circumstantial stuff. I gather that's what bothered Abbie?"

"More than a little. But what really bothered her was the gun."

"What gun? The woman hung herself!"

"Yes, she did. But she had a loaded thirty-eight revolver in her bedside table, inherited from her father. It was registered to her and she'd taken the gun safety/training course before getting the permit."

"Yes. I begin to see Abbie's difficulty."

Arnie said it for him. "Why would Marie Lynne go through all that pain and trouble when a simple twitch of her index finger would have done the job?"

Family History

Robert Harris Owens III did not like his name. None of the three nouns felt comfortable to him and stringing them together made him sound like a law firm. For him, tacking on the Roman numeral III was simultaneously pretentious and – in his mind – misleading, connoting a distinguished lineage and hinting at family wealth.

His freshman college roommate saw his initials and labeled him simply "Rho," and he used that as a surrogate first name ever since. For a short while, he exploited the fact that it was a Greek letter and a mathematical symbol as a conversation starter with sorority types, but dropped that when someone pointed out that Rho was the symbol for "density" in physics.

He thought of his lineage as "the family of only children." His grandfather was an only child as well as an outright scoundrel. He chose the name Robert Harris Owens as part of his reimaging project when he immigrated to America from Australia in 1925. He left Sydney as a very small time and unsuccessful crook– his specialty was housebreaking and mugging – named Clarence Dalman, a descendant of English convicts transported to Australia during the late 19th century. He entered into America, thanks to a venal immigration official in San Francisco, as Robert Harris Owens, declaring himself to be an "import-export broker" with mysterious connections to even more mysterious but highly placed buyers and sellers. He launched his business career by impregnating and marrying the youngest daughter of the head of the Italian mafia family that controlled key ports in Northern California. The Owens business flourished, featuring products that were "diverted" in the course of stevedoring operations.

He died in 1942, just one month before Rho's father, another only child, was born. He was killed when a shipboard crane 'accidently' released its load – a British-made printing press – from directly over his head. Local speculation had it that his gangster father-in-law could stomach his flagrant "skimming" but finally could not overlook the insult to his beloved daughter caused by his frequent extra-marital affairs. In any case, his still-young widow was comforted to learn that a million-dollar life insurance policy had been taken out three weeks before he was killed. She named her son after his father, saying modestly, "It's what he would have wanted."

Rho's father downplayed the pompous name. He became "Bobby" in the family and "Junior" to outsiders. He acted out the Hollywood script for the first-born son of an ill-educated immigrant of dubious descent. He excelled in school all the way through, completing a Harvard Law degree and starting his own firm in San Francisco, specializing in Mergers & Acquisition. Largely through Junior's own example and the inevitable editing that goes with the passage of time, the family's shady history was slowly sanitized, becoming part of the colorful history of early California. The father's misdeeds morphed into examples of bootstrap capitalism.

Junior married a local socialite just long enough to produce Rho, another only son. The name -- Robert Harris Owens III – was one of many contentious subjects. His father understood the burdens of having the same name as an undistinguished father and favored something less patrician, but he was overruled by his then-wife. She argued, "It's what prominent families do."

Rho's parents were divorced the year after he was born and lived the rest of their respective lives as if to demonstrate the wisdom of their separation. His mother divided her time between Paris, Sicily and San Francisco, seeming to view her son as an under-educated travel companion rather than as a child to be nurtured. Rho's lasting impression of her was that of an ambitious governess, a publicly solicitous presence constantly on the lookout for a more upscale family with a more promising, or less demanding, child. She married and discarded another three reasonably eminent husbands before dying at age sixty of cardiac arrest while hiking on Mt. Kilimanjaro. She simultaneously dominated and scandalized the upper crust of local society with her serial romances and views that -- even in San Francisco – were referred to politely as "outspoken," or impolitely as "libertarian bullshit." She bequeathed to Rho several million dollars, access to well-connected relatives, and an exotic heritage. All of these had proven useful to him.

Rho's father never remarried, focusing most of his attention on his law practice and raising his son. He was a quiet, unassuming man. He preferred camping in Yosemite to European Grand Tours, walking to his office rather than calling the limousine, self-parking to valet service. He always over-tipped and never raised his voice. He developed a reputation in the Bay Area business community for absolute integrity and was the "go to" person for the exploding high-tech business community, hungry for introductions to financing and creative relationships. He died of an aneurysm three years ago, as quietly as he lived.

Rho's extended family consisted of exactly one surviving member. His great uncle Sal, youngest brother of his grandmother, continued on as the only remnant of his grandmother's large and raucous Italian-American family. It had a history of mob connections, although recurring gang wars and the ongoing civilizing of Northern California led to its slow gentrification. By the time Rho was off to college, the family's involvement in criminal activities was reduced to almost nothing. However, even today, Rho would hear stories of corrupt politicians, protection rackets, and the occasional mysterious death or disappearance of an acquaintance.

The stories were vague about names and dates and for a long time Rho assumed they were apocryphal, motivated by a need to have a colorful past. But then there was Uncle Sal.

Sal was a diminutive seventy-year-old throwback that lived alone in a Pacific Heights mansion with killer views of the Golden Gate bridge. Rho spent much of his childhood in that house, fascinated with its dark corners and multiple levels. It had an actual elevator and a turntable in the garage, so that Sal's enormous 1962 Cadillac could always launch itself directly onto the street. For Rho, Sal's house was his bat cave. Today, Sal divided his time between chess games in Golden Gate Park, golf at the Olympic Club and evening hours at the Pacific Union Club, usually in an overstuffed chair in one of the gloomier nooks of the "reading room."

Sal seemed to take a special interest in Rho's assimilation into the San Francisco business scene and they would schedule an occasional "keep-in-touch" dinner on their own. Most of their conversation was about old San Francisco, viewed through Sal's prism, heavily laden with obscenities and a total lack of concern for political correctness. To Rho, he was a charming old fogey from a romantic past, the last of a kind.

Then, one evening, Rho got a call from Sal.

"Hey kid! I hear you have a problem with Cardozo in the Planning Department. Bunch of stupid assholes!"

Rho wondered how Sal knew about that. Cardozo had slapped a "Stop Work" order on a construction project that was part of a remodel of Rho's offices. The project was fully permitted by half-a-dozen city agencies, but Rho suspected that one of the City Council members had complained to Cardozo because Rho had hired an out-of-town contractor to oversee the work.

"Not really a problem, Sal. They just get nervous about making decisions when there's more than one possibility. They'll come around eventually."

"Eventually can be a long time when you're my age. I know you think it's old fashioned, but I have some ways to speed up the process. If you like, I'll be glad to help. You know... Make them an offer they can't refuse?"

Sal's use of the famous Marlon Brando line from 'The Godfather' triggered a long-dormant memory of Rho's grandmother telling him stories about Uncle Sal's rough-and-tumble early days organizing dockworker's unions on the California coastline. The memory amused him and made him brash.

"Something involving envelopes with unmarked bills, or baseball bats and kneecaps, maybe?"

Sal was silent for a long time and Rho wondered if he had offended the old man. He was surprised by the absolute seriousness of the response, as though Rho's suggestions deserved serious consideration.

"Let's give them a chance to do the right thing first. I'll give the Commissioner a call. If he doesn't see the light, there are other ways to get their attention."

Rho wasn't sure if it was Sal's flat intonation, or the inflection he put on the words "other ways," or perhaps just an overactive imagination carried over from his grandmother's stories, but suddenly his image of Uncle Sal changed from a scrawny old man lacking both past and future into something much more menacing, an offendable gnome capable of viciousness after the sun went down.

Two days later, Cardozo, the infuriating petty bureaucrat who was blocking Rho's construction project, simply lifted the "Stop Work" order and signed off on the entire project. That same day, Rho saw Sal walking on California Street near the Fairmont. When he honked and waved at him, Sal waved back, smiled and then simulated a baseball swing, at an imaginary ball at about knee level.

The Assassin

Zachariah Kovacs was an emotional void. He did not experience anger, fear, hate, love, irritability, impatience, anxiety, loneliness, patriotism, exhilaration, loyalty, or envy. Not one of the countless forces that washed through the lives of ordinary people, leading to aberrations ranging from the merely eccentric to total dementia. He was supremely rational and, at the same time, morally insane. In terms of temperament and personality, he was the ideal assassin.

Born of psychopathic Hungarian parents in Chicago, he spent his childhood in a series of increasingly harsh foster homes, leaving in his wake a series of social workers rethinking what they had been taught about abnormal psychology and the innocence of youth. He joined the Army at age sixteen and spent the next five years in Viet Nam practicing how to kill people. He was dishonorably discharged when he posed for a New York Times photographer wearing a necklace of Viet Cong ears and an expression of utter disinterest.

He spent the next three decades as a free-lance mercenary, operating in Africa, Southeast Asia, Central America and – finally – central Europe as the country once called Yugoslavia broke up into vicious, warring factions. He became known for his ability to hunt down and kill designated targets, both civilian and military. This skill was in demand on both sides of the regional conflicts that drew him. He sometimes worked for the insurgents and sometimes for the government-in-power; but, whichever side he was on, he was a shadowy, unofficial agent – thoroughly "deniable" if he was exposed.

Outwardly, Kovacs was unremarkable in all but one respect. He looked like any other sixty-three-year-old tradesman bored by his job. He was of average height and weight, clean-shaven with thinning hair, with better posture and more scars than most males of his age. He dressed drably, in off-the-rack black and grey garments that obscured his outline and made him hard to see on a dark rainy night. If asked for a quick one-word impression, most casual observers would say "harmless."

His only distinguishing features were his eyes. They stood out; large, so dark as to seem almost black; more prominent because they were set closely together under thin, almost invisible eyebrows. They were empty of expression, cold, conveying no information whatsoever about thoughts or feelings. They did not change if he smiled or frowned, as if what he was seeing was irrelevant to what he was thinking or planning. They signaled nothing particularly human.

His eyes were memorable, therefore a handicap in a profession where anonymity was vital. So he hid them behind sunglasses and tended to look away from whomever he was talking to, down at his feet or across the room, making him seem shy or diffident to the occasional person he interacted with, emphasizing his apparent harmlessness. However, when he thought it was important to be taken seriously, he would stare directly, unblinking, and you would be acutely aware that the person before you was special, someone that did not live by the same social or moral codes as most people.

Kovacs was tired. The shrapnel from Vietnam, lodged near his spinal cord; the bad knee from an interrogation in

Kosovo; the two missing toes, courtesy of "friendly fire" in Afghanistan; it was as if all of them had found a voice and were chanting in unison: "You're too old for this." He was thinking more and more about retirement, somewhere far from any active war zone. He had about three hundred thousand Euros spread around in bank accounts in Europe and could always supplement his income with an occasional well-paying assignment.

His one vanity was that he believed that he could not be impressed, that he had seen every variety of human possibility, both good and bad.

Then he met Walter Morrison.

At the time, Kovacs was working for Viktor Volkov, a Russian oligarch and one of the more rapacious ex-KGB officials that magically wound up controlling a significant part of Russia's natural resources after the collapse of the Soviet system. He employed an entire stable of thugs and used them frequently. But he liked to use foreign contractors for particular assignments, usually the more complex cases. Kovacs had worked for Volkov once before, a straightforward assignment to eliminate two rivals bidding for the state assets being auctioned. Volkov was pleased by the results.

Kovacs did not like Volkov. He was a peasant, elevated by animal-like cunning and sheer luck to his present condition. He underestimated his enemies and had no subtlety. However, he paid well and Kovacs was content to listen to his rants while waiting for him to miscalculate.

His present tantrum was one that Kovacs had heard before. The Russian was proposing a unilateral modification of a joint venture contract with a Western mining consortium, a change that would transfer twenty percent of the assets and profits from the Westerners to Volkov without any compensation. The Western group objected and had sent a five-man delegation of executives to Moscow to assert their rights under what they referred to as "the rule of law." Walter Morrison led the delegation.

Volkov had a different view. "Americans! They wave their contract and talk loudly about their 'rule of law'! In Moscow! They know nothing about power ... which we shall teach them!"

Kovacs thought of many responses, none of which would make the slightest impression on the man. He merely asked, "What do you want me to do?"

"Kill one of them. You know Americans better than I do; you pick the one of the five that is best to get our message across."

"Are you sure you want to do this? These are important people ... connected people ... and not just in London and New York." *He still hasn't realized that the world has changed; that there are easier ways to get what you want than by killing people.*

"Just do it! And make it look like a mugging gone wrong. Everybody that matters will get the message but we can blame it on the street thugs."

The delegation was staying at the Ritz-Carlton, in the Tverskoy District of Moscow. The meetings were scheduled in an ornate conference room at the same hotel, for each of the next five days. Kovacs did some elementary research using newspaper archives and the internet. He quickly ruled out three of the five delegates. Two of them were minor functionaries whose death would not cause much notice and another one was a high-ranking State Department official whose death would demand a detailed inquiry with excessive political fallout. That left Morrison, who was the primary negotiator within the Western consortium, and one other, an English barrister named Townsend who was managing the legal arguments during the meetings.

The oligarch used his KGB connections to arrange for a fake ID. Kovacs reserved a room at the Ritz Carlton as Alex Mathers, a Canadian journalist. The first day, Kovacs checked out the surroundings and observed the delegation as they entered and left the conference room. Neither Morrison nor Townsend left the hotel, cycling between the meeting, the restaurant and their rooms. Neither had any visitors as far as Kovacs could tell. Given the short time frame, he decided to act at the first opportunity. It came on the second day.

Morrison and Townsend left the meeting together and stood waiting at the lobby elevator bank. Kovacs got in first and stood in the corner behind the two men, but he was certain that both of them had noticed him. That meant a surviving witness. He decided on a variation that would facilitate Volkov's scheme and amuse him as well. The two men got off at the same floor, still deep in conversation, and walked together down the ornate hallway. Kovacs followed and when Morrison opened his door about halfway down the hall, Kovacs moved quickly. He shoved Morrison forcibly into the room and showed Townsend the gun to convince him to follow Morrison. Once all three of them were in the foyer, he closed the door behind them.

Kovacs was using the silenced version of the Makharov handgun. It was an impressive all-black, elongated and deadly looking instrument. Both men stared at it and then at Kovacs. What they saw – or didn't see – in his eyes was even more frightening than the Makharov.

He watched them closely, waiting for a sign. He must kill one of them, but which one?

They were clearly different from one another. Townsend was exhibiting the expected behaviors, the alternating of outrage and fear, the frantic eyes casting about for help that wasn't there. Kovacs had seen it many times. Morrison, however, was calm, looking at Kovacs as though he was a slightly distraught job applicant to be mollified.

Kovacs thought, *He's the dangerous one to leave alive. He'll be able to describe the assailant, right down to the gravy stains on my necktie ...*"

This was confirmed immediately. Morrison asked, almost conversationally, "What do you want?"

"I have to kill one of you. Nothing personal. Just a form of extended negotiations when in Moscow." Kovacs spoke as though he was commenting on the unusually warm Russian weather.

As he spoke, the Makharov's silencer traced a lazy arc traversing the two men standing close together. Townsend's eyes were locked onto the gun, part of his look of growing horror mixed with puzzlement as Kovacs' words began to sink in. On the other hand, Morrison just nodded thoughtfully.

"I'll give you one hundred thousand dollars if you shoot *him*," said Morrison, inclining his head to indicate Townsend.

Kovacs smiled, partly because he was pleased to find that he could still be surprised. And partly because of Townsend's expression, gaping at Morrison, still trying to comprehend what he had heard. He closed and opened his mouth again and again, searching for a response that would restore the urbane world that he was used to. Instinctively and predictably, he settled for outrage, drawing himself up and starting to say. "Morrison! What are you –"

Morrison interrupted, speaking to Townsend with a barely detectible note of exasperation, as though to a subordinate who was slow to catch on. "It's simple, Townsend. One of us is about to be shot. I prefer that it be you."

Kovacs watched the exchange and then looked inquiringly at Townsend, wondering if he would realize the utter seriousness of Morrison's offer and attempt to outbid him, but somehow knowing that he would be disappointed. Townsend would be the righteous Englishman to the end.

When Townsend continued to splutter and look around for some magical escape, Kovacs raised his arm, putting the tip of the Makharov silencer about three inches from the bridge of Townsend's long nose, and fired one shot. The man fell with his head resting on Morrison's left foot.

Kovacs turned to Morrison, bending his arm to rest the pistol on his shoulder, the muzzle pointing up at the ceiling.

"You owe me one-hundred-thousand dollars. How do you propose to pay me?"

Morrison was looking down at Townsend, marveling at the small hole in his head and the large pool of blood already forming. He gently pulled his foot from under Townsend's head. Without looking up, he said distractedly, "However you like. I presume you'll want cash. I'll need a day or so to gather it up."

"Do that. Get the cash and keep it handy. I'll pick it up from you, probably back in the states within the next week or so."

Morrison had still more surprises for Kovacs. When Kovacs turned to leave, Morrison said, "Actually. I'm looking forward to seeing you again. I'd like to talk to you about doing some work for me."

Kovacs thought about it. Instead of a direct answer, he extended his arm and gently laid the muzzle of the gun against Morrison's left cheek and said, "Some of my clients don't like the non-cancellable clause in my standard contract. They look for a way out. Especially if they can save a hundred-thousand dollars."

Morrison raised his arm very slowly and very gently pushed Kovacs' gun to the side, away from his face, saying, "I'll wait five minutes and then call for help in a very distraught voice. I'll tell the Moscow Police that we were mugged by an overweight and tall man in a black leather jacket who spoke very poor English with a heavy Russian accent. A Chechen, I think. Poor Townsend was shot when he tried to resist. The mugger ran away without taking anything."

Kovacs nodded. He removed the silencer and put it and the pistol back into the gaudy tourist bag with the Canadian maple leaf on its side. He looked around to make sure he hadn't touched anything and turned to leave.

"One more thing," Morrison said. "Please don't tell Volkov about our conversation."

When Kovacs asked tonelessly, "Who's Volkov?," Morrison just smiled.

Two days later, while sitting in the First Class Lounge for British Air at Heathrow, Kovacs came across an article in the Financial Times reporting on the mining consortium's negotiations in Moscow. All parties had agreed that the original contract terms were quite clear and could not be changed lightly. "The rule of law" was a frequently used phrase. The Western consortium team was returning home earlier than planned due to the tragic death of Arnold Townsend, a random victim of the street crime infesting the new Moscow. In the last paragraph, it was noted that Viktor Volkov was being investigated for crimes against the state, probably tax related. It was rumored that Putin himself had initiated the inquiry.

Zachariah Kovacs found himself looking forward to his next meeting with Walter Morrison.

A Quiet Patriot

Walter Morrison was many things, but first and foremost, he was a patriot. Not the common sort, the overloud kind who mistook bigotry for patriotism and held America up as the shining example of enlightened governance. Morrison simply felt that America was the last and best chance for a world spinning out of control.

He was a product of his time, tempered by his education and experience. He believed passionately in the rightness of American dominance, the specialness of its culture and values, its self-assigned role as the defender of democracy and personal freedom. Inevitably, he was a Republican and a devout capitalist. He believed in competitive markets, free enterprise, free trade, globalization, and – perhaps most importantly – a limited but activist government based on values, a necessary condition for allowing the whole collective ecosystem to sustain itself.

He had not read the Ayn Rand books, but he would have admired the fictional John Galt. Given his choice, America would be run as an aristocracy rather than a democracy. And he dedicated himself to achieving that end, albeit covertly.

He was realistic about the limitations of the American form of capitalism. He respected the creative power of self-interest, but feared its corrosive effects in the absence of countervailing forces. He knew about corruption, arrogance, self-dealing, egotism, cruelty, indifference; all of the moral hazards of unchecked power. And he understood the other side of the coin: the futility and occasional peril of unfocused charity.

He accepted that his world-view would require his country to occasionally act as a bully, but only and always for the greater good.

He was not an outspoken advocate for his value system, leaving that to shrill talk-show hosts and the omnipresent candidates for higher office with their one-dimensional views and simpleminded solutions. He despaired at the way that opinions substituted for analysis and that the validity of an opinion was measured by the fervor of the speaker. At dinner parties, he limited himself to asking questions rather than making declarative statements. He might ask "Who better than America?" or "What economic system would you choose in place of capitalism?" when some particularly outspoken and insistent critic emerged. Such tactics rarely worked, however. Patriotism and moderation seemed to have become incompatible species.

He was also a superb entrepreneur, in many ways a caricature of the Texas oilman. Beginning as a wildcatter in East Texas, he built the Morrison Group into one of the best-known engineering design and consulting firms in the world through a "rollup" of similar firms wherever he found them. Their current list of contracts included design, engineering and construction for multi-billion infrastructure projects on all seven continents, including highways, airports, refineries, ports and telecommunication networks in all stages in completion. Much of their business was for defense purposes and highly classified. It was the largest privately held firm in its industry, although the coming IPO would take away that distinction while making him a billionaire several times over.

Morrison's quiet but passionate patriotism and his global business platform made him into a highly effective unofficial diplomat, particularly in the cauldron of Middle Eastern politics. He served on several corporate boards and would occasionally act as a minister-without-portfolio for the administration, both Republicans and Democrats. He had been a key part of the back-channels that negotiated hostage releases, disarmament deals, and various cease-fire arrangements in several dirty little wars around the world.

It was true that the Morrison Group was usually a beneficiary of his political ventures. But that was inevitable given how deeply they were imbedded in all phases of development. The Group made money in the run-up to the invasion of Iraq and Afghanistan as ports and airports had to be made ready. Then they made money again in the reconstruction of the infrastructure facilities that were destroyed due to the invasion. Leftist groups in the U.S. and conspiracy theorists around the world saw sinister plots at work, and Walter Morrison was often cast as a "Daddy Warbucks" prototype. But the truth was simpler: Morrison was simply a patriot, a true believer in the rightness of America.

He was one of those rare individuals that pop up every few generations: an enlightened capitalist with a commitment to public service; the businessman-statesman that can serve as an ambassador on demand, capable of working across borders and cultures without losing sight of the bigger picture.

It helped that he looked the part. He was tall, with broad shoulders and salt-and-pepper hair that was just unruly enough to suggest a boyishness that appealed to women. He was in his mid-sixties, but still athletic-looking and with a ready smile. His appeal spanned the social and cultural spectrum in a way that politicians envied. Twenty years ago, a gossip columnist for the New York Times described him as "the only Texan who had ever been accepted by San Francisco society." He fitted in equally well at the opening night gala for the San Francisco Opera and in the middle of a construction zone in hard-hat and coveralls.

He was neither introspective nor religious. When he thought about it these days, he viewed his own life as an arc with three discontinuities; points in time where his life's trajectory was radically altered, diverted into a new and unpredicted channel by external events, like an express train being shunted onto a previously unknown track.

The first shock was twenty years ago, a direct result of the first Iraq war, the one he thought of as "the good war," a killing ground justified by Saddam Hussein's naked aggression and horrendous miscalculations. At first, everything about it reinforced his pride in the US. It became a war-fighting clinic put on by the U.S. military. Its only flaw, in Morrison's view, was that the coalition forces did not finish the job, but left Saddam in place.

There were only one-hundred and forty-eight U.S. military casualties. But his only son was one of them, a second lieutenant with the Marines, whose Humvee ran over a mine. Two months after that, his wife of thirty-five years died, mostly from grief. The losses and his subsequent solitude changed him, leaching away much of his idealism and leaving a suppressed bitterness in its place. Friends dropped away, and he worked to fill the time, rather than with any greater purpose in mind.

He slowly morphed from being a rational optimist into a fatalistic pessimist, still fretful about the decline of America.

Like many of his contemporaries, his dissatisfaction led to his exploration of ways to use his wealth and influence to change the course of events.

The shift in perspective required him to become a criminal.

If asked, Morrison would have said that his criminal acts were designed to achieve a more efficient allocation of resources or to achieve a greater good. And it is true that he did not personally benefit to any great extent, although those 'reallocated resources' were dedicated to those causes that he deemed just.

At first, he violated the laws that he deemed to be either stupid or irrelevant, like a late-night motorist turning left on a red arrow when there was no traffic in sight. His first crimes were relatively victimless, corporate in nature and in defiance of distant and faceless enforcers – federal or supranational authorities who were easy to disdain and elude. He traded on inside information, funded junkets for DOD procurement officers; classified political contributions as tax-deductible marketing expenses; created shell corporations to move large amounts of money around the world without calling attention to the recipient.

Not surprisingly, his criminality focused on energy policy and the Middle East, seeking ways to maximize American influence and facilitate democracy in the region.

He did not keep score. But to his certain knowledge, his relatively benign criminality in those early days diverted millions of dollars to gray-area projects that would have failed otherwise. He knew of discrete acts that could not have happened without his assistance: the assassination of a dictator, an arms deal that kept a rebellion alive, a disinformation campaign in an ex-communist state, and the opening of a new oil field to compete with OPEC.

Perhaps he would have been satisfied to play that role out, that of a behind-the-scenes benevolent uncle to extralegal fringe organizations whose mission was to preserve and extend the American way. But then the second shock occurred.

September 11, 2001 and its aftermath changed him – and the character of patriotism -- forever.

Morrison watched with fascination as a dramatic act of terrorism galvanized the U.S. into lashing out in all directions like a petulant Greek god spewing moral outrage and pursuing a "war on terror," setting forces into motion that would radically alter the world order in future decades. For Walter, "Nine-Eleven" clarified America's moral responsibilities and weaknesses and made abundantly clear who her real enemies were. It jarred the nation into finally being realistic about the decline of American power and dependence on Middle East nobodies because of their damnable oil.

It was obvious to Morrison that the Middle East was irrevocably altered by the U.S. response, although it would take decades before the outcome would reveal itself. It was chaos theory on a grand scale. He shifted his influence efforts to supporting clandestine and extra-legal efforts to achieve limited but well-defined outcomes, to sustain the momentum created by 9/11.

Now, ten years after the attack on the World Trade Center, he was dismayed to watch as the U.S. was clearly losing its stomach for the hard choices, reverting to complacency and acceptance of a declining role in world affairs. A fatal softness was settling in. He began to speculate on ways to restart and sustain the moral outrage.

He considered running for the Senate or seeking a cabinet post in the new administration. He toyed briefly with funding a think tank or foundation to push for new approaches in foreign policy. However, both his instincts and the formal feasibility studies that he commissioned left him skeptical of conventional approaches. He had spent too much of his life lamenting the behavior of lobbyists and politicians to seek to become one.

Then the third and last discontinuity appeared without any warning. It was just ten months ago, a fulcrum in time when the brainstorming became active planning. It marked a tipping point, where he became the Western equivalent of a fanatical imam crouched in a cave in Northern Pakistan.

Five years ago, his annual physical at the Mayo Clinic detected the onset of CLL – chronic lymphocytic leukemia. He was assured it was manageable, that his life expectancy shouldn't change. Then, ten months ago, he got the call from his oncologist after his annual examination. Dr. Weber was the world's best, according to Morrison's own research. He remembered Weber's terse announcement, "The leukemia has morphed into a new and highly virulent form. It's deadly."

Walter's time horizon shrank to twelve months. Given such news, most men would review and rethink their so-called 'bucket list.' And Walter did. He made a plan for his end-game; a simple four-point "to do" list.

The first three items were classic strategies, as useful for growing a large-scale criminal enterprise as for General Foods launching a new cereal product. First, leverage the substantial expertise and global reach of the Morrison Group. Second, identify and enlist a small group of likeminded and powerful allies. Third, bequeath enough money to the right groups to sustain – without him – the transformation of the Middle East.

His fourth and last initiative was not taught in business schools and did not have a corporate equivalent. Not surprising, given that it was inspired by a small group of fanatics armed with mere box cutters who demonstrated the power of unleashed moral outrage. But it was the culmination of the other three parts of the grand strategy, the element that would jumpstart a new world.

Create a cataclysmic incident.

His recognition that this might require the killing of thousands of innocents did not lessen his resolve. Rather it enabled the next stage of his criminality, a quantum jump from genteel white collar crime from far behind the lines to massive personal violence once removed, like Bruce Wayne transforming himself from a timid daytime philanthropist into the sinister nighttime Batman.

Another Cocktail Party

Walter Morrison was attending his forty-seventh cocktail party in the last six months.

The glitterati -- that's how he thought of them – were all here, their smiles in place, their tag lines carefully rehearsed. Each of them carried a checklist in his head – who they had to get close to and the message that had to be sent. The targets were coded as "primary" or "secondary," the former being the high-value-but-hard-to-get-at movers and shakers. A congressperson was automatically a primary, as was a high-level regulator such as the head of enforcement for the SEC that had just entered the room.

The so-called "secondaries" were the nice-to-have-but-not-essential fillers, to be used as placeholders while stalking the primaries, or as concession prizes for those who never made contact with a high value target, like a bomber pilot trying to find a place to drop left-over ordnance on the way home from a mission.

An overhead camera would show it clearly, he thought; like an x-ray examination using injected dyes. The primaries would be stationary points spread throughout the room, approximately equidistant from one another, each circled by a slowly rotating band of petitioners. The seekers would resemble a tidal current moving continuously through the room, slowing and forming human eddies at each cluster to seek entry. A successful encounter would be easily detected, marked by any pair walking at speed, cutting across the current in a straight line, to the periphery of the room, signaling their intention to talk without being overheard or interrupted.

One could write a pattern-recognition algorithm … program a video camera … to measure the success of a Washington cocktail party. Or, even better, to see who's susceptible to influence. Social espionage … the latest way to get the edge.

The thought caused him to wonder if any of the various clandestine services already had such a device. The Deputy Director of the FBI stood just ten feet away talking with the New York Times bureau chief and he thought briefly about asking him his opinion of the idea. *Limited to domestic surveillance only, of course!*

He accepted that he was a "primary" within this taxonomic system. This was both an objective and an accurate assessment. Arrogance was not in his nature. But he recalled his phone call from Dr. Weber and thought, *Not primary for very long though. I am the ultimate version of the 'lame duck' politician.*

As if to confirm his present status, two of the more remarkable people at the cocktail party approached him. To any observer, the convergence of the three of them would seem a perfectly casual encounter, a momentary and completely natural pause in the flow of dark-suited and distinguished men around the crowded room.

Avraham Mosel – 'Avi' to his friends -- was a small, trim man who looked exactly like what he was, a high-ranking diplomat. All of his features -- the erect posture, elegant clothing, salt-and-pepper hair and, above all, his regulated speech -- reminded his friends of a certain age of David Niven, sans mustache.

"Walter. Always a pleasure. But, tell me, last time we talked, you were very concerned about one of your companies. A leak, I believe. I hope you've solved the problem."

"Hello, Avi. Good to see you again. And yes; the problem is fixed. I found some outside expertise, exactly the right specialty. The problem no longer exists... quite literally."

Farley Purcell, the third person in the momentary group, was the opposite of Avi. He was large in every respect, an inverted triangle of a man who stood out in the crowd, even without the dress blue uniform of a three-star general in the U.S Army.

"Good evening Avi. And Walter. I'm glad to hear your problem has been solved. I wish that the rest of our institutions worked as smoothly in solving problems."

Avi sounded amused. "Surely you're not referring to the American military."

"Actually, I'm not. I was thinking of our legislature and their incessant pettifoggery."

Walter smiled, but without any real warmth. "A great word, Farley, and it certainly fits well. But shouldn't you – a senior military office in our civilian controlled defense infrastructure – be more careful about using such disrespectful language. Remember what happened to MacArthur."

"A rare patriot. He should have been president."

Walter and Avi looked at one another with identical and pained expressions, a non-verbal exchange that was ended by an extremely thin woman in a bright red dress who fastened both hands onto Avi's forearm and – smiling insincerely at the other two – pulled him away and back into the general swirl of people.

Purcell watched him go, with a quite transparent expression of distaste. "I wish we were not forced to deal with such people."

Walter wondered which 'people' he was referring to as represented by Avi – Jews, diplomats, Israelis, foreigners or civilians. He suspected that Farley would be opposed about equally to each of the categories. *Time to rethink the composition of our little group. The good general lacks the nuance required to carry this off.*

Glancing around to insure he could not be overheard, he looked directly at Purcell and said, "He wants the same things we do, just for different reasons. You need to keep the objective in mind rather than worry about the pedigrees of your associates. Wasn't it your beloved MacArthur who said, 'It is fatal to enter a war without the will to win it'?"

Purcell started to respond, but Walter was already headed for the Deputy Director of the FBI. He really did want to ask him about the use of algorithms for domestic surveillance.

Strategy 101

It took months for Walter to build his coalition of likeminded change agents in the U.S. He did not keep a list but he personally knew every one of the dozen-or-so members. If he had drawn an organization chart – which he didn't – it would resemble a spider web. The organization had no name and its members were not even aware of their membership, but they all subscribed to the same set of core values, centered on using covert American power to shape the Middle East. Like Walter, they would not be embarrassed if labeled 'a patriot.'

He had identified them over the course of his business and diplomatic dealings. Some worked for the U.S. government – a member of Congress, senior civil servants at Defense and State, a few retired military officers, and a pair of CIA veterans. Civilian members included business executives, a couple of university professors specializing in Middle Eastern geopolitics, and a leading expert on terrorism. Walter's main regret was that this extraordinary group of individuals – they were all men – must remain hidden, not only from each other but from the public that they served.

They paid dues to Walter's hidden organization in the form of information and services. The kind of information that was not publicly available; about emerging State Department policies, insurgency-fighting capabilities, shifting tribal loyalties in Afghanistan or Pakistan, overstated oil reserves in certain regions. The services were "personal favors," the kind of gestures that powerful friends can make for a friend pursuing a good cause: intervention in a regulatory hearing, a file erased here and there, a job offer for a "friend" of Walter's.

The men were realists as well as patriots, which is not often the case. Their views had been formed through experience and disappointment. Their advice and cynicism immediately altered his thinking and gave shape to his strategy in two major respects.

Early in his search, while having dinner with a Middle East expert who became one of his recruits, the discussion focused on the proposed U.S. withdrawal from Afghanistan. Walter asked, "How many innocent Afghan civilians will have to die before we get serious about taking real military action against the Taliban?"

His dinner companion smiled the most cynical smile Walter had ever seen and said, "You're *almost* asking the right question. The real question is how many *American* civilians will have to die?"

Perhaps it was at that point that Walter began to think of himself as a terrorist. To his credit, he recognized the hypocrisy of his thinking. If he was going to kill thousands of innocent Arabs, he was a patriot. If it was thousands of Americans, he was a terrorist.

He decided not to worry about the distinction.

The second shift in his planning came from another dinnertime conversation, this time with a group of retired military officers, one of whom was a two-star general. Walter was a passive observer, listening as they compared notes from the several "war games" exercises they had participated in centered around a hypothetical Middle Eastern crisis scenario. The clear consensus was that "game" was the right descriptor.

"It's all bullshit!" The two-star exploded. "We're eight-thousand miles away, begging Tajiks, Kurds, Bahraini's and fuck-all others to *please, please* let us fly our goddam expensive airplanes over their god-forsaken desert so that we can fire a million dollar missile to hit a target that is either gone or the wrong one! Then we train their soldiers and police, so that they can kill us before we leave out of sheer fucking disgust!"

A week later, Walter scheduled another dinner with the general and reminded him of what he had said. "It's an old problem in logistics, isn't it? The war's over there; our troops are here. What's your solution?"

The general looked at him for a long five seconds. "It's simple. Get your friends to help."

"Our friends? The Brits? Europeans?"

The general was derisive. "Their military forces are obsolete, unmotivated and a long way off. And even worse, their governments are pussies. They'll authorize a hospital ship or two, maybe a 'peacekeeping mission,' and then insist on a joint command to make sure nothing actually happens!"

The general leaned back in his chair, clearly about to give a lecture. Walter recalled that he had earned a Ph.D. from Princeton, specializing in Middle Eastern politics.

"Name all the countries in the world that fit all of the following six criteria. No exceptions."

He counted them off, a finger at a time. "They are physically close to the Middle East conflict zone. They are secular democracies. They have a strong military capability. They are severely threatened by Islamic fundamentalism. They have a lot of anti-terrorism experience. And they like America. "

Walter smiled. "Israel." After a brief pause, he added, "And Turkey."

The next morning, Walter instructed his Administrative Assistant to arrange an extensive Middle East itinerary for him. The official purpose of the trip would be to visit as many of the Morrison Group's local subsidiaries, vendors and customers in Israel and Turkey as could be scheduled. He also gave her a handwritten list of nine government officials in Israel and six in Turkey that he had worked with on diplomatic ventures in the last few years and asked her to check on their availability.

It was not until he settled into his first class seat on El Al that he acknowledged the implausibility of his mission. *How does one recruit a traitor? Distinguish between treason and patriotism in cultures and languages that I do not understand? Sell terrorism as enlightened public policy? Demonstrate that I am not insane?*

I do not know the answers to any of these questions ... but I know the place to start looking for the answers.

The Second Conspirator

It was not surprising that Avraham Mosel and Walter Morrison became friends and co-conspirators. Much of their affinity was personal, as they were alike in so many ways. Each had started in poverty and worked his way to enough wealth that he could do as he pleased. Like Walter, Avi's wealth came from building things. He had founded and subsequently sold what was now the largest commercial construction company in Israel. They were both trained as engineers and they shared a preference for theories, data and analysis over intuition or hunches.

Each of them lost his only son in a questionable war so one-sided that a casualty was viewed as more of a statistical anomaly than a personal tragedy. They did not talk about their grief, but sensed in one another the same void. In the last ten years, each of them moved with ease into diplomacy on behalf of their respective countries, although Walter was "unofficial" contrasted with Avi's ambassadorial posting to three different European countries up until his retirement.

But these biographical overlaps were much less important to their relationship than were the strong views they shared about right and wrong in the cauldron called "the Middle East." Those views almost always clashed with the actions of their respective governments, which were becoming increasingly dysfunctional, marked by polarization along the classic liberal/conservative fault lines and exaggerated by a very strong fundamental religious minority that exercised political power far beyond their numbers. Decisions were made very slowly and even then reflected a crazy-quilt pattern of compromise that made them palatable to a bare majority but worse than useless for coherent policy.

For Avi and Walter, it was an easy migration from shared political dismay to their joint realization that doing nothing was intolerable. They agreed that it was far better to be condemned as a well-intentioned traitor than to go quietly along on the wrong course.

Avi's network of highly placed friends and covert activists in the Israeli government and intelligence services was the equivalent of Walter's U.S. coterie of advisors and informants. Even better, his diplomatic experience enabled him to access likeminded leaders in other Middle Eastern locales.

Like most Israelis, Avi held a mixed bag of opinions about Americans in general. He admired them for their optimism and straightforwardness; envied them their wealth and relative freedom from care; respected them for their power while scorning them for the hesitant way they exercised it; feared them because of Israel's dependence on them; and, finally, liked them.

However, he viewed his opinions as a luxury, fully aware that – for good or ill – the Americans would determine the course of history in the Middle East for the next couple of decades whether he liked them or not. In one of their early meetings, he suggested as much to Morrison, who began shaking his head before Avi finished talking.

"Much too strong, Avi. Nobody – Israeli, American, Arab, or anybody else – can control what is going on. You've got a bunch of children playing with matches inside a fireworks factory, while so-called responsible adults are standing around debating the merits of alternative parenting models."

Avi smiled gently, in the manner of someone who had thought about the question in advance. "We could take away some of the matches."

When Walter just looked at him, Avi continued, "For example, deprive Iran of its nuclear capability?"

Walter scoffed. "Neither of our governments has the guts to do that! There's no leadership. And none can emerge given the current political ecosystem. Policy is reactive, a series of knee-jerk responses to stimuli!"

"If you're right – and I think you are – then whoever provides the stimuli shapes policy."

Avi leaned forward and spoke very quietly. "On depriving Iranians of nuclear warheads, for example ... Suppose I said that I know a small group of people that is intending to do just that. All they need is enough money."

Later, Avi came to realize that their criminal relationship really began when Walter responded instantly, "Exactly how much money do they need?"

From that meeting several years ago, the relationship between Walter and Avi quickly became a close working partnership, tacit in all respects but with clearly agreed upon goals and protocols. The division of labor was a natural one. As a wealthy American heading a global firm with a significant scientific capability, Walter was responsible for financing and materials. Avi, with his familiarity with Middle Eastern politics and players, coordinated and monitored the distribution of funds. They collaborated fully on strategy and intelligence, each of them serving as the linkage to their respective cabals in their countries. Avi created an Israeli corporation -- TACA – to serve as a conduit for those funds and Walter began diverting his wealth and the resources of the Morrison Group toward underground Israeli and other Middle Eastern interests that were aligned with their clandestine mission.

Walter was amused by the parallels between what they had created and what his Fortune 500 cronies were talking about at their golf outings. *Avi and I have created a classic application of modern organizational theory; an entirely virtual organization with goal alignment from top to bottom. With the additional advantage that most of the members are unaware of the existence of the organization itself.*

All of that was before Dr. Weber's call and the shortening of Walter's time horizons.

The critical moment had come at a dinner meeting, this time in Beirut. Thinking back on that meeting, Walter realized that they had danced around the issue repeatedly, but always backed away from any explicit acknowledgement of the real purpose.

It's time. The clock is running down. He thought of a country-western song from his Texas days, with a lyric about a cowboy at the bar. *It's closing time and you haven't got a date yet.*

The inane thought made him smile and Avi picked up on it. "That's a rueful smile if I ever saw one, Walter."

"Did you formally propose to your wife, Avi? I mean, was there ever a moment when you were in a state of terror as to whether the answer to a question was 'yes' or 'no'?"

"Rachel never in her lifetime answered a question with a simple yes or no. She would have made an ideal Rabbi in that respect."

He considered Walter closely. "What is it that's bothering you, Walter? I'm sorry that I seem to have the power to worry you so much about what I might think."

Walter took a deep breath, and then said in a rush, "I'm thinking of staging a major terrorist incident and I'm wondering if you'd like to participate."

That was easy. I said it. Clear evidence of psychopathic and delusional thinking.

Avi's reply was instantaneous and so casual that Walter stared closely at him, wondering if Avi had heard what he had actually said. Avi stared back at him with the same polite expression of interest and asked, "What's the objective? Of your so-called major terrorist incident?"

They must teach that in ambassador training school ... to respond to raving madmen as though being asked the time of day.

"I want the U.S. government ... No, I want the American people -- to get outraged enough at the Middle Eastern mess to use our highly touted 'policeman of the world' status to actually do something about it."

Avi waved dismissively, but the intensity of his gaze did not change. "It's been done. As I recall, almost three-thousand Americans died on September 11, 2001; which led to the start of the Afghan and Iraq wars and, some say, subsequent 'Arab Spring' revolutions in Egypt, Libya, Syria, Yemen and other Arab states."

Avi's expression did not change during his recitation of historical events. Walter had the feeling that he was the one being auditioned for a key role, not the other way around. *All this time and all these words ... to get to this point!* He took another deep breath.

"Actually, that's my working model ... the destruction of the World Trade towers."

He watched Avi closely as he recited the simple words. Even to him, they sounded horrific, a monstrous confession. But Avi's expression merely shifted from polite to thoughtful.

Walter went on quickly. "But it lacked sustainability. The outrage dissipated. Too much was left to chance. So I have two improvements I want to add."

Avi raised both eyebrows.

"We've got to broaden the base. We've proved the Americans can't do it alone. We've got to enlist our likeminded friends in the Middle East – that's Turkey and Israel, by the way -- and work in a concerted way. And we've got to dedicate real resources – money, planning – to covert operations after the incident. To make sure the effort continues in the right directions instead of fragmenting and dissipating."

As he listened to himself, Walter realized that this was the first time he had talked openly of his vision. He had just given his 'elevator speech' on how to upset the world order. *I've said enough in the last two minutes to warrant a trial in The Hague.*

And he's still listening.

Avi shook his head, "Speaking as an Israeli – and, I think, channeling my Turkish colleagues -- eing sympathetic is one thing; sending troops another thing. The attack on the World Trade Center and your death toll earned you massive worldwide sympathy, but your so-called friends in the Middle East still did not go to war with you."

"I know. But they will next time."

"What will be different?" Avi asked the question as if he already knew the answer.

"Because I'll kill Jews and Turks as well as Americans."

The two men sat looking at one another for a full minute. Avi was the first to speak. "Just for the sake of argument … I think it will be hard to do. Security is off-the-scale in all three countries. Car bombs are easy, but they kill a couple of dozen random bystanders. Your plan requires scale. Or assassinations. Unless you have one of those suitcase nukes?"

Avi's last question had a curious inflection, as though he was hoping for a positive response.

"No nukes. No nasty microbes. No rogue satellite lasers. No doomsday machines. Let's just say for now that I have sleeper agents already in place; agents with massive destructive powers."

"Walter, why are you telling me these things?"

"Because I need … I want … you to help me."

Avi nodded slowly. The conspiracy was now two-thirds complete.

Their immediate problem was to find their third partner, the Turkish arm of their unholy triumvirate. Turkey was the working model for their future Middle East – a secular democracy with a large Muslim population, Eurocentric and western-leaning, an economy not dependent on energy. More importantly, it fielded a large and professional military and its present government was positioning the country to play a leadership role as U.S. influence faded.

However, the problems were serious. The ruling party was Islamic, although publicly committed to secularism. The relationship with Israel, although historically a very strong one, was at the moment contentious. The Turkish opinion leaders – business, military, political – were experiencing a serious approach-avoidance conflict over joining the

European Union. And then there was the continuing struggle with the fifteen percent of the population that was Kurdish. A small but vicious war was still being waged with the PKK in Eastern Turkey and was threatening to spill over into the newly independent province of Kurdistan within Iraq.

Avi was clearly troubled by the prospect of bringing in a Turkish partner. "Two worries: First, the agendas are really murky. In America and Israel, if you call someone a "patriot," you pretty well know what you're dealing with. In Turkey, everyone is a so-called "patriot," but that doesn't tell you much about their real feelings on Islam, secularism, the Kurds or Israel's right to existence."

"What's your second worry?"

"We will be really dependent on our Turkish ally, whoever he is. You and I? We can blow things up, kill quite a lot of selected people in designated locations all at the same time. That's your cataclysmic event. But once that happens, the blame must fall on the right people. For that, we need someone who has connections with extreme Islamic groups, the jihadists; someone who can leave a trail to their door."

Walter added, "Or someone who can convince them that they should claim credit for it, even though they had nothing to do with it. They may be sufficiently fanatical to believe that they can use the outrage for their own purposes … to ride the tiger, as it were."

And what if they're right? What if we slaughter our own citizens and all it does is to further the causes of our worst enemies? A question that I shall not think about, I think.

Walter added, "Even then, we need to provide a plausible chain of evidence, a lot of what the press calls 'smoking guns,' at the very least."

What a strange world we live in, where people are eager to claim credit for mass killings. Where confessions lack credibility, so that terrorists need to be able to prove that they are the ones!

Two weeks later, Avi called Walter late at night. "I have our third partner, I think."

"Excellent. Tell me about him."

"I can't. That's his absolute condition for participating."

Walter's first reaction to the words was a pervasive sadness. *So much for co-conspirators!* He realized that he had unconsciously begun to believe in 'honor among thieves' as he and Avi had worked together. His second reaction was harder to characterize; a premonition, perhaps, that an unraveling had begun; one that would eventually doom them and their quixotic venture.

He shook the thoughts off and simply asked, "What can you tell me?"

"The good news: He's like us. He wants what we want. And he's willing to get there in the nasty way we propose to get there. And he's connected to the right people, on both sides of the fence – generals, politicians, jihadists."

"And the bad news?"

"How do you Americans put it? He's from the other side of the tracks. He's not a particularly respectable individual. There's a very strong streak of paranoia, particularly if he's dealing with foreigners. At the moment, this translates into his demand for anonymity. Effectively, we would deal with him by cell phone and – maybe – an occasional meeting."

"Can it work?"

There was a long hesitation. "If you trust me to speak for both of us."

The Turk

The Turk liked to describe himself as "a simple man." And it is true that he affected a style of dress and vocabulary such that he could easily be taken to be an ordinary laborer on the docks at Kusadasi; or a low-level administrative functionary in the halls of government in Ankara; or an ex-NCO in the Turkish army; or a chemistry teacher in a Kurdish madras. In fact, he had been all of those, and more.

His physiology even reinforced the first impression of peasant heritage. He was a large, barrel-like figure with a silhouette suggestive of a Bulgarian weightlifting champion. Most men felt small next to him and he liked to get quite close to whoever he was talking to, as though using his bulk to give added weight to his words.

Although he was rich, he did not seem so. He lived modestly in a small house when he was at home. His wife and children did not have any obviously expensive habits and they tended to be a reclusive family, staying to themselves. Even when he was the public head of a major company in Istanbul, he drove himself to and from the office in an entry-level Mercedes. He was on a first-name basis with those of his employees that he saw frequently. He attended every game of his beloved Black Eagles, the Besiktas soccer team; and was among the loudest in the bedlam that was a Turkish football stadium.

To label him "simple" was in many ways a default choice for observers. He shared nothing about himself with others, believing – probably correctly – that uncertainty was his friend, given the circles that he moved within. The multiple layers of his existence were subterranean and invisible, displayed selectively to an audience of his choosing.

However, the image of simplicity that he liked to convey was illusory. He could trace his family back several hundred years and his ancestors included both petty criminals and sultans; and he was pleased that his blood contained trace elements of both. His father had served on the staff of Ataturk and two of his uncles currently were high-ranking officers in the Turkish military. As though to maintain some kind of cultural balance, another uncle and two of his brothers were legbreakers in the Turkish underworld.

If you asked his closest associates to describe his behavior (something you would not presume to ask), and they did (which they would not dare to do), they would start and end with stories of his legendary changeableness, his sudden whiplash reversals in emotion that would leave observers wondering what had just happened. They would tell of the time he shot a dog that would not stop barking, and then carried it in his arms to the veterinarian to treat the wound; or when Mahmet asked for his permission to marry his niece and he beat the man senseless before hugging him tearfully and agreeing to the marriage. If they had been there to see it (which they weren't), they would tell of the time he slit the throats of Ehud's Kurdish wife and three daughters while Ehud watched, and then gave him one-thousand acres to grow poppies.

Indeed, the Turk was a man of considerable complexity.

A Billionaire on Paper

Littleton really is very good. If things were different ...

Morrison grimaced at his own incomplete thought. *Things are not different; they are what they are.* Somebody's epigram popped into his mind: "You must give up hope for a wonderful past."

He was a passive participant in a meeting in the Group's boardroom, watching Marcia Littleton lead five investment bankers exactly where she wanted them to go. The issues on the table were about the timing and pricing of the IPO. *And they think the ideas are all theirs*, Morrison marveled. *And for that, they get a fee of almost a hundred million dollars.*

Listening to Littleton describing the company he had built, Morrison felt pangs of something; not quite regret, more like nostalgia, a remembrance of simpler times. He had singlehandedly built the Morrison Group from scratch into a recognized leader in its field by being smarter and meaner than those that he competed against and eventually acquired. Once at that pinnacle, he became bored and began his double life. On the surface, he devoted most of his time to public service, to bringing influence to bear in visible ways. In reality and in the dark, he was executing his own agenda for a new American model for the Middle East.

Early in his corporate life, he aspired to be the world's youngest billionaire and selling the Group would be his means to that end. However, it quickly became apparent to him that the Morrison Group could be a clandestine vehicle for real change as long as he maintained control. So, despite the urging of his friends and advisors, the Group remained private. To ensure his control, he deliberately recruited mediocrities as managers at the corporate level, while the subsidiaries and the projects were staffed with the best engineers he could find. But the good managers stayed in the field, far from headquarters. He made Carlton a figurehead CEO with day-to-day responsibility and an outrageous salary to look the other way when Morrison used the business for his extracurricular activities. The Group was his personal weapon in a private war.

But then his timelines changed, bringing new priorities. He needed a critical mass, and he needed it quickly. He could not control the human and physical resources of the Morrison Group from beyond the grave; nor could he hand it off to anyone that he could trust to use it appropriately. *It must be monetized. Converted into the most powerful of all change agents: Cash!"*

Two years ago, when he thought he had decades to go, his rough bookkeeping indicated that he was spending a hundred million dollars or so each year furthering his private geopolitical goals while creating minimal risk for the reputation of the Morrison Group. He calculated that he had doubled that amount simply by sharing some of the classified research findings in GSI with some key allies. The impact was a twofold win. He generated more cash and helped those allies with similar goals. The danger to the Group would ratchet up, but could be controlled and – in any case – deferred until it no longer mattered to Walter Morrison.

This shift changed both the quality and the quantity of his criminal activities. Arguably, he was engaged in terrorism, espionage and treason. The contracts *were* classified and *did* involve technologies that could shift the balance of power in unstable regions. He was the cause of the deaths of individuals that he knew, murder once removed. He was aiding and abetting known gang members in several different countries, some of who trafficked in arms, drugs and flesh.

However, his beloved market economy offered a much greater one-time opportunity. As a private entity, the Group had a net worth of just under a billion dollars and Walter owned 98% of it. However, if offered to the public, it was estimated to be worth about five billion dollars. An IPO would leave Walter with most of that amount, all to be dedicated to his subversive agenda.

But in order for an IPO to happen, he needed to professionalize the corporate echelon, and quickly. The SEC's listing standards made it quite clear that the Group was going to need a significant makeover. The irony was exquisite. He needed Marcia Littleton. He brought her in to make the transaction happen. Now, she was the primary threat. *We're OK ... if she doesn't get too curious about the extracurricular stuff before the IPO. After that, it doesn't matter; the money will be scattered all over the globe.*

"How does that sound to you, Walter?"

He became aware of an expectant silence that had settled over the group. Snapping out of his reverie, he saw Littleton and the bankers looking at him curiously.

"I'm sorry. I was thinking of something else. What is it you asked?"

The lead banker – a highly groomed stereotype in a pinstripe suit and power tie – cleared his throat and started again. "So Walter, Ms. Littleton and all of us agree. We recommend pricing at $120 per share and we should be ready to go on May first. You personally should clear about $5.2 billion in a few hours. If that meets with your approval, of course?"

A Call to the Middle East

Walter stayed in his place as Littleton and the bankers left the room, thinking about the accelerating timetable. A slight frown became apparent. He took a cell phone from his pocket and pressed a single key.

A very large man with a dark complexion answered the call on his special cell phone. He was at the moment in a limousine stalled in extremely dense traffic near the middle of Cairo. When he saw the caller ID on his screen, he leaned forward and pushed the button to raise the glass partition between him and the driver.

"Yes?" The accent was pronounced. And there was a two-second delay because of the intricate scrambling protocols built into the phones.

"We may need to speed up a little bit. Will that be a problem?"

"No. Assuming you can deliver what you promised, I expect to have the product in place and ready to launch well ahead of our present target date. But is there a problem?"

The hesitation was very slight. "We have some final testing to do, but we're 98% done on this end. There are some, shall we say, personnel issues that must be dealt with."

"Do you need some help? Imported talent?"

"No, but thank you for the offer."

"Anything else?"

There was a lengthy pause, sufficient to cause the dark man in the limousine to wonder about its cause.

Walter resumed with the same assured tone. "I am confident that we can do this. I have personally directed every aspect of the preparation. The world will be enraged and will be seeking an outlet for that rage. But ..."

The man waited, knowing what was coming, but wondering how Morrison would try to shape it.

"I apologize for my words. But the rage is only half of what we need. It must be channeled. And I have only your assurance that it will be directed in the proper direction, focused on the right people."

The man was amused and briefly wondered how many men he had butchered for expressing the slightest doubts about the value of his promises.

He responded calmly enough. "I repeat. I will provide four individuals with impeccable – and traceable – jihadi credentials. The three in the Middle East will position themselves as close to their assigned site as possible without arousing suspicion. Each of them will be carrying the highly specialized electronic devices that you are so confident about and will activate them at precisely the same time. Our fourth operator – the one in your country -- will perform his part on the same timetable. Immediately after the ... incident ... they will be found dead, surrounded by bits and pieces of evidence that will tie them quite clearly to Islamic fundamentalist movements and known terrorist groups. Someone claiming to be an al Qaeda leader will call Al Jazeera and claim responsibility for all of the incidents."

"And they – these four individuals – they will know nothing about why they're doing this?"

"No. They are motivated by fear, greed and religion. A very powerful combination of forces, in my experience."

"If I were a defense attorney looking for holes in your story, I would say that it sounds too pat."

The dark man scoffed, "The rage of defense attorneys means nothing." Then his tone changed to one of quiet reason. "But think how a prime minister or one of your Texas congressmen will react when CNN provides close-ups of body parts and our wonderful internet blossoms with all of the details of another al Qaeda plot."

There was a long silence. Each of the men was aware that what was said next would be important.

Walter started. "I apologize for my questions. Avi has assured me of your competence, but I am cursed with this need to know the details ... and the people."

"You do not need to apologize. In my world, one lives or dies because of details ... and people. And Avraham has told me much about you."

Walter took a deep breath. "I would like to meet you."

The man in the limo looked out at the chaotic street scene, thinking about loyalty and a son in San Francisco that admired the man, even though he was American, rich and an infidel.

He said, "Yes. I think it's time that we meet."

"Are you able to come to San Francisco on short notice?"

"Yes."

"I'll be in touch. Stay well."

"Insha'Allah."

Ends and Means

Marcia was beyond bored. *I hate this part* was the refrain that ran on a continuous loop in her consciousness, even as she smiled her way through her assigned role. For the evening, she was cast as part saleswoman, part financial guru, co-starring with Walter Morrison in a private room at the Ritz-Carlton in Manhattan. *Still better than the bad early days, where I was trotted around the room as the token woman executive.*

It was the end of a very long and tedious day. *Another thirty minutes and I can get back to my room and slog through two hundred emails.* She was amused to realize that even that prospect was more appealing than the meet-and-greet bit that she was engaged in at the moment. *God! Terminal introversion has set in! No wonder I can't get a date.*

The so-called "road show" was a carefully choreographed series of presentations to investors and analysts, a corporate blitzkrieg designed to create exposure for the upcoming IPO. The CFO of the company was usually a fixture at such events, but Marcia had very carefully groomed her assistant Ben Creed and given him the title of VP of Investor Relations so that she could skip most of them.

She couldn't avoid this one. Walter Morrison had called her very early this morning.

"Marcia, I need you to be in New York by the cocktail hour for the Morgan/Chase hosted analysts meeting. I've got the Gulfstream headed your way now. I know you don't like these events, but there are some specially important people in this audience that will feel put down if we put Ben Creed in front of them rather than you."

She hesitated, mentally reviewing and rearranging her schedule for the day. She knew that she had no choice, partly because the Chairman was asking, but also because she felt guilty about delegating what is a traditional role of the CFO.

Her hesitation enabled Walter to show his diplomatic side.

"Please. It would be a personal favor for me. I really would appreciate it."

She made it to the meeting room barely in time for the presentation and took a major role in the Q & A that is a staple of these affairs. Now, almost an hour into a cocktail hour with the thirty or so guests, she had yet to identify anyone that cared very much about whether the CFO or her number two showed up. She made a mental note to ask Walter who it was that needed her particular attention.

She was trying to edge away from the two hedge fund types that were far more interested in getting her into bed than they were in the Morrison Group IPO. She had begun to plot her escape from the room when Morrison came to her rescue. He winked at her as he insinuated himself between her and the two men, nudging them away and talking with great animation about the demand for new issues. *That was gallant of him. He must feel guilty about dragging me to New York.*

She was almost to the door when she was approached by a distinguished looking man, about sixty, casually dressed in blazer and slacks. For some reason that she could not isolate, he didn't seem to fit with the crowd. *A major money guy? Investment bank? Hedge fund, maybe. But I know all the major faces. Not him.*

"Ms. Littleton. It is my pleasure to meet you. I am a long time admirer."

She held out her hand. "Thank you, Mr. ...?"

"My name is Avraham.   But 'Avi" is both easier and friendlier."

"Indeed. And whom are you representing?"

"A number of investors, mostly foreign. But they have two things in common."

Marcia glanced at the door, but her companion clearly wanted to tell her something. She sighed inwardly, hoping that her fixed smile and direct eye contact would mask her desire to be out of there.

"The first is that they control ungodly amounts of money and are quite anxious to find opportunities such as the Morrison Group IPO presents." He spoke as though referring to a group of in-laws that had overstayed their welcome.

Not the usual money manager at all. Or he's hoping that cuteness will get his foot in the door. She was dismayed when her reply came out much harsher than she intended. "I think that's true for everybody in this room. What's the other feature they have in common?"

"They believe – they believe very strongly – in American exceptionalism."

For the first time, Marcia looked closely at the man she was talking to. *Good looking. No ... actually quite handsome, almost movie-star caliber. Deadly serious, but covering it up with that little self-deprecating smile.   A very slight accent, maybe middle European. Really good tailor. And for whatever reason, he wants me to hear what he has to say, and I don't think it has much to do with IPO opportunities.*

"Mr. ... Avi... The oldest and best piece of advice I ever got about talking to strangers at cocktails parties was –"

He interrupted and finished her sentence, "Never, but never, mention religion or politics." Then he added, with that same ambiguous smile, "Good advice ... for mediocre people unsure of who they are or what they want."

Neatly done. If I decline to pursue the line of conversation, I reveal myself to be a morally vacant and insecure person. OK, let's see where this goes.

She smiled, but only to emphasize the deliberate coldness of her tone. "Whatever American exceptionalism is or isn't -- and the concept itself is certainly exceptionally ambiguous -- I think it clearly blends the two taboos – both religion and politics – making it a double no-no for discussion."

Avi's cryptic smile clarified itself into an expression of delight. "Ms. Littleton. You have just elevated my opinion of the American CFO by several notches."

He moved a half-step closer and said, "A very elegant and sophisticated epigram ... that reveals absolutely nothing whatsoever about your personal views as to the underlying subject."

He paused and when he spoke again, both his voice and his expression were different, much more serious. "The individuals that I represent believe that America is the last and best hope for our interconnected future, that we need to enable – to free -- your institutions to do what they do best."

Her retort was immediate. "But that's precisely what our market does. Money seeks its highest and best use. Your investment fund, for example, can be a most effective enabler by channeling resources to those causes you favor, American or otherwise."

He responded immediately and with passion. "But it's limited. Hedged about with rules and regulations that are irrelevant or – what's worse – counterproductive. Enforced by bureaucrats with checklists rather than an overarching strategy. My colleagues and I want to use our financial resources to create leverage ... to do the right thing the right way, to use a homespun phrase."

"Funny. The phrase that comes to my mind as I'm listening to you is, 'Does the end justify the means?'"

"And how would you answer that question yourself?" The intensity with which he asked made quite clear to Marcia that this was not a casual conversation; that this man really wanted to know her views on ancient moral and ethical questions.

She paused long enough to signal that her reply was not a casual one. "I am a situational relativist. I believe 'right' or 'wrong' is determined by context; that absolutes are neither useful nor trustworthy. This makes me very distasteful to fanatics, but a great conversationalist at cocktail parties."

She went on before he could speak again. "And you, Avi? Will you use your substantial means, financial or otherwise, to do what you deem to be the right thing the right way, regardless of the consequences?"

"Ms. Littleton, I think -- "

"That's a little vague of me." She interrupted, her voice raised. "Let me put it this way. If you become a major investor in the Morrison Group, will you use your Board influence to violate the spirit of the rules while observing the letter of the rules? In pursuit of your particular revealed truth, of course."

Listening to herself, she wondered what had triggered her sudden aggressiveness. Avi was looking simultaneously thoughtful and offended. *This is why my daddy warned me not to talk about religion or politics at cocktail parties.* Without being aware of it, she and Avi were standing toe-to-toe with their shoulders braced, within a few inches of one another. Marcia was surprised at how quickly she had become so publicly passionate about abstract ideas.

He provoked me. Quite deliberately. Why?

She realized that she wanted to hear his response to her challenge. But something had changed in the atmosphere around them. She suddenly realized that the crowd had thinned out in the room. Morrison and a group of four or five guests were the only ones left in the room with them. He was clearly disengaged from whatever his guests were talking about and it was clear to Marcia that he was watching her and Avi intently. Perhaps because their voices had risen in volume.

The moment passed, each of them suddenly aware of the space around them and their sudden prominence within it. As she watched, Avi began to fade back into the urbane and distinguished gentleman she had originally encountered just a short time ago. The smile again became ironic and his posture more relaxed. She stepped back and held out her hand. He took it and held on.

"Ms. Littleton. You are a formidable debater. I look forward to another opportunity. I wish you well. I am glad I had the chance to convey my belief that the Morrison Group is a prime example of the American exceptionalism that you find so ambiguous."

For one brief moment, she had the distinct impression that he was about to bow and kiss her extended hand. But he simply turned away toward the small group by the window. Marcia walked out of the room, feeling Morrison's eyes on her the whole way.

As she left, Avi and Morrison met in the center of the room. Morrison looked at Avi inquiringly.

"Not a chance," Avi said, shaking his head.

"I thought not. But it was worth a try."

"Walter. You're right about her. She's smart, and highly principled, even if I don't much like those particular principles. That – and her access to what we're doing – make her quite dangerous."

Morrison smiled sadly. "I know. It's quite ironic. The longer I know her, the better she looks, the more admirable she becomes ... and all it does is shorten her life expectancy."

Contract Negotiations

Zacharias Kovacs met Walter Morrison for the second time, in Morrison's suite at the Drake Hotel in downtown Chicago. Morrison had a few minutes before he was to make his appearance as the keynote speaker at a conference on "Global Energy Prospects" in the hotel ballroom. He answered the door immediately when Kovacs knocked.

"Mr. Kovacs. Nice to see you again. We seem to always meet in hotel rooms."

Kovacs was startled. This was not a good beginning. Part of it was that Morrison displayed no surprise or uneasiness to find an assassin standing in his doorway. The other jarring fact was that he greeted him as 'Mr. Kovacs.' As far as he knew, no one knew his real name. *Nobody still alive, anyway. I think maybe this meeting may have a slightly different ending than either of us had envisioned.*

Morrison picked up on the slight frown and guessed correctly as to its cause. "I did some deep research on you after our meeting in Moscow. You have a very impressive resume. Entirely an oral history, of course. You could qualify as an urban myth in today's culture."

When Kovacs frown deepened, he added, "No need to worry. I have much more to lose than you do if our relationship is exposed to public view."

Kovacs' expression remained stony. "My business model does not contemplate *any* losses, regardless of their magnitude relative to my employers."

"Yes, I know. But there are three factors that you need to include in the calculations you're making at the moment."

Kovacs' uneasiness ratcheted up another notch. *He didn't have to disclose that he knew my name. He's threatening me quite deliberately. And he's not the foolhardy sort.* Although he would not admit it, even to himself, Kovacs was bothered by Morrison. If he knew his reputation, he should be a little nervous, maybe even fearful. Morrison was neither; he seemed indifferent to what Kovacs might think or do.

Morrison went on, "First – and please forgive the cliché – I've arranged for your identity to be disclosed to various police agencies if I should die an untimely death or if anonymous accusations start showing up. Second, and by far your strongest assurance of my silence, is my need to maintain my public image. If it became known that I consort with assassins, I would lose everything I care about. Finally, you would miss out on more of this."

He handed him a small black canvas book bag. Kovacs opened the Velcro strap to see that it was filled with U.S. currency.

"The $100,000 I owe you. Unmarked, non-sequential bills. And I can offer you a means of tripling it if you're interested."

"And if I decline?"

"For me? I find another vendor, although surely one inferior to you. For you? You walk away to wherever you want to. I have no hurt feelings. But why would you do that?"

Kovacs stared at Morrison for a long ten seconds. Then he shrugged and said, "Tell me what you have in mind."

Death of an Auditor

The first phone call had come from a mousy underpaid administrative assistant at the Pentagon. She received one thousand dollars in cash every Friday afternoon, slipped into her apartment mailbox in an ordinary white envelope. That amount, combined with her intense dislike of her boss, was sufficient to overcome the twinges of uneasiness that crept into her consciousness. All she had to do was to call a certain number if a particular contract was scheduled for DOD audit in the next round.

Five weeks had gone by, five white envelopes. No phone calls required. But now she had to make the call. She dialed the number very slowly, as if her reluctance somehow mitigated the sense of guilt that she could not quite suppress.

"Yes?" The voice had no inflection whatsoever.

"This is –"

"Never mind that. I know who you are. Why are you calling?"

"The GPR contract has been scheduled for review – an on-site visit – next week, beginning on Monday."

"Donnelly?"

"Yes."

The line went dead. *What have I done?* The question made her look around furtively, as though the act of making a phone call was somehow suspicious. Then she thought of her arrogant boss and the lousy pay. *I'm going to miss those white envelopes on Friday afternoon!*

The second phone call followed immediately. The man set aside the cell phone that he had just answered and picked up another one. He dialed with a single touch of a button and was answered immediately.

"Yes?"

"Consider the contract to be active."

"What level of urgency?"

"Before the start of work on Monday."

Both parties hung up simultaneously.

At the other end of the call, Kovacs frowned and began sorting through alternatives. He had followed his target intermittently for a week, looking for habits and opportunities that could lead to an unremarkable death, assuming that the client could make up his mind. No good solution had presented itself.

David Donnelly was unaware of being followed. After a week of watching, Kovacs suspected that he was completely oblivious to other people or his immediate surroundings. He did not know if it was because Donnelly was an American living in a gated community in Marin County who had never encountered a threat, or if it was his sedentary occupation that conditioned him to a spectacular unawareness of his external world.

Donnelly was apparently some kind of a process-oriented consultant. He seemed to spend most of his time either generating or contemplating complex, multi-colored flow charts or in interminable meetings with likeminded professionals. He worked sixteen hours a day, ate in fast food restaurants, and had no visible friends or non-work relationships. He was one of the most colorless people that Kovacs had ever encountered.

Time was running out. The client had specified, "Leave him alone unless I give a definite go signal." Once activated, the mandate was to, "terminate as soon as possible." But the new schedule ruled out the two or three highly imperfect "accidental" scenarios that he had concocted. This would have to be one of those *ad hoc* ventures, the kind Kovacs didn't like. But he'd taken the job on those terms. Three hundred thousand dollars compensated for a lot of job-level stress.

Kovacs picked him up in the semidarkness of early Monday morning as Donnelly left his home, following him to a multi-story parking ramp in South San Francisco. Kovacs drove past the entrance and parked in the lot of a convenience store across the street. He quickly walked toward a side entrance to the ramp. He noted with interest the homeless guy sleeping on the grass just outside the concrete wall of the parking ramp, half-covered by a blue tarp and with his heaped grocery cart and an empty bottle in plain sight. Kovacs picked up and put on the tattered overcoat lying on top of the grocery cart as he entered the three-story concrete parking ramp. He smiled, visualizing the coming series of events. *Like improv theatre, except we don't want an audience.*

Once inside and in the shadow of one of the supporting pillars, he stopped and watched as Donnelly spread out one of his flow charts on the hood of his car and spent a couple of minutes tracing lines with his index figure, as though reassuring himself of what was there. He watched as Donnelly pinned the chart to the hood by carefully placing his index finger on a particular point, while using his free hand to laboriously fish out his cell phone from an inside pocket and start dialing.

Kovacs was a hundred feet away, but Donnelly's behaviors clearly indicated that he was about to communicate something of interest to somebody else. *I don't know what you've found or whom you're talking to. But I'm willing to bet that my client might appreciate a termination of that particular call.* He scanned the area but saw only one other person walking directly away from them and about sixty yards away. *This is as good as it's going to get.*

Donnelly had the cell phone pinned between his ear and his shoulder, keeping his hands free to roll up his charts and put them in the briefcase open on the car roof. Kovacs did not move away from the pillar until the other person had entered the stairwell and was out of sight. He approached Donnelly quickly, the pistol held in the pocket of the vagrant's smelly overcoat. The weapon was a ridiculously unreliable "Saturday Night Special" he had bought near Union Square from a fifteen-year old-Latino gang member for fifty dollars.

Donnelly was unaware of Kovacs until he was only twenty feet away and even then, his glance revealed no interest or curiosity. *The incredible arrogance of Americans! They cannot conceive of the idea that someone might wish them harm!* Kovacs fired five times as rapidly as he could from about ten feet away, placing his shots very precisely. The first shot was in the thigh, the second in the stomach, the third carefully placed in the heart. The last two shots were high and right, hitting only the concrete support column well to the side of Donnelly. He hated to look like a rank amateur, but the improv scenario called for it.

The noise of the shots was somewhat confined by the surrounding concrete, but he moved as quickly as he could. He checked to make sure there was no pulse, took Donnelly's watch, wallet and briefcase, ignoring the five spent shell casings at his feet. He walked quickly to the side exit and then along the wall to where the vagrant was sleeping. He placed the gun next to him on the blue tarp and threw the overcoat, wallet and watch on the ground next to the sleeping man. The briefcase was upturned next to him, but Kovacs scooped up the flow charts that Donnelly had been scanning and took them with him. He stepped back and looked at the tableau, trying to see it through the eyes of an LAPD street cop.

Finally, he prodded the sleeping man with his foot. As soon as he began to stir, Kovacs quickly walked away, diagonally across the street and a half-block away. He used the telephone outside the convenience store to call 911 to report a shooting "by some guy with a beard, wearing a dark overcoat." He gave the location and hung up. He retrieved his car and drove around the block to a position where he could see the scene. He was pleased to see the vagrant sitting up and holding the gun and looking in the wallet. When the sirens got close, he drove away.

Smoking Guns

His phone rang, the caller ID indicating that it was Huggins.

"Hey Rob. How's it going?"

"More interesting than last week. Thanks to the Morrison assignment."

"That sounds ominous. I thought it was your vanilla strategic analysis slash reengineering contract. The kind where you tell the client what they already know and then send a large bill."

"So young, and yet so cynical! But in this case maybe justified. I asked Velma to sit in on the team looking at the General Accounting systems and structures. I think you should listen to what she's come across. Can you come to the conference room?"

"Velma, huh? Why doesn't that surprise me? I'll be right there."

He thought about Velma on the way to the first floor conference room. *The walking counterexample to The Corporate Human Relations Handbook!*

There is a conventional script for building a corporate career. First, do well in a good college, preferably majoring in economics, engineering or one of the more applied offshoots of the so-called 'liberal arts.' Then get an entry-level job or an internship with a prestigious consulting or Wall Street firm. Work for a few years and then enroll in one of the top three or four MBA programs in the country. Do well in that program and you're launched, one of the elite that will be fast-tracked in whatever firm they join, whether it's on Wall Street or Main Street. Equally important, in the course of executing that plan, you will have built a network of influential and well-placed peers, a club that will look out for its members as they rise in their various organizations.

Oh, and it helps considerably if you're physically attractive. One study of (male) MBA's from one of the top MBA programs in the U.S. found that the single most important predictor of post-graduation success was how tall you were!

Velma Scranton violated almost every one of these conditions. First, she was a female. She was short, with a stocky build that her indifferent wardrobe accented rather than disguised. She seemed to own more sneakers than high heels. Her features were ordinary, unremarkable in part because she wore no makeup and combed her hair infrequently. She graduated from a small Midwestern college with a major in International Studies and she had little or no interest in taking two years off for a graduate program that – as she put it – *would try to teach me a lot of stuff that I already know or would never use.* She rode a motorcycle to and from work, giving rise to rumors about her sexual orientation. As far as anyone knew, she had no friends and scoffed at the idea of "networking" as a way to get ahead.

About the only thing going for her was her almost psychic sense for finding patterns in complex data arrays. Or, even better, anomalies in those patterns. Rho likened her to a superhuman music critic that could detect a micro-second delay in a single quarter-note imbedded in a symphony played by an eighty-piece orchestra. Her closest parallel was

Mr. Spock, the half Vulcan-half human logician from the Star Trek series. The big difference was that she was real.

She was the firm's point person on fraud investigations. Her data sense matched up nicely with her belief that corporations were riddled with self-interested materialists that would find ways to exploit their insider status by fiddling the numbers for their own benefit. It was depressing to Rho that she seemed to be right more often than not. *Either she's really good, or most of our clients are crooks!*

"Hi Rob. Velma. I take it that you've once more found some malfeasance in the world of commerce?"

Velma spoke first. "Smoking guns is as far as I would go at the moment. But I'll bet next year's raise that DaVinci Associates is not what it seems."

"As I recall, we gave you next year's raise two years ago. In any case, you and I both know that you're not motivated by money. Let's hear the evidence."

Velma opened her laptop and Rho realized that she was about to launch a presentation.

"Whoa! First, tell me about DaVinci Associates. All I know is what Littleton told me when we negotiated the contract."

Velma closed the laptop, sat back in the high-backed leather chair and spoke very quickly, using a monotone that left Rho with the distinct impression that she thought he should have come to the meeting better prepared.

"A highly successful and exotic company, in existence for five years, based in South San Francisco. Their specialty is materials testing. They do a lot of failure analysis, stress testing; generally concerned with the applications of new types of materials for conventional buildings and infrastructure projects. 'Lighter but stronger' is their corporate motto. They've got a whole bunch of patents on new technologies. One of them is a scanner hooked up to a backpack that can predict if a cantilever bridge will fall down anytime soon; that sort of thing."

"Who's their customer? How do they make money?"

"Any of the design/engineering firms engaged in designing or managing the construction of large infrastructure projects views them as essential to a cost-efficient completion. The Morrison Group has been about 10% of their revenues, according to the Wall Street types who have tried to get at the numbers. Which is hard to do, by the way. They're one of the more secretive private companies around."

"Why would they sell out to the Morrison Group?"

"Officially? You'll hear all the buzzwords – strategic fit, synergy, vertical integration, product complementarity. The real reason is the same old thing: money, lots of money. Those same Wall Street boffins think that Morrison will end up paying about twice the 'real' value of the company, although god knows how that's calculated. It'll show up as "Goodwill" on the balance sheet and be written off down the road, long enough in the future that the shareholders won't scream foul."

Huggins broke in. "There's one other reason for "why sell now?" A guy named Rahm Izak was their CEO until a month ago. He's an Israeli who came to this country about thirty years ago and was the real driver for the company. He was a rare combination of a brilliant engineer and an exceptional manager. Think Steve Jobs with a personality transplant. Once he was gone, DaVinci Associates became a target for the big boys."

"Did he quit?"

"Nope. He was in the wrong place at the wrong time. He was killed by a bomb in the ballroom of an Egyptian hotel, along with thirty-four other Americans and Brits attending a scientific conference. Some jihadist group claimed responsibility."

"What's the status of the deal?"

Velma took over. "The Morrison Group has completed its due diligence. Lawyers are haggling about the details, but it should wrap up within the next few weeks when the Boards vote. Rob and I agree that all the dust should be settled and the deal closed by mid-April, just before the IPO."

"OK. So, Velma, I'm curious. Why are you poking around in DaVinci Associates if you're really interested in reengineering the General Accounting function within the Morrison Group?"

"You know me, Rho. I just go where the bread crumbs lead. Rob's got a three-person team analyzing the workflow within the accounting department. Standard dull stuff. We've already learned that it's not your usual service unit in a closely-knit organization with a unified set of policies and procedures. It's more like an outside bookkeeping firm dealing with a large number of distinctive and unrelated clients. The real controls – the checks and balances that make sure money goes where it's supposed to go – are at the operating units, the ones that authorize payments and deal with vendors and customers."

"There are hundreds of those to choose from within the Group, aren't there? And DaVinci Associates won't be one of them until the deal closes?"

"Sure. And Rob's team will sample from them. But I wanted to look at DaVinci Associates for a couple of reasons."

"First, Rob told me to start with GSI – sorry, Geophysical Sciences Inc. – and that quickly led me to DaVinci Associates."

Rho glanced at Rob. He nodded and said, "Remember Cannell's outburst in our meeting? About keeping our twerps away their DARPA contracts?"

Rho nodded, "He was quite sensitive, as I recall."

"Given his sensitivity, I figured that would be a good place to start. Not just because he's an asshole, but because it's precisely those kinds of customer relationships that will be the trickiest to fit into any kind of organizational redesign."

"And...."

"It turns out that more than half of those contracts are in the subsidiary called GSI ... for Geophysical Sciences Inc. It's a bunch of eggheads and geeks, mostly engineers and programmers, who work on underground structures – storage caverns, support beams for skyscrapers, crude oil or gas reservoirs, that sort of stuff."

"Sounds properly dull."

"Not if you like working underground. They're known as 'the mole people' in the rest of the company."

"It doesn't sound like the kind of thing DARPA or DOD would be particularly interested in."

"You'd be surprised. Think missile silos in North Dakota. But, as it turns out, their single biggest source of funding is for GPR."

Rho grimaced and simulated an intense thinking process. "I know ... I know ... Don't tell me ... Grade Point Retrogression? Yes! Gravity Protected Rockets!"

"Not quite, but a spirited try. In the real world, it's known as Ground Penetrating Radar."

"Now that sounds sufficiently far out to be of interest to the Star Wars types. The very stuff of science fiction."

"Actually, it's been around for quite a while. It's widely available and quite useful. Used by archeologists for mapping digs, police for finding bodies in shallow graves, geologists for finding oil & mineral deposits, etc."

"So why is DARPA interested, if you can buy the technology off the shelf?"

"The existing technology has some limitations. The most serious one is the effective mapping depth is determined by a number of factors, particularly the type of soil you're trying to penetrate. Clay or rocky soil, for example? You might see about a foot underground. Not very revealing. And the existing technology works best with ground level antenna moving very slowly over a relatively limited surface. Finally, the resulting "maps" require a lot of expertise to interpret. All-in-all, it's not a very user-friendly technology."

"And GSI is trying to make it more friendly?"

"What if I had a bunch of eggheads and geeks that could enable me to map structures and caverns up to five-hundred yards underground in any type of natural or man-made material – think concrete or rocky desert soil – by using an airborne antenna, with AI-based software to generate three-dimensional maps that any sixteen year old high school dropout could read …"

"That's what the geeks would call a paradigm shift."

"Better than that, it's something your average Senator on the Intelligence Committee could relate to. Finding cave systems in the Bora Bora mountains? Secret nuclear plants in Iran? Drug smuggling tunnels from Mexico into the U.S.? Hardened missile silos? Buried communication cables?"

Velma had been sitting quietly during this back and forth. Now, she leaned forward and took over from Huggins.

"That's one reason why I went to GSI. Once there, there were two more factors that got me to DaVinci. First, DaVinci represents some ten to twelve percent of GSI expenses, so it makes sense to single it out for that reason. They're the biggest single vendor."

"All related to GPR testing?"

"A lot of it, we think. But that's just a guess at the present time."

"You said two reasons you started with GSI?"

"The other one is that the General Accounting department had already done a lot of analysis that I could piggyback on. The manager of the department – a woman named Marie Lynne Broder – had participated in the due diligence of DaVinci and her administrative assistant thought I could use her analysis. As far as she knew, nobody within the Morrison Group had seen it yet."

Rho said, "That's the recently deceased Marie Lynne Broder, I presume?"

Both Rob and Velma looked at Rho with a newly suspicious expression. *I have to remember to brief them on my side-deal with Littleton.*

For now, Rho just looked at Huggins with some real concern. "Rob, can we defend this to our client if they ask us why we're reanalyzing data already collected on a yet-to-be-concluded acquisition?"

"Absolutely. I will tell them the same things I just told you. And one more thing between the three of us. As you said when we started this, our real value to the Morrison Group may be to help them get in shape for the IPO and the brave new world of being a public company. What better way than to use their last and best acquisition as the testing ground?"

Rho stood up and stretched.

"OK. You two have given me a nice little tutorial on GSI, DaVinci, and GPR. Assuming I've mastered all of the acronyms, remind me again why you asked me to come down here … I seem to remember an impression that there was some skullduggery?"

Rob and Velma looked at each other.

Rob said, "Skullduggery? Such a nice word if you're talking about run-of-the-mill wrongdoing. But how about treason?"

An Accounting Exercise

Treason?

Velma stood up and opened the laptop, projecting a blank Powerpoint slide onto the large screen at the front of the room.

"I'm going to show you some numbers from Marie Broder's analysis that trouble me. But there's some qualitative background that should come first."

"Marie Lynne – that's what everyone calls her – had great difficulty getting these numbers. She was stonewalled by both the GSI managers and then by DaVinci Associates. I think she finally got past them by citing some SEC regulations about due diligence and transparency. Even then, she got pulled off by the CEO himself."

"Carlton?"

"Yep. Told her he needed her for some internal study on transfer pricing. Turned out to be a make-work analysis that the mail clerk could have done."

Velma clicked the remote, and a slide appeared on the left half of the screen, an Excel worksheet with three columns and about twenty rows.

"This is what Marie Lynne started with. These were the last six months of billings that GSI had received from DaVinci Associates, sorted by date. They add up to about six million dollars. All of them were invoiced to GSI, personally approved by Carlton or Morrison, coded as "Test Expense," and paid promptly."

She clicked again, and a similar looking Excel worksheet appeared on the other half of the screen.

"This is from DaVinci's records. The first thing Marie Lynne looked at was the revenue stream for DaVinci. This worksheet is a listing of their bank deposits for the most recent six months. It shows – she used the laser pointer to indicate columns on the right hand side of the screen– the date, payee and amount. She called this Worksheet #1."

"Marie Lynne doesn't sound very imaginative in naming files. But why start there – with DaVinci revenues?"

"Two really good reasons. First, she could cross check their accounting against what she already knew – the checks coming from the Morrison Group." The laser pointer indicated the column of numbers on the other half of the screen. "Second, by far the most common accounting frauds involve revenue accounting one way or another. It's a natural starting point for any due diligence team."

Rho walked to the front of the room and stood alongside the screen. "OK. I can see an invoice of $149,250 here – from DaVinci to GSI," pointing at a row about halfway down the left hand side of the screen. "And here's a $149,250 million deposit shown in the DaVinci deposit list," indicating a row on the right hand side of the screen with a "GSI" label. "So they match …billed and deposited … No hanky-panky there."

"Nope. And you see the little tick mark alongside both items? I'm sure that's where Marie Lynne matched them up and concluded the same thing as you."

Velma paused, and Huggins broke in. "See anything else interesting in those DaVinci Associates numbers, Rho?"

"Accounting was never my strong point, but ...," and Rho walked away from the screen and then stared back at it for about thirty seconds.

"Well. Based on the number of times the GSI label shows up on that deposit list, it looks they were a relatively important customer for DaVinci."

Velma said, "About thirty percent of their total deposits during the six months."

"And I only count six other names on that listing – none of which I recognize -- so DaVinci's business apparently is concentrated within a very small set of customers."

"A grand total of fourteen customers in the last fiscal year."

Huggins pressed Rho, "Anything else?"

"What is this? A Rorschach test for accountants?" Rho stared at the screen for another thirty seconds.

Rho shook his head. "Apples and oranges, isn't it? What's on the screen? Deposits at DaVinci vs. billings to its customers ... A listing of transactions with two different customers during a six-month period, for different services for different companies on different dates, with different amounts. What am I supposed to conclude?"

Velma smiled as though he had just confirmed something. "Neither Rob nor I picked it up either. And – as you know – I'm pretty good at this stuff. But Marie Lynne did, and she left us some bread crumbs."

She used the laser pointer to pick out one of the names in the DaVinci list of deposits – "TACA." Then she clicked the remote again and said, "Here's Marie Lynne's 'Worksheet #2.' It's a simple comparison of deposits from TACA and GSI payments to DaVinci."

"This column shows the time difference – the number of days – between the GSI payment and TACA deposits, and this" – the pointer slid to the final column – "the size of the GSI deposit relative to the adjacent TACA item, expressed as a percentage."

Rho said, as though talking to himself, "So it seems that DaVinci Associates always received a payment from GSI six days after a TACA deposit ..."

Rob and Velma stared at him approvingly, like a pair of teachers showing off a star pupil.

"... And the amount of the GSI payment is always and precisely eighty-five percent of the TACA deposit."

Velma closed up her laptop and shut down the projector.

Rho thought for a bit. "That's beyond coincidence. There's got to be some connection between the work DaVinci does for both TACA and GSI. Did Marie Lynne have a theory?"

Rob said, "Those worksheets are all that remain of Marie Lynne's professional existence. All of her files, both paper and electronic, have been expunged. Carlton indicated that it was 'company policy' in the case of ex-employees." This last statement was expressed in a voice that conveyed a strong cynical undertone.

"So, how ..."

Velma interrupted. "She had these worksheets on a thumb drive that she gave to her secretary for printing. The secretary forgot, not very surprising given the chaos following Marie Lynne's suicide."

Rho turned to Rob. "Have we approached anyone at DaVinci or the Morrison Group about this?"

"No. First, we aren't sure what all this means and given how prickly Carlton is about these GSI contracts, we thought we needed to bring you in on this first."

Rho said, "This doesn't look good, does it? You've got a classified Defense contract as the apparent linkage. Assume you're a DOD auditor and you came across this. What kinds of questions would you ask to satisfy your curiosity about these 'coincidences,' a euphemism if there ever was one"?

Velma said, "We've played that game with ourselves. The first obvious question is 'What's TACA'?"

"And …"

"We don't know. Among other possibilities, it's the name of the national airline of El Salvador. Assuming it's an acronym, there are an amazing number of matches. You know Google! Everything from 'Tacoma Area Community Association' to 'Talk About Curing Autism' to the 'Turkish American Cultural Alliance.'"

"What about how DaVinci treats the deposits for accounting purposes?"

"That we know. The first worksheet shows the account code. They classify their payments from TACA as 'Royalties.' It fits, given their proprietary technology and licensing arrangements. The GSI payments show up as 'Test Services Revenues.'"

"One more question: Who owns DaVinci Associates?"

Rob answered, "We don't know. We've done enough checking to know that the ownership group is carefully disguised. There are multiple layers and numerous offshore shell companies employed."

Rho steepled his fingers, leaned back in his chair and swiveled to look out the window. After a moment, he stood up.

"OK. For right now, let's keep this strictly between the three of us. Velma, I'd like you to look for more bread crumbs, but do it from the Morrison Group end of things. See if you can find out what kind of testing they're contracting out and where the end product – the GPR gadget or whatever – is headed and what state it's in. If you get any kind of resistance, back off and let me know."

"Rob. Focus on our consulting mandate – the need for an overarching strategy. Within that, look at their decision-making processes with respect to acquisitions, vendor selection and corporate level controls applied to subsidiaries. The general rubric should be 'How decentralized do we need to be?' And, the same as Velma, if you get pushback from Carlton or his henchpeople, smile politely, say 'yes sir,' and then give me a yell."

Velma and Rob stood up and headed for the door. Velma went out, but Rob paused, looked at Rho as if to challenge him, and said, "It's very sad about Marie Lynne … committing suicide, I mean. … terribly unhappy in her personal life, I suppose…"

"Sad? Absolutely. Suicide? Maybe. Very mysterious. Could be a Hitchcock movie … 'Death of a Bookkeeper' or something like that …

"I've got a better title than that."

Rho waited expectantly.

"'Requiem for a Whistleblower' … and the good guys don't win in the end."

"I'll miss that one. I like movies with happy endings."

Rob turned to leave, but Rho stopped him. "There's another sub-plot that you should know about. Did you see the article in yesterday's Chronicle about the shooting in South San Francisco?"

"No. I'm a sports and business page only kind of guy."

"The victim was a guy named Donnelly. He's a DOD project auditor. He's been reviewing Morrison Group contracts for the last two weeks. He was shot on Monday morning, the day that he was scheduled to begin his review of the GPR contract."

Rob just stared at Rho. Then he sat back down.

I think it's time for me to bring Velma and Chip up to date on the various side deals I've struck with Littleton.

He talked without stopping for the next ten minutes. Huggins sat quietly, but a look of concern was quite evident when Rho finished.

"So, on that note, watch out for Velma. As I recall, the bread crumbs led Hansel & Gretel to a witch's cottage and a near-death experience."

A Murder, But ...

Rossotti picked up on the first ring.

"Hey, Rho. Another questionable suicide?"

"Hi Arnie. No. This is a quite unequivocal case of murder most foul. Of Mr. David Donnelly, recently deceased in our fair city. I'd like to know a little more than what's in the public domain. I'm hoping you can -- "

Arnie interrupted, "I know the Donnelly case. More than I'd like to."

He paused, clearly thinking, and went on, "Look, Rho. This one is going to be real sensitive. And you're a civilian. I'm not sure I can help."

"C'mon Arnie, you know me. I'm not a tabloid reporter."

When Arnie remained silent, Rho continued, "And I may be able to provide a new slant for you to work with."

The silence lasted for another twenty seconds. Then Arnie said, "How about that long-promised beer? Say the Tosca on Columbus in thirty minutes?" He hung up without waiting for Rho's reply.

The popular North Beach bar was at its rowdy best when Rho got there. Arnie already had a booth, with two beers sitting in front of him.

Rho sat down opposite Arnie. "This worries me. You actually bought the beer?"

"I figure if you can do pro bono work for the city, I should be able to treat you to a bottle of beer every now and then." He handed Rho the bottle and they clinked them together. "Here's hoping word doesn't get around about my sudden generosity. My creditors might regain hope."

Arnie sat back and looked at Rho with an expression that reminded Rho of someone about to open a birthday gift that he knew he wasn't going to like. "What's your interest in Donnelly?

"Same as with Broder. He was doing some work for one of my clients."

"The same client? It seems to be killing off its employees fairly fast.

"It's a big company, so they've still got some slack. Actually, Donnelly is – was – not an employee. His job just brought him into contact with my client. It's pretty indirect.

"Look, Arnie. I don't want to put you on the spot. The newspaper coverage provided a lot of details about Donnelly's killing. I just wondered if the police were satisfied with the nice neat way it's worked out. But what's your problem? You used the phrase 'real sensitive.'"

"A can of worms. It's the kind of case where nobody comes out looking good. Think about it: homeless veteran shoots ordinary citizen. This is a city where homeless veterans mingle with ordinary citizens all the time. Who's safe anymore? And maybe our notoriously liberal legal establishment will get upset because we're railroading homeless veterans through the courts just to keep our tourists coming."

"The newspapers make it sound pretty clear-cut."

"This is all off the record, right? Way off ..."

Rho just nodded.

"He was at the scene, holding the gun that fired the shots. He had the victim's watch, wallet and briefcase in his possession. Both he and his overcoat test positive on the gunshot residue test. The DA could sleep through the trial and still get a conviction."

"His name is Jacob Marley –"

"I saw that. The same as Ebenezer's Scrooge's dead partner. The press loves it."

Rho looked puzzled. "I still don't get it. It doesn't sound like the kind of story that would have any legs. The evidence is pretty damning."

Arnie gave a deep sigh. "There are some inconvenient truths. First, Marley says he didn't do it, that he was sleeping until somebody poked him and dumped the gun and other stuff on him."

Rho shrugged. "To say "I didn't do it" is not much of a defense, is it? Any witnesses?"

"None that help either way. Nobody saw Donnelly or anybody else in the ramp. A couple of locals – including a cop driving by -- saw Marley sleeping at the base of the parking ramp wall, but that was thirty minutes before the shooting. The first cop on the scene after the shooting said that Marley was confused, like someone just waking up. But he was holding the damn gun and going through the wallet!"

"What about the 911 caller ... surely a witness there?"

"Very brief, and quite anonymous. Said there had been a shooting, by a bearded guy with a dark overcoat ... And, yes, Marley is bearded and owns a dark overcoat. Now speckled with GSR."

"Any of that 'soft, circumstantial stuff'? The kind that Lieutenant Abbie was worried about in the Broder suicide?"

"There's his record. Marley has no criminal history other than a couple of loitering charges; no history of civilian violence of any sort. The other street people that he hung out with are pretty sure he didn't have a gun. But, on the other hand, he kind of floats in and out of reality. Short term memory doesn't work worth a damn. He's been treated at the Vet Hospital for PTSD."

"Arnie, I don't get it. This is one of those run-of-the-mill urban tragedies … even in San Francisco."

Arnie looked depressed. "Three things … the kind of little puzzles that defense attorneys love."

Rho waited. Arnie held up three fingers.

"Marley's fingerprints were not on the briefcase or cell phone. How did those objects get from the shooting scene – fifty yards away – to where they found them?" He folded the first finger down, leaving two.

"And the briefcase? It had nothing in it. Who carries an empty briefcase around with them?" One finger remained.

"And …"

"Marley was an ex-Navy SEAL, highly skilled with all kinds of weapons. He was within ten feet of his target. How come he sprayed five wild shots around the place like a hopped-up gangbanger?"

Escalation

Kovacs was sitting in Golden Gate Park feeding the ducks a half-loaf of Wonder Bread when his cell rang. He flipped it open, noting the caller ID, and said simply, "Yes?"

"The front entrance in thirty minutes. Can you be ready?"

"Yes."

"Remember what I told you. It must be – "

Kovacs hung up before the sentence was complete. *Why do I work for stupid people?* He thought about that question briefly, but it changed form. *How do such people rise so far up in the world?* Then, finally, he answered his own question. *Because they are willing to employ such people as me.* He looked at his watch and then started dialing his cell phone. The ducks waited patiently.

When his call was answered, he said, "You need to be in place in twenty minutes."

He listened to a response that went on long enough that his expression of distaste became quite pronounced. He interrupted. "The arrangements are made. You do what you have promised and we shall do what we have promised. Your family will be wealthy." After a pause, he added in a tone totally without any affect, "And if you do *not* do what you have promised, we shall also do as we promised. Do you understand me?"

He closed his phone and resumed feeding the ducks.

Rho waited outside the ornate open-air front entrance of the Morrison Group office building for his scheduled meeting with Marcia Littleton. The Group headquarters occupied the first ten stories of a new office complex in a prime location, at the foot of one of San Francisco's famed hills. Normally, it was a quiet street, but there was a traffic snarl at the top of the hill, leading to a lot of horn honking and racing motors as the uphill-bound cars were reminded of gravity. A dump truck loaded with torn-up asphalt had doubled-parked at the crown of the hill, forcing both directions of traffic into a single lane. Rho was glad to be on foot.

Even better, he had commandeered a spot on a bench only a sidewalk width's distance from the Morrison Group entrance. He was sharing the bench with a diminutive bag lady in a bright red raincoat, one hand tightly grasping a shopping cart piled high with her dubious possessions. She smiled brightly, revealing several missing teeth. Rho smiled back and offered his opened bag of potato chips for her to share. She said 'Thank you' and took the entire bag from him, rolled up its top carefully, and put it into a canvas shopping bag that dangled from her shopping cart.

That's OK, I guess. Redistribution of income of a sort. Potato chips are not a healthy snack anyway. Littleton can buy my lunch.

The street scene and all of its elements made Rho think once more how much he loved this city. *San Francisco at its diversified best. And I'm about to spend a couple of hours with a beautiful and smart woman. All's right with the world for a brief moment.*

Looking into the atrium and across the lobby, he saw Littleton just getting off the elevator and heading for him. She looked directly at him, but was talking on her phone and clearly distracted. She stopped across the sidewalk from his bench, just inside the atrium, still talking. He stood up and waved, but she held up one finger, a signal that he read as "Wait," so they stood twenty feet apart.

Rho heard a yell from up the hill and glanced up. For half-a-second, the world seemed normal. Then he realized that the white dump truck was careening down the hill out of control. It was massive and getting bigger by the second. He could see the driver hunched over the wheel, but there was an eerie absence of engine noise and no apparent braking. The rapidly increasing velocity of the huge vehicle was the inevitable effect of gravity at work. Rho pivoted to look down the hill, at the busy intersection that the truck was about to sail through. He moved away from the curbside, knowing there was nothing he could do except watch the crash.

But when he looked back, he froze. The driver had changed course. Fifty yards uphill, the truck jumped the curb, smashed through a row of newspaper vending boxes, and headed straight for the Morrison Group building, still gaining speed. From Rho's curbside perspective, it seemed to be nothing but a bright metallic rectangle of grillwork. The driver still held the wheel, close enough now that Rho could see the panic in his eyes. Rho guessed he had the brake pedal pressed to the floor.

Littleton was directly in the path of the truck. She had turned toward the noise and was holding her phone as if to ward off the truck, seemingly transfixed in place.

Later, Rho could not recall why he acted as he did, nor could he remember the details of the next three or four seconds. He sprinted the twenty feet between he and Littleton, viewing her much as he did the tackling dummies on the athletic field at Stanford. He hit her as hard as he could, wrapping his arms around her and still driving forward. He could not recall any sounds. The only thought was of the monstrous truck bearing down on them. He thought he was too late and every cell in his body braced for impact. Then there was massive noise, steel meeting concrete and glass at high speed. It seemed to go for a long time. When it stopped, he heard the screaming.

He was lying on top of Middleton, sprawled face down in the atrium. A very fine concrete dust cloud was slowly drifting downward onto them. She was still holding her phone.

Time seemed to restart. He looked behind him, first seeing one of her shoes, still recognizable even though it was the thickness of a sheet of cardboard. To his left, ten yards away, he saw the rear of the truck imbedded in the café that formed the streetside corner of the building's atrium. Glass, tile and concrete cascaded around and over the cab of the truck. Beneath the center of the truck – easy to see from his floor-level perspective – there was an indistinct mass. It slowly revealed itself to be a crumpled and fully-loaded shopping cart. The remnants of a red raincoat were a part of the mass.

As he stared, still absorbing the last few seconds and slightly surprised to be alive, he realized that the redness was spreading.

The world slowly moved back toward normalcy. Marcia Littleton probably had broken ribs. Rho chose to believe that the injury was caused by hitting the floor rather than by the force of his tackle.

The bag lady and two elderly women who were drinking tea in the café and were directly in the path of the truck were emphatically dead. Rho overheard the paramedic attending to Littleton say, "No open coffin services for those three" and remembered the gap-toothed smile

The truck driver had only minor injuries. He was belted in and the massive front end of his truck protected him well. He was barely coherent, saying over and over, "The brakes failed! The brakes failed!" He said that when he started down the hill, he could not depress the brake pedal, that he stomped on it repeatedly, but it wouldn't move. Gravity, combined with his heavy load of asphalt and the steepness of the hill, made a wicked combination. Halfway down, he thought it best to sideswipe some buildings rather than wipe out a dozen cars in the intersection. *Probably not a bad decision – except for the three women who didn't get out of the way.*

The cops didn't touch the truck, waiting for the accident investigation team to run the show. The first investigator on the scene looked in the cab, took some quick photographs, and came out shaking his head.

"There's a Starbucks coffee mug – stainless steel – wedged under the brake pedal. I'll bet that it was loose on the floor and when he started down the hill, it rolled under the pedal."

The driver was a thirty-seven year old Turkish immigrant named Turgai Beyh. He owned the truck and was working free-lance, mostly suburban trash hauling and occasional construction jobs. He had a perfect driving record. He confirmed that it was his coffee mug and that he had stuck it under his seat earlier that day.

Incredibly, the cops had a video of the runaway from start to finish. A tourist from Omaha was taking a video of the street to show to his flatlander cronies in Nebraska. He filmed the truck as it gently started down the slope until its high-speed immersion in the atrium. The driver was visible throughout the entire video, his posture rigid, at first focused on steering a straight line down the narrow street and then a slight turn to the right when he changed his mind. A few frames included Rho's headlong dash and tackle of Littleton. Those same frames showed the bag lady in her bright red raincoat disappearing under the truck.

Loose Ends

It was nine PM. Morrison was in his tenth floor corner office looking out at Treasure Island and the Bay Bridge. He viewed each of these manmade objects with considerable nostalgia, as huge – 'monumental,' in the strict sense of the word -- demonstration projects proving that design and engineering could reshape the world, that geography can be overcome. He had built the Morrison Group on that belief system.

I wonder how much time is left. He had called Dr. Weber this morning, ostensibly to get the results of the latest round of blood samples that Weber had drawn last week.

"I feel really good for a person that's dying. What do you see in your microscope?"

He was proud of the matter-of-fact tone that came through. No hint of the recurring hopefulness that was always there. *Maybe the lymphocytic whatchamacallits have stopped multiplying, or stopped doing whatever it is that is killing me in such a kindly fashion.*

Weber nevertheless heard the subtext quite clearly. Perhaps that is why his response was extra-clear, harsher than it should have been. "No change, Walter. I'm sorry. Remember, I told you that you'll feel fine – maybe a little more tired than usual – for awhile. And then you won't. It's zero-one, not a gradual slide. How long? It's hard to tell, but it's weeks, maybe a couple of months; not years."

It's strange how little I care.

He turned from the window and joined the three other men in the room, seated around the conference table in his office. He placed a complex-looking phone in the middle of the table.

"I'm going to call our primary contractor. I want the three of you to listen, because I want your opinion of his advice.

He engaged the speakerphone and dialed a number that was answered immediately.

"Yes?"

"First, I want to congratulate you on your creativity. It was an ingenious plan."

"Plans are for shit. The woman is still with us. And?"

"Second, you failed. That's not acceptable."

"It happens. Not very often, but it happens. Do you want me to try again?"

"That would be too obvious. In fact, now we need to be sure that she stays alive for a while. Let's put that one aside. I'm going to try to divert Ms. Littleton another way. But I'm wondering if your agent – the truck driver who failed – should be put on your "to do" list?"

The reply was instantaneous and emphatic. "Absolutely not. Turgai Beyh did what he said he would do. It's not his fault that an American hero came along at precisely the right moment. And he will continue to honor our agreement. He'll probably get a few years for vehicular manslaughter and he'll do the time without a peep."

Morrison sat back in his chair, staring at the phone. *So Kovacs has an honor code of sorts. That's very interesting.*

The disembodied voice on the phone read the silence correctly. "Morrison. Don't do something stupid. Send the money through channels to Ankara. If you don't, we're done.

And you don't want that." After a short pause, he added, "I promise you: you don't want that."

"I surely don't. The money will be there tomorrow. Enjoy a day off."

He punched the 'end call' button and swiveled around in his chair to face the other three men. He held up his hand to forestall any comments, saying, "One more call" as he redialed, leaving the speaker on.

"Marcia. It's Walter Morrison. I apologize for calling after hours."

The tone in which Littleton answered conveyed both surprise and curiosity. "That's not a problem, Walter. What can I do?"

"Nothing, actually. I just wanted to tell you how glad I was that you weren't hurt this afternoon. That was a very scary incident."

"Worse than that for the three women killed."

"Of course. It's tragic."

"And we need a new atrium."

"Involuntary urban renewal. And no problem if you own a construction company, as we do. But, Marcia, the main thing is that you're all right. Aside from my personal affection for you – which is considerable – the Group needs you."

"Well, I'm slightly damaged goods. The ER just released me. It turns out that I have some cracked ribs. Nothing that should interfere with daily life very much."

"I am sorry to hear about your ribs." Morrison's tone shifted to a different register, a warmer and more personal voice. "But there I can help in a tangible way. I want you to take some time off. Get away and recuperate. A couple of weeks, even a month, somewhere with a beach and really bad internet connectivity. The Gulfstream can deliver you anywhere in the world. Take a guest of your choice along. Just tell me when and where."

There was a long pause. The four men listening around the conference table all leaned forward attentively, their eyes fixed on the phone as if her answer would contain visual cues.

"Walter, I … That's very generous of you. But I can't take the time right now. We're at a critical point and too many balls would fall to the ground if I'm out of the picture. I'll gladly take you up on your offer when the DaVinci Associates deal is put to bed and the IPO is a done deal."

"You're sure? One thing I've learned the hard way is that nobody – not one of us -- is indispensable."

"It's more about sheer stubbornness than ego. I just want to see it done, and done right."

"An acquisition is an acquisition. We've done a hundred of them." He went on in a carefully neutral voice, "Or are you seeing anything particularly unusual about the DaVinci deal?"

Again, the four men around the table focused intently on the phone.

One advantage of a telephone conversation over a face-to-face encounter is that the absence of visual cues and body language forces a concentration on slight shadings of tone and pitch. There was a long pause, and when she spoke her voice had changed. It was carefully modulated, with a deliberateness that telegraphed a sudden wariness, as though being cross-examined under oath

"We're on schedule. So far, all the financial stuff looks good. Frankly, Daniel's been more involved in the details of pricing, strategy and DaVinci operations than I have, so I'm probably not going to be the one to get nervous."

Three of the men in the lamp lit room all turned to look at Daniel. He in turn looked at Morrison with a raised eyebrow.

"Marcia, once more – I'm really glad you're OK. No more close calls, OK? Are you sure you won't take me up on that vacation offer – two weeks, a month, all expenses paid, corporate jet at your disposal, drinks with umbrellas in them?"

"Thanks, Walter. I really do appreciate your concern, and your offer. But now's not the time."

"Goodnight then. I'll see you in the office tomorrow."

The room was silent, each of the listeners processing what they had heard. Carlton was the first to speak

"She smells something. She's becoming a real threat." Then he added, "It's too bad that truck missed."

The very large and dark man spoke in heavily accented English. "It would be good if she was not on the scene."

Morrison responded. "We've tried. In a variety of ways, actually. Avi tried a covert approach to see if she could be coopted into a more sympathetic attitude. His assessment was exactly the opposite." All eyes shifted to Avi, who simply nodded. "And you just heard our most recent attempt – an enticement to go away for a couple of weeks."

Carlton said, "I knew that wouldn't work. She doesn't have a life outside of work!"

"I thought that today's near-death experience might have made her susceptible. They say that a sudden confrontation with one's mortality often changes your perspective about what's important." *A hypothesis that I can offer some evidence on.*

Carlton snorted. "Not Littleton!" When nobody spoke, he continued, "I think we should tell our mysterious contractor to try again, and do it right this time!"

Morrison's sarcasm was undisguised. "What? Another staged accident? We might as well call the SEC, the FBI and the Justice Department. Tell them to start formal inquiries!"

Avi asked, "So we let her operate with a free rein?"

"We only need a couple more weeks. Daniel, you and I can keep her busy on other things to some extent without making her more suspicious. As she said, she's got a lot of balls in the air. We can direct her to focus on some of them that don't rub up against DaVinci Associates or GSI. Like the two Owens projects. Those are classic CFO turf. Keep her busy and away from the smoking guns."

He thought but did not say, *And there's always Kovacs.*

Carlton spoke up. "There's another problem."

The other three men simply looked at him.

"Owens, the guy Littleton hired on the strategy & reengineering projects? He seems to have another agenda."

"What's bothering you about this extra agenda?" Morrison asked.

"His firm is doing a textbook job. They've got their consulting associates all over the company and seem to be asking the right questions. I'm getting a report every couple of days and it's going well. It's what Owens is doing himself that bothers me."

"He's spent most of his own time this past week at three of our business units. Guess which ones?"

Morrison's tone was quite testy, "Daniel ...."

"GSI, DaVinci and SS. And he's asking about precisely those contracts and vendors we don't want him asking about.

Somehow, he knows we have business dealings with TACA and AA, even though he doesn't know what they are – yet – or who owns them."

"Can he find out?" Walter asked.

Carlton looked thoughtful. "A couple of years ago – when we set them up – I would have said 'no.' But now? They've been on the grid, fairly active now that they're living off of our money. There are trails, and a really diligent web crawler could follow them."

"And if you like coincidences, my office got a call from the SFPD yesterday wanting to know what Donnelly was working on just before his death. I think Owens may have stirred that up."

"Any problem about Donnelly?" This came from Avi.

"No. He was reviewing our vendor files, checking off forms. He hadn't started looking into the DaVinci or GSI contracts yet. And the police already have what they think is the killer. Our contractor set that up quite nicely."

Morrison raised his hand to cut off the discussion. "Same as Littleton. We'll watch and wait. Daniel, instruct your people to report on any of their conversations with the Owens group. That's enough for now."

When Carlton and the dark man left the room, Walter turned and looked at Avi. He sighed deeply.

"Remorse, Walter?"

"Far too late for that, isn't it? No, an emotion more akin to frustration, I think. We can kill people, but all it does is to expose us to more risk. It doesn't solve the problem."

"Owens is dangerous. On several dimensions. Once the IPO closes, TACA and AA disappear. But until then, we need them to stay invisible."

Avi paused, folding his arms over his chest, his chin down and the fingers of his right hand rapidly tapping on his forearm. Walter had seen the body language many times and knew that Avi was engaged in a dialogue with himself. He waited patiently.

Avi stood up abruptly. "Owens must go."

"I think so too," agreed Walter. "And his unfortunate death will give us a perfectly good excuse to suspend the consulting agreement. After all, it was Mr. Owens' opinion that we valued."

A Thank You Note

Rho was at his customary bench on the Marina, latte cooling beside him, more or less forgotten. For once, he was oblivious to the jogging women and the constantly changing view of the Bay. It was as if the amount of attention required for the recurring questions cycling through his consciousness – and probably his subconscious as well – did not allow for extraneous cognitive activity.

He was startled when someone sat down next to him, and then amused by his sudden sense of entitlement about bench space. He was even more startled when his new bench mate said, "Celia said that I could find you here…. One-hundred yards south of the entrance to the Yacht Club."

"Ms. Littleton – "

"Please, call me Marcia. I think such familiarity is appropriate. Last time I saw you, you were lying on top of me."

Rho felt himself blush, the first time in a long time. "I was running like hell to get away from a truck and you got in my way. How are the ribs?"

"It hurts to sneeze. Other than that, a good excuse not to exercise."

A silence settled in, each of them content to look around them and let the awkwardness dissipate.

She was first to break the silence. "I understand you're here most mornings."

"Yes, although if you ask me 'Why?' I doubt if I could answer. For sure, Celia and I will have different views as to my motivation."

"I know what you mean. I grew up in Montana and every morning I'd go out on the back porch and look at the mountains. It was a mandatory start to every day, summer or winter. I'd have a hard time explaining why I did that, even to myself."

"Ms. Littleton ... Marcia ... I think we need to rethink the scope of this consulting assignment. It's gone in some surprising directions."

Marcia looked startled, and Rho realized that she had expected a different line of conversation.

Nice move, jerk. She wants to talk about the aesthetics of the outdoors and you bring up a business arrangement! She feeds you lines that open all up kinds of possibilities and you just watch them sail by! No wonder you live alone!

"Business arrangement? I agree, but not here and now ... another time and place. I just wanted to say 'thank you,' and I thought this would be a good venue to do that."

"I didn't do – "

"Yes, you did. If you hadn't, they would have had to clean me out of that Peterbilt grill with a wire brush."

"I was only -- "

She put her hand on his forearm. "Rho, you saved my life. Thank you." And she leaned close and kissed him on the cheek, very gently.

Celia would be horrified. Or would she? She told her where I was ...

An old geezer with an even older dog was watching from a nearby bench. He gave Rho a big "thumbs up" and grinned. Even the dog seemed amused.

"OK. I accept your gratitude. If you're free next Saturday night, you can buy me dinner."

"I am free at that time, and I will buy your dinner. But you're letting me off cheaply. In some tribal cultures, I would have to be your slave for life because of what you did. Obey your every wish and all that."

Once again he found himself wondering if she was fully aware of the import of what she was saying, words freighted with innuendo and eroticism. His rational self took one view: *She's just being playful, trying to lessen my embarrassment. Don't read anything into it.* On the other hand, his more primal self argued, *This is a fully self-actualized modern adult woman. She is quite aware of the multiple meanings -- and possible consequences -- of her actions and words.*

He played it safe. "It's simpler than that. Next time we find ourselves in the path of a runaway truck, it's your turn to save me."

She smiled and stood up. "I'll see you next Saturday night. We can talk about the scope of your assignment then."

I wonder what she means by that. Rho shook his head. And then, *I wonder what I want it to mean?*

The Sales Pitch

The wind was omnipresent in this land, like gravity in its constancy and force, unbroken by trees or walls. It molded the land, structures and the character of the people who lived within its reach. Outside, it altered a man's posture and caused him to speak louder, to choose different destinations. Women in their burkhas pulled them tighter around them and took smaller, quicker steps when walking downwind. Entering a building caused men to stand straighter and to appreciate the wind even more because of its momentary cessation. Even then, the dry wind seeped into houses, appearing as a faint stirring of the air or as a barely perceptible whisper. It caused visitors to the territory to experience a vague uneasiness that they could not trace to its source and it made them irritable.

The Turk did not like the wind. Nor the type of men that inhabited this land. But he understood them. They were ruthless and elemental because the harshness of their environment demanded it as the price of subsistence. Their tribalism, Sharia law, and anti-Western fanaticism flourished in a world where softness was fatal. *I wonder what they would be like if the wind stopped blowing.* The thought was the only sympathy he permitted himself, knowing that his life was forfeit if they thought him weak.

It had taken him three weeks of careful negotiation to reach this forlorn village on the edge of the Northern Territories. The location was unimportant by itself. The meeting could have been in Karachi, Dubai or any of several other urban settings. What was important was the group of four men that had gathered to hear his proposal. They were not the leaders, but they were those who had access to the leaders of al Qaeda and the Taliban. Avi and Walter had assured him that the American Predator drones with their Hellfire missiles would not be a problem for the three-hour window of this meeting. *And if they are, I won't have anything to worry about in any case.*

The thought triggered another. *If they don't like my proposal, I wonder if they will allow me to leave here alive?* So far, he was accepted in these circles because of his decades-long role as their conduit to the European addicts who were dependent on the poppy fields of Afghanistan and Pakistan. He also brokered several major arms shipments and assured an occasional safe passage for one of their couriers. They viewed him as reliable and trustworthy, even though he lacked the fervor for jihad that made their followers so malleable. But this was new.

Three weeks ago, after Avi had briefed him, the Turk had teased them. "I can give you the means to go far beyond September 11, 2001. The infidels will see what 'shock and awe' can truly be like!"

When their intermediaries pressed him for more, he simply said, "Ask your leaders if they have enough courage to kill the leaders of their enemies in their homes, along with thousands of their followers; at the same moment in time."

When they returned again, asking for still more, he said, "Take me to your leaders." This is why he found himself in this god-forsaken place with his life in the balance.

The ritualistic tea was served. The elaborate formalities were observed. Then the room was emptied and only the four men remained with the Turk. They looked at him, and he began speaking.

"The Americans and their allies have lost their stomach for their war on terror. Now is the time to strike a great blow. To change the course of history. I have access to a new and terrible weapon that is already in place, waiting only for the right moment...."

An hour later, the Turk was still alive. As he was leaving with his Taliban guide, the senior member of the group of four men spoke to him. "We must discuss your proposal. I believe it has great promise. And great risk. We shall let you know of our decision. Travel safely."

"Insha Allah."

As he left the village, the wind gusted and a dust cloud enveloped the car, reducing visibility to a couple of car lengths. *I wonder if it is an omen.*

Inklings and Oddities

"Do you believe in synergy? The two plus two equals five theory?"

Rho and Marcia were having their scheduled Saturday night dinner. She had picked the spot – a very expensive Japanese Fusion restaurant close to the financial district. Rho's question came just after they had ordered an aperitif.

She smiled. "Yes, except for mergers, in which case it's badly overvalued. And I'm not sure it even exists in the case of marriages. Is there such a thing as negative synergy?"

"Oh my yes! It's a common outcome of committee meetings, for example."

"So what motivates your question?"

Rho began. "It's about what's going on at the Morrison Group. You know a lot of stuff from your inside view and I know a lot of stuff from wandering around and asking a lot of questions. I was thinking that maybe if we put it together, we might actually get some useful conclusions out of the combination."

She grinned. "Kind of like the 'you show me yours and I'll show you mine' game we played as kids?"

"Yeah, but with different outcomes in mind."

She turned serious. "OK. I'll start. One of my puzzles is around those DARPA contracts. What I know is that we've got two separate subs – three, if we include DaVinci -- with highly classified defense contracts. Each of them is paying a hard-to-track vendor called 'TACA' for vague services and the payments seem to be somehow connected with progress on specific contracts. The payments are being authorized by our Chairman, Mr. Walter Morrison, rather than through normal billing channels."

"My turn," Rho said. "A related puzzle. We know of two suspicious deaths -- Broder and Donnelly. Just before they died, each of them was looking into either the sources of those very payments you just mentioned –"

She broke in. "And the CFO of the Morrison Group, the person most likely to stumble on such information, is the object of an accident that may not be an accident."

Rho continued, "We also know that the vendor – TACA -- is a consulting or advisory firm based outside the U.S. and is privately owned by individuals who badly want to be anonymous."

"Time for the synergy test: What does this tell us?"

Rho thought for a minute. "There's some kind of funny business involved in those contracts. It's possible that the research results are being shared with an unauthorized buyer with deep pockets."

Marcia added, "And someone really wants to keep it a secret, maybe even if they have to kill a few people in the process."

He added, "And Walter Morrison has to know what's going on."

Marcia was quiet, focused inward as though viewing some inner video. Rho let the silence go on. She looked up and said, "There's something else. I don't know if it qualifies as synergy … more like too many coincidences to be coincidental."

Rho raised his eyebrows, trying for a quizzical expression.

"The Group has two major events about to happen, the kind of deals that change the entire trajectory of the company. The DaVinci merger and the IPO. But Walter is paying no attention to them. No, that's not right. He is intent on the *timing*; he's obsessed about them being closed within a few days of one another and not later than two weeks from now. But all the other stuff – people, price, technology, who's on the boards – he's positively indifferent to."

"Maybe because he won't be involved after the IPO? "

"But he will be. The management structure won't change, and he'll still get a mega-million dollar bonus by staying in place."

Rho sat up straighter. "That's quite interesting. Huggins mentioned another set of odd coincidences as well. You've got three major turnkey projects that are being pushed to completion at about the same time – two weeks from now – for no apparent reason. The project managers all commented on it and said Morrison was checking with them daily to make sure timelines are being met."

"Why?"

"We don't know. But I think we can add another – what shall we call it – 'informed guess,' maybe, to our list."

They looked at each other, as though each of them thought the other one had the solution to a common problem.

Finally, Rho said, "Two thoughts. First, Morrison is working very hard to achieve a particular combination of events at about the same point in time, two weeks from now. And he doesn't much care about what happens after that. And, second, whatever it is, it isn't good."

An Accident Investigation

"Uncle Sal. Good to talk to you again. How's that arthritic knee?"

"Hello, nephew. Didn't you know? The docs can replace any part now. I have a new knee, and I'm shopping for a new hip. With the Viagra, I can do anything you can do!"

"I'd challenge you to prove it, but I could never live it down if I was outpointed by an octogenarian."

"You clearly have a better vocabulary than me. Whatcha need? Time for another lunch?"

"We're overdue, but right now I'm looking for a referral."

"For ...?"

"That's the problem. I don't know." Rho put it as succinctly as he could. "I need to find out if a one-man trucking company is a legitimate operation."

"What do you know?"

"It's local. The truck is a dump truck. It was loaded with asphalt. Its brakes failed and it crashed into a building, killing three women along the way."

"I know just the guy. Wait for a guy named Derek Riordan to call you. He owes me."

Derek Riordan called the next morning and agreed to meet later that day. He said, "I owe Sal, and he says I can trust you. But this has to be strictly confidential. As the politicians say, this is not for attribution."

Riordan had read the newspaper account of the accident with great interest. He described himself as an ex-official of CDTOA, the California Dump Truck Owner's Association. He did not look or sound like he belonged in the trucking industry. He was small with a slight build, dressed by Tommy Bahama, and he spoke in whole sentences. Rho thought, *I need to stop stereotyping.*

Riordan did not need an extensive briefing. "I know Turgai Beyh. He's a good man and I was sad to hear what happened. Sal said you wanted to know if he ran a legit business and I can tell you that he did. He's honest, hard working and totally dedicated to his family. I often thought that he was seriously overqualified for a one-man trucking company."

"What about the so-called brake failure?"

"It wasn't a brake failure. First of all, brakes don't fail all at once like that. Second, it seems that a coffee mug got wedged under the pedal. He couldn't push the brake to the floor. That truck was purely coasting!"

"How do you know that?"

"I read the accident report." When Rho looked skeptical, he quickly went on, "I do some free lance investigation, mostly for insurance companies who are skeptical of certain claims. Mostly commercial stuff. I have a lot of contacts in the DMV and DOT.

He paused. "And Sal added a little weight for me."

"Is that plausible? That coffee mug bit?"

"I've heard of it. And it's easy to imagine. Remember all the dealer recalls because of the floor mats that jammed the accelerator pedal and caused crashes? Sudden acceleration syndrome, they called it."

He went on. "You were a witness. Based on what I read, you gave the clearest account of what happened during the ten or so seconds that truck was headed downhill. You only missed one key detail. Between your and Turgai's testimony, it sounds like pure chance at work – an unfortunate accident. But he'll almost certainly face charges of vehicular manslaughter and will probably have some serious jail time. I visited him at the County jail just before coming here. He says he doesn't want a trial and will plead guilty to whatever charges they bring."

"But ..." Riordan paused, clearly thinking hard about whatever he was about to say. "But there are some, shall we say, 'anomalies' that aren't in the accident report and wouldn't be deemed relevant to any legal proceedings."

Anomalies! Such a nice word. I'll bet this is going to sound a lot like Lieutenant Abbie talking about Broder's suicide, and Arnie's listing of what he called 'inconvenient truths' around Donnelly's murder.

He said nothing, waiting for Riordan to proceed.

"Turgai works with an older cousin. His name is Ahmed... arrived from Turkey about six months ago. He answers phones, schedules loads, does the bookkeeping and does pick-and-shovel work for Turgai when he needs an extra hand. Maybe a few days a during a month. I talked with Ahmed."

"It seems that Turgai was not taking any jobs for the last few days. Said he was waiting for some big contract that would make lots of money and he didn't want the truck to be tied up when the call came. Ahmed said that kind of dead time was not unusual."

Rho shrugged. "So?"

"But then he proceeds to take on a load of junk asphalt – barely within the weight limit -- and let it sit on the truck during that time. That doesn't make any sense.

"Then there's the location thing …"

Rho looked at Riordan, waiting for him to explain.

"There was no reason for him to be on that particular street with a load of asphalt. It's not a truck route and there sure as hell isn't any place to dump asphalt before the street dead ends at the Embarcadero.

"And one more: why was he double-parked at the top of the hill?"

Rho broke in. "Those are good questions. What does Turgai say?"

"First, the promised 'big contract' kept getting put off. He was going to give it one more day. Why that street? He says that he had come off the bridge headed for 101 and was trying to avoid the business district. Double-parking at the top of the hill? He says you're wrong; he only stopped for twenty seconds or so to adjust a mirror."

Rho thought for a few seconds. "You said I was a good witness, but I missed one detail. What was it?"

Riordan shrugged. "Not your fault. You don't know Turgai or his little idiosyncrasies. Remember, the guy drove a dump truck. And he was Turkish, very proud of his heritage; always talking about how the Turks had conquered half the world. In short, he is a very macho kind of guy. Anyway, for whatever dumbass reason, he never wore his seat belt."

"But he did on that day. I saw it. And it shows up in that tourist video."

"I know. It makes me wonder if he knew he was going to crash before he ever started down that hill."

A Call to Ankara

Rho sat with his leather chair reclined at the maximum angle with his feet on his desk. From that position, about all he could see was the pointed tip of the Transamerica building in the financial district.

He called Derek Riordan. "Mr. Riordan, I think I'd like to talk with Turgai Beyh's cousin. I think you said his name was Ahmed. Could you help me set that up?"

"I could. But Ahmed's gone back to Turkey. He left yesterday. I was trying to find him to see if I could refer some business his way."

"What about other family members? You said that Turgai was a dedicated family man."

"I did, and he is. But the family's all back in Turkey, Ankara area I think. He was sending them any money that he could, but it wasn't much. The impression I got was that his parents are professionals of some sort, but poor. Turgai told some wild stories involving political persecution. There's a couple of sisters as well."

"Thanks, Riordan. You've been very helpful. I'll tell Sal the same thing."

"Thanks, and let me know if you need a dump truck."

What the hell! Time to cash in some of that political clout. He called Celia into his office, saying in a pompous tone, "Get me the U.S. Ambassador to Turkey." He was disappointed that Celia simply nodded, her expression unchanged.

One of Rho's best friends was Benjamin Appleby. Ben was older, much wealthier and far more passionate about the

Democratic Party than Rho. He served as the Northern California rainmaker for political donations during the last two presidential elections and was rewarded by being named Ambassador to Turkey last year. They had not talked since his grand sendoff party, but Rho had kept up with his progress and was impressed by his apparent enthusiasm for the job.

Celia buzzed him five minutes later. "The Ambassador is on line two."

"Rho. I hear you're a hero, rescuing beautiful damsels and such. Congratulations."

"My God! I made the Turkish headlines? Globalization is proceeding faster than I thought."

"Not quite. Facebook, actually. And a few Tweets from some mutual friends. It sounds horrific. I'm glad you weren't hurt."

"Let's just say I was sufficiently lucky to compensate for my usual stupidity. But that incident is why I'm calling. One of the principals is a Turkish immigrant with his family still there in Turkey. I'm wondering if the embassy can help me get some basic information about them."

"It depends. But if one or more of them has immigrated to the U.S., we should have something. Why don't you hold on and let me get one of my deputy assistant under something-or-others to take the details? I'll get back to you as soon as we can gather some details."

"Thanks Ben. I really appreciate – " But Ben was gone, replaced by music; at least it sounded like some form of music. *Local folk music, I guess.* He amused himself by trying to think of a major Turkish composer. He had yet to think of one when a woman's voice broke in. "Mr. Owens. I'm

Victoria Ambar. Ambassador Appleby has asked me to take the information you have for him."

Rho recited the little information he had, saying he thought the family was in the Ankara region and that he would appreciate whatever information the embassy could share. She promised to do her best and said that she would call back.

It took less than two hours.

"Mr. Owens, this is Victoria Ambar."

The name was strange to him at first. Then he recalled his call to the American Embassy in Ankara. He sat up straighter and then laughed at himself. "Ms. Ambar. Thank you for calling back. And I appreciate that the time difference is working against you at the moment." He calculated that it was well after the dinner hour in Turkey.

"Not a problem. Can you hold on? The Ambassador would like to speak with you."

The high-pitched music – he thought of it as wailing – came back on, but only for about ten seconds.

"Rho. This is Ben. And this call is entirely unofficial. In fact, you haven't heard from me since that slightly drunken party in San Francisco."

What's going on? "I'll forget I ever knew you, if you like." Rho stared at the phone as if the instrument itself was at fault. "Look, Ben. I thought I was making a perfectly ordinary request. I would have called your embassy for this kind of question even if I didn't know you."

"Your request was quite ordinary, very run-of-the-mill stuff. Questions like that keep folks like Victoria quite busy. But it seems that any interest in the Beyh family is of interest to other people as well."

"What other people? And doesn't an ambassador have enough in-country clout to ignore them? Can't you pull rank?"

"Not on these people. I've learned that the hard way. Actually, there's quite a lot of useful information that they didn't share with us in our ambassador orientation program. I know which fork to use and the proper way to wear my sash, but they forgot to tell me about the darker side of office politics in far off places."

"Are you in trouble?"

"Nothing that can't be sidestepped. But remember, this call –"

"This call never happened. Absolutely. Since we're not actually talking then, what can you tell me about the Beyh family?"

"The immediate family of your man Turgai lives in Ankara and consists of five other individuals – his parents and four children, two of each gender. They live together in a quite small house in one of less desirable sections of the city. To all appearances, they are quite poor. Apparently, they live off of the money that Turgai sends home."

"To all appearances … ?"

"Yesterday, they apparently received a large amount of money. The father quit his job and bought a car. According to the neighbors, they won a lottery. But the local newspapers publish the names of winners. They aren't mentioned."

"With all due respect to the paranoid, Ben, this doesn't sound like the kind of information that needs to be hushed up!"

"It's not. The problem is not Turgai; it's the other Beyh, his cousin Ahmed."

"His father – his name is Sedat – has some very interesting connections. Just a year ago, he owned a bank, a private medium-sized commercial bank centered in Istanbul. It mainly provided loans to construction and transportation companies. The government shut it down, apparently because the loans funded what they called 'criminal enterprises.' All of the visible assets of Sedat and the other board members were seized to pay off depositors."

"And why does my knowing any of this make somebody nervous."

"I don't know. But yesterday – the day after you dodged Turgai's truck – Ahmed's entire family showed up here at the embassy and applied for U.S. green cards."

"Aren't they hard to get?"

"Extremely. But they applied in a special category. I quote, 'Foreign entrepreneurs who invest half-a-million dollars in a commercial enterprise in a targeted employment area that will benefit the U.S. economy and create at least five full-time U.S. jobs.' "

"Doesn't that require a lot of documentation and layers of approval?"

"Normally, it does. But they showed up with a readymade, highly professional business plan and a certified eight-hundred-thousand dollar cash balance in a New York bank. All the stateside red tape has been taken care of."

"Pretty good for someone that's just had all his assets expropriated by the state. Do you remember the kind of business they are proposing to invest in?"

"Something to do with providing labor services for construction companies. The working title for the proposed company was Reactra, or something like that."

"Will the application be approved?"

"It already has been. By someone way above my pay grade. I've been told to expedite the process as much as I can, but I'm not to ask any questions and to forget whatever I happen to know about the Sedat Beyh family."

"Have you seen anything like this before?"

"Nope, but I'm new on the job."

"What's your guess? The family must have some high level connections to bypass your embassy."

"They know somebody important, that's for sure. And whoever it is can put pressure on somebody high up in the administration – cabinet level, probably at State – or in Congress. Or it could involve some covert back-channel deal between the Turkish government and ours. There are a few of those in play, given all of the Middle East politics. Turkey's at the epicenter and our best friend in this neighborhood, next to Israel."

"Or, it could … " Appleby paused long enough that Rho was about to prompt him. "It could be a CIA operation.

"Look, Rho. One piece of advice. Don't push any further on this. I've been around long enough to know that there are big players in the game, and they'll run over anyone that gets in their way."

Rho laughed. "That sounds faintly sinister, like the back cover blurb on one of those thrillers I see on the airport newsstands."

"If you become a nuisance to the people I'm thinking of, you'll be dodging something more accurate -- and lethal -- than runaway dump trucks."

Organizational Analysis

The Owens firm hired the best and the brightest and it equipped them with state-of-the-art computers and software. Rho was continually amazed by their facility at retrieving and displaying enormous quantities of esoteric information. They made him feel obsolescent, like he was trapped in some pre-technology time warp. However, he was often dismayed at their inability to draw meaningful conclusions from the incredible clutter of facts, data and opinion that they pulled from the ether. Part of it was the difficulty of seeing the big picture, literally. Their electronic screens were too small.

Therefore, almost every project team at some point in their project would say, "Let's go to the wall."

The main conference room in the Owens offices featured a whiteboard covering a wall that was ten feet tall and twenty feet long. Small tables at either end held marking pens of all the primary colors, color-coded magnets with flow-charting symbols, snap-on grids for graphical work, colored thread for linking nodes, and various other tools whose purpose was not clear. One third of the wall surface served as a gigantic electronic tablet and – at the press of a button – would print out a multi-colored image of whatever had been written or drawn on that section or export it to a hard drive or LCD monitor halfway around the world. There were two five-foot stepladders to insure that every inch of the board was accessible.

Both Rob Huggins and Velma Scranton were practitioners of the "Post It Note" school of organizational analysis. Although they would never admit it, even to themselves, they derived great satisfaction from filling the entire wall with their little multicolored scraps and would debate at length before placing one more piece among the hundreds already in place. They were engaged in such a debate when Rho walked in.

To Rho, the wall looked like a gigantic piece of modern art. *Genre? Clearly a collage ... Mixed media. MOMA class. Title? Maybe 'Neural Inner Space' or some such thing. Artist? Certainly deranged. Pollock squared.* However, he had learned the hard way that he must treat the wall displays with respect. To do otherwise would be like laughing at the finger painting that your five-year-old daughter brought home from her first kindergarten class.

He gestured at the wall. "I presume I'm looking at the Morrison Group organization chart. Looks like you've done a lot of work. But be gentle with me. You're going to have to walk me through it."

Velma sat down. Rob picked up a wooden pointer – another throwback that he preferred to the laser pointer – and moved to the far left of the wall.

"What we have here" – and he waved the pointer at the wall – "is the end result of about one-hundred person-days of research." He added with a grimace, "About half of which is billable to the client."

"Even allowing for its international scope and its fixation on being decentralized, Morrison is an exceptionally complex organization. They have about five thousand legal units, subsidiaries. Most of them are shells, designed to limit the parent liability and – in many cases – to limit their tax bill. We think we've identified all the subs, but we've left out the ones that don't have anything to do with operations. They're over here." He pointed to a strip of overlapping yellow post-it notes that filled up a three-foot vertical strip at the left edge of the wall.

"The subs that matter in the chain of command are these." And he ran the pointer along a row of about a dozen larger pink squares that ran half the length of the wall, along the very top. "Most of them are distinct geographic units, countries or regions of the world – North America, Europe, etc."

"These" – indicating the last four post-it notes in the row, all blue – "are specialized subs. They are global in scope and focused on a function or product or a customer, instead of geography. Three of them – GSI, DaVinci and Special Services -- handle most of the classified DOD contracts."

"The major players in the design/engineering industry, the dozen or so biggest firms including Morrison, work in well-defined industry categories. These are shown here." The pointer moved slowly down a column of larger captions on the left side of the wall – energy, infrastructure, telecommunications, transportation, military, and unclassified.

Rho said, "Pretty straightforward, so far. It's your classic matrix organization – a geographic dimension, your top row of subs, and an industry/market dimension, your left hand column."

Velma said, "More or less. And that's the simple picture that they present to the world. And it's the starting point for our analysis. But the real guts of the Morrison Group is the rest of those post-it notes.

Rob's walked his pointer the length of the wall, indicating the sea of squares that seemed to fill the entire space. "These are projects, contracts – well-defined tasks to design and/or build a particular structure in a particular place for a particular customer. This is how the Group makes money."

"Here, for example," – he picked a single post-it note at random, the pointer resting on a square in the approximate center point of the wall – "a contract to design and build a dam for the Republic of Yemen, in the Tihamah region of the country, scheduled for completion within six months."

Rho said, "OK. So we've got hundreds of money-making projects. What's the color-coding? I see red, white, and orange. And some of them with a big check mark."

"First, most of what we've talked about so far is public information. It took a lot of digging, but it's all there for anyone who wants to slog through all of the official filings country-by-country. But from here on –"

"It's Rob and I exercising our considerable professional judgment," Velma broke in. "It comes from the Morrison Group files and our discussions with a lot of lower-level operating people."

"And I don't think the Group really wants us to know all this." Rob waved at the wall once more. "My meetings with Carlton have been difficult. He wants to keep us in a windowless office at headquarters looking at written policies and org charts. I think he's afraid we're going to cost him his job if we really understand how screwed up the place is."

Rho knew it was possible. Two or three times, the firm was hired by a CEO who wound up getting fired when the firm made its final report to the board. *That's not the case here. It's not his job security that's bothering Carlton.*

"I gather -- I hope -- you haven't actually stayed in the office at headquarters."

Velma laughed out loud. Rob merely smiled. "Nope. And Littleton's been as subversive as we have. She's pushing us to go precisely where Carlton doesn't want us to go. I've never seen a CFO with so little respect for her so-called superiors."

"OK, now tell me about these color codes."

Velma said, "I'm mostly responsible for the white squares, so I'll take them." Rho estimated that the white ones were probably two-thirds of the total.

"First, it's important to know that these kinds of projects have two distinct phases – design, and then build. Each of those is in turn a composite of many sub-processes. For example, "design" can include permitting, architecture, engineering, etc. They are huge contracts with long time lines, calling for different types of experience and expertise. Therefore, most of them are carved out and assigned to different firms, or joint ventures are formed to bring together the necessary resources."

"The white post-its are those contracts where Morrison has a relatively minor role. Perhaps limited to "design" only, or maybe in a joint venture with a much bigger local partner." Velma's voice shifted slightly, signaling that she was transitioning from lecture mode into a more subjective zone. "It's a judgment call, and I could be wrong. Sometimes what looks like a minor task on paper can be the critical step in getting a project done on time and under budget."

"I trust your judgment, Velma. And if I'm understanding you, I can ignore the white squares. Right? So what are the orange squares?"

Velma shrugged. "That's what left over; the major projects. The ones where the Morrison Group is the major, maybe even the only, contractor. As you can see, they're a player in a lot of countries and in a lot of industrial sectors."

Rho noted that the orange and white squares were spread out all across the wall, occupying most rows and most columns.

"And these red squares? " Rho went to the wall and indicated a small cluster of red tags.

Rob said, "Those are the so-called turnkey projects. Contracts where Morrison has responsibility for the whole job from start to finish. The idea is that they do everything and then just hand over the completed thingamabob – highway, dam, airport, refinery, whatever – when the job is 100% complete. Only the biggest and best of these firms get those kinds of deals."

Rho said, "It's like I hire a contractor to build a house for me, hand him the plans and say 'tell me when it's done."

"Yeah. He may even draw up the plans for you."

"Most of them are in the row you call 'Energy.'"

"That's the sector where Walter Morrison grew up, and where they're the strongest relative to the competition. And that means that Morrison is also big in the Middle East, because that's where the jobs are. Not surprising to see the clustering."

"OK. One more graphics question: What are these check marks for?" Rho indicated three of the red squares that had a large black check mark in one corner.

"Those are projects that are scheduled for handoff within the next month. Combined, that's an unusually large chunk of business. It's the first time they've ever had that much work ending at the same time. And the field supervisors we've talked to told us that they've been under pressure to make the time lines work. It's important to someone that these top out at the same time."

"How do you manage hundreds of projects like this simultaneously?"

"You don't, really. At least not simultaneously. These contracts are spread out in time, some of them over ten years. There are long periods where work is routine, repetitive stuff. Think of building a hundred mile stretch of interstate highway or a pipeline. So-called management is getting a good foreman."

"For the bigger, more complex projects, or for the critical phase of some otherwise ordinary construction job, Morrison has a cadre of key people – no more than thirty or forty within the entire company – that they send in. Almost a SWAT team approach. And if it's turnkey, they've got one or more of their really good people on top of it the whole time."

"Have you talked to those folks?"

"Whenever we can. So far, we've run into them "sort of by accident" when we've been touring a job site."

"What about all those joint ventures and local partners? Any patterns there?"

Rob and Velma looked at each other and smiled simultaneously. Rob said, "Glad you asked that question, boss." He nodded at Velma. She went to the wall and started arranging magnets and colored threads. She worked for about three minutes, her body blocking whatever pattern she was concocting. Rob said nothing.

She stepped back. The overlay of colored threads on the multicolored matrix of post-it notes was severe sensory overload for Rho's first glance. *It's a wiring diagram for a motherboard on a main frame. Maybe a map of the London Underground.*

She said, "Actually, we also have this particular diagram on the computer as well, set up so that we can expose it one thread at a time. This is a little overwhelming."

Rob grinned and said, "She did this to me too. She won't admit it, but she's showing off again. The queen of pattern recognition!"

Rho conceded, "I give up, Velma. It's very impressive, but I have no idea in hell what I'm supposed to see."

"Obviously, I've added more players to the wall." She indicated six colored magnets near the top in one of the few empty spaces. Each was about two inches in diameter and each of them was holding down the upper end of a cluster of colored threads. The threads diverged, each of them terminating on various post-it notes scattered within the matrix.

"These black magnets" – and she indicated a cluster of four with threads running directly to the red squares – "are large construction companies working on the indicated projects. Morrison is a design, engineering and consulting company. They provide construction support, but often co-venture with a pure construction company to do the actual building. These are their partners on the indicated projects. The two in the Middle East are Turkish and Israeli companies."

Her pointer moved again, stopping at a pair of blue magnets. "Each of these is a key vendor to the Group, but not a construction company. The white thread runs from the vendor to the particular subsidiary that is being billed." Each magnet had white threads running to three of the "specialized" subs of the Morrison Group – DaVinci Associates, GSI and one labeled "SS."

"SS stands for 'Specialized Services.' It's a hodgepodge of products. The two biggest revenue areas are demolition and research into new forms of composite materials, usually involving concrete at some level."

"Demolition? In the middle of a *construction* company?"

"Not your ordinary wrecking ball operation at all. Think of decommissioning a nuclear generating plant; or breaking up an aircraft carrier; or removing an eighty-story skyscraper from downtown Tokyo. Who better to do that sort of thing then the people who build them?"

"Sounds plausible. OK, what about those black threads?"

"The black thread indicates cases where the sub seems to be passing on those vendor costs to various contracts, via intercompany billing." All three of the Morrison subs had black threads running between them and the turnkey projects.

"If I understand you, then it seems that these two vendors – your blue magnets -- are both providing significant services to three of the specialized subs, and those costs eventually are being passed on to the projects and presumably reimbursed by the ultimate customer."

Rob nodded. "Yes. Pretty standard stuff. But one of those vendors" – She paused, and her pointer hovered over one of the two blue magnets – is named TACA. The same hard-to-pin-down bunch that has some connection to a very highly classified DARPA contract at GSI."

"Well, well … And the other?"

"Just as obscure and hard to track down. The name on the invoices is AA Ltd. But it sure as hell isn't Arthur Anderson, American Airlines or Alcoholics Anonymous!"

"I wonder if our friendly CFO could check to see if there are any correlations between the vendor's billings and the intercompany payments? Like the ones from TACA to DaVinci to GSI?"

"She's already working on it. Herself. She didn't want to delegate that to an accounting clerk. She's still got Marie Lynne on her mind, and maybe on her conscience."

Rho stood up. "Rob, Velma ... Great work. I'm not sure exactly what we've got but I'm going to find out. For right now, keep going on the official consulting project. This..." and he waved his hand at the board, "is all relevant to our reengineering and strategy initiatives and I'd build it into your next presentation to Carlton."

Huggins looked highly dubious. "Are you sure about that?"

Rho thought for a moment. "No, you're right." He waved at the wall. "Everything there except Velma's work with magnets and threads is pretty ordinary. Delete that bit before showing it to Carlton."

At the door, he turned and said, "I need a photo of that wall, just as it is." And, by the way, if you take the picture with a large format camera, I think you'd have a decent shot at getting a MOMA placement!"

An Airport Conference

Rho met Littleton in a reserved conference room at the first-class lounge for United Airlines at SFO. They had two hours before her flight for New York.

Rho arrived after Littleton and saw her through the floor-to-ceiling glass wall. She was sitting and talking on her cell phone. As soon as he entered the room, she stood up and held out her hand, saying, "I'm glad you could make it. This is the only time window I've got this week and I need to know how our project is going."

He shook her hand and sat down opposite her, remembering their meeting on the Marina bench and the tantalizing ambiguity of her parting comments. *Today, another incarnation: the thoroughly professional gender-free business executive. Maybe that's the norm and I've just got an overactive imagination.*

"I'm sorry to drag you out here, but I don't have much discretionary time. Carlton's got me running all over the place."

"Is that unusual?"

"He's always left me alone. The truth is, he's scared to death of finance and would happily have nothing to do with it. He likes to sell stuff. That's OK, but I've never seen a CEO of a major company who knows so little about numbers."

"So what's changed?"

"I don't know. Everything he's asking me to do is important, but he insists that I should handle it myself, not

184 | Thomas Hofstedt

delegate it to a staff member. Says we're in a critical stage, blah, blah, blah."

She said emphatically, "I don't like it, or him!" and stood up quickly, as though her frustration required a physical expression. She clasped her hands behind her back and did some kind of isometric, twisting stretches that made Rho wonder if she played golf. *An economy of motion*, was the unbidden thought as he watched. She was completely unselfconscious, although Rho for his part was acutely aware of the way the fabric of her tailored suit stretched across her chest and the curvature of her hips as she rotated her shoulders through ninety-degree arcs in both directions. He couldn't decide whether to watch her or to look away and finally settled on looking at his cell phone, as though waiting for an important message. He felt extraneous.

He said, "I gather the ribs have healed."

"I'm ignoring them." She sat down at the conference table and said, "Enough about me, tell me --"

"Bear with me for a moment," he interrupted. "Before we get too far, I'd like to ask you about some curiosities we've come across, see if you know anything about them before I start to bias you with a full-fledged briefing."

"Kind of like the free-association technique of a psychiatrist?"

"Kinda, but no demeaning diagnosis at the end."

She sat back down, her back straight, her hands folded on the table before her. A model student ready for the quiz.

Rho started with, "GSI & GPR"?

"Didn't we cover this ground at dinner on Saturday? OK. GSI is the Group's subsidiary, mostly defense contracts but some commercial stuff for major customers. Bunch of nerds and geeks with Ph.D.'s. GPR could be anything, but given that you've paired it with GSI, I'd guess it's a one of the million DOD acronyms that the nerds and geeks throw around."

"How about 'TACA'?" He spelled it out letter by letter.

"Nope. But if we were playing one of those word games, I could come up with a really cute approximation. How about The Alliance for Cultural Assimilation?"

Rho didn't smile. "A Turkish name – Beyh?" Again, he spelled it out.

"Nope."

"An American name – David Donnelly?"

"Nothing particular. I know a few Donnelly's, but none named David. Unless you're referring to that DOD auditor whose name came up in the Executive Committee. I don't recall his first name."

Rho kept on. "How about a local startup company called 'Reactra'?"

"No."

"That morning you almost became one with the dump truck … Who knew when you'd be leaving the building?"

She thought for a moment. "Carlton. He set up the meeting that I was headed to. My AA. That's about it."

"That's the end of the free association – "

"Wait. Reactra?" She reached beneath the table into her briefcase and pulled out an iPad. After about thirty seconds of keypunching and scrolling, she looked up and smiled.

"I feel like the class dunce who finally got one right. The name rang a bell. Our Investment Committee just approved an 'angel' investment in the company, part of our very limited 'alternative investment' portfolio."

"How much was it?"

"Eight hundred thousand." She scrolled again and added, "For a 19% share." She continued to look at the screen with a puzzled look. "Says nothing about who holds the 81% piece, which is interesting."

Rho started to ask another question, but was interrupted. She said, "Let's reverse roles for a bit. I gather from this series of questions with a lot of proper nouns that you have in fact begun to turn up some...what did you call them? ...'curiosities,' I think. Why don't you tell me what you know, or suspect?"

Rho talked steadily for the next thirty minutes. He told her what Rob and Velma had turned up from Broder's USB drive; about the linkage between the driver of the runaway truck and the Beyh's expedited application for green cards; about his discussions with Arnie of the investigations in Broder's and Donnelly's deaths. She asked a few factual questions, but other than that did not interrupt his narrative.

When he finished, she said simply, "Wow!"

"That's an apt comment, I think. Nothing is quite what it seems. We've got a mare's nest of contradictions, puzzles, and question marks."

"Yes, but I think there are least three major and disturbing themes beginning to emerge from the mess."

Rho sat back in his chair and spread his hands out, signaling that he was waiting.

"OK. But before I start, you need to know I feel slightly silly, like I've spent too much time locked up with one of those conspiracy theory nuts."

She took a deep breath. "First, we have lethal force being applied very discreetly, apparently with the intent of covering up something; something that someone doesn't want known. It has expressed itself as a suicide – Broder, an apparently random murder – Donnelly, and an accident – that damn truck we dodged."

He nodded. "Each of those has been made to seem disconnected from one another and from the Morrison Group. In each case, all we have are some vague and highly subjective doubts, leading us to wonder if they're linked."

She shook her head. "Not if I'm right about the second emerging theme. The Morrison Group is somehow connected to each of these incidents. And not as an innocent bystander!"

She ticked off the points. "The GSI/TACA connection identified by Broder; Donnelly's ongoing audit of GSI contracts; and -- now -- the Group's investment in a company to be run by the family of the man who drove the runaway truck."

He spoke, his brow furrowed. "Nice deductive reasoning, Sherlock. But I must admit I don't see your third theme."

"It's a bit of a reach. But the way I would phrase it is, 'They're afraid of what I might know.'"

"Two quite direct reasons for thinking that. First, Morrison pushed hard for me to take two weeks off. Offered me all kinds of inducements. Second, Carlton is clearly trying to keep me out on the periphery of the company with all of these suddenly-important assignments that only I can do."

"What are your indirect reasons?"

"At a road show – an investment presentation – last week in New York. Walter insisted that I go. At the closing cocktail hour, a very suave fellow – he said his name was Avraham, but call him Avi – was very persistent about talking to me, wanting to know how I felt about American exceptionalism. How patriotic was I? Would I cut corners for the greater good?   That sort of thing.   Looking back on it, I think I was being auditioned.   And I had the definite feeling that Walter set it up, that that's why he wanted me in New York."

"The other indicator?   Remember when I hired you?   I was puzzled by something I overheard Morrison say to Carlton."

"Yeah, I remember."   Rho recited, "Maybe it's time to get rid of Littleton."

Marcia wrapped her arms around herself, as if feeling a sudden chill.

"They weren't talking of firing me.   I think they had something more permanent in mind."

New Lines of Inquiry

Rho dialed Derek Riordan.

"Derek, this is Robert Owens ... Rho. I have a proposition for you."

"I'm listening. Until I hear the word 'risk free,' 'annuity' or 'money back guarantee.'"

"You said you were doing some work as an investigator. I need someone who knows how to find out things about people who don't want things found out."

"Eloquently stated. But you need to know I'm not a detective. I don't have a license, don't have any interest in wayward spouses, rebellious teenagers or small time hoods who don't make their court appearances on time. And I don't use telephoto lens, wiretaps or phony business cards."

"None of which I need."

"Why me?"

"First, because I think you're interested in Turgai Beyh; and some of what I need to know is about him. Second, because I need someone who knows about construction and can talk to the whole range of people involved in that business. Third, I think you're smart. Last but definitely not least, because you're at least a little bit afraid of Uncle Sal, so I figure I've got some leverage if I need it."

"You run a major consulting firm. All that is is investigative work by people who wear better suits than I do. You've got lots of bodies with lots of smarts. And they're more afraid of you than I am of Sal. Why not just delegate?"

"I am using them where I can. But they lack an essential trait."

"Age?"

"No. Sneakiness."

"I understand this is crass. But how much will you pay me?"

"Two thousand per day, and all expenses. And a bonus of undetermined amount if all goes well."

"Mr. Owens … Rho … I accept. What is it you want me to find out, and from whom?"

"Let's start with this new company, Reactra." Rho spent the next forty-five minutes briefing Riordan on what he had learned from Appleby about the Beyh's history, new business interests and impending move to the U.S. "See if you can find out what the business is going to do and who the majority owners are. In particular, what's the connection to the Morrison Group?"

"And Riordan," Rho put extra stress on the words, "don't let anyone know who you're working for. It might get complicated otherwise."

As soon as Riordan left, Rho called Velma.

"Velma, I need you."

"Boss, this is an open line. We need to be careful how we talk!"

Rho grinned broadly. *So much for that very expensive workshop on "Managing Diversity in the Workplace!" Neither of us seems to have learned anything except better repartee!*

"Let me rephrase. I would like you to devote your considerable data mining skills to finding out who the hell really owns these things called TACA and AA, Ltd."

"What's the priority level? I've got lots of –"

Rho cut her off, "Move this to the head of the line. I think it's key to several other puzzles that we have."

Globalization at Work

Rho picked up the phone.

"This is Riordan. I have some information on the Beyhs and what they're up to. It's very interesting. Do you have some time?"

"I'm free all afternoon. Can you come by at two?"

"Sure. Keep the coffee hot. And I'm bringing another person with me."

The other person turned out to be Uncle Sal, who smiled innocently when Rho was clearly startled by his appearance with Riordan. "What's the matter, nephew? Last time we talked, you said that we were overdue for a catch-up meeting?"

Riordan broke in before Rho could think of a rejoinder. "Who do you go to when you have an oddball question about a particular time and place, the kind of question where there is no Britannica Encyclopedia or Farmer's Almanac?"

"Google. Of course."

"Of course. Well, Sal *is* Google if you're interested in the seamier elements of San Francisco."

"And I'm family too." Sal looked – Rho could think of no other word – cherubic. "And Derek had no choice. He owes me too much. Oh, and if you're worried about the fees? I'll work free – 'pro bono' is what the goddam lawyers call it."

Riordan talked nonstop for the next thirty minutes, describing a search pattern – mostly via the internet and telephone -- that ran from San Francisco to Washington D.C. to Istanbul to Tel Aviv to Los Angeles and included extensive conversations across the social spectrum -- congressional aides, construction industry executives, banking regulators and Wall Street analysts. "It's amazing how much people will tell you if you promise not to disclose the source." At the lower end, "among the people who actually work for a living," as Riordan put it, he apparently visited with common laborers, merchant marine crew, truck drivers and – on a three-day trip to Istanbul – cops and taxi drivers. Rho was beginning to envision DeToqueville on a global scale. *What have I started?*

"The expenses are substantial; and almost everything I've learned is deniable. " Riordan said without the slightest hint of guilt or uncertainty, "but I think you'll find it a good investment."

"So. What expensive and deniable facts do we know that we didn't know before?"

"First, the Beyh family – Ahmed's, not Turgai's. The patriarch – Sedat – is in fact entrenched within the Turkish mafia. 'Mafya' if you're Turkish. His holding company was a front for widespread drug-related lines of business, money laundering – which goes along with the drug business – and massive corruption in large scale construction projects, mostly in the eastern part of Turkey."

"I thought the government shut him down?"

"Yes and no. It gets a little fuzzy at this point. Most experts agree that there is active collaboration between certain government officials, high-ranking military officers, the mafia and some of the major corporates in Turkey. Each of those groups has an agenda that's only partly about money. Religion and history are huge drivers over there. Every now and then, usually after some public outcry, the police announce a major anti-corruption campaign and there are some showcase arrests. Sedat Beyh and his bank were one such case. He paid enormous fines but escaped criminal charges.

"But …," Rho prompted.

"But it was a sweetheart deal. If I used sports metaphors, I'd say 'He took one for the team.' Behind the scenes, he still has substantial assets, cash flow and – more importantly – clout within the Mafia hierarchy. The betting is that the move to the U.S. is part of the deal; that he's being kicked upstairs and into semi-retirement. That preapproved application for the green cards? They're for him, his wife and two daughters. He wants to turn the Turkish construction companies over to his sons and nephews."

"Truck drivers?"

"Well, that's another interesting feature about the family. Ahmed has a master's degrees in civil engineering and a doctorate in chemical engineering. In fact, he's got about ten years of solid professional experience in designing and testing new composite materials."

Rho filed that away for the moment.

"OK. What about Reactra?"

"I'll let Sal talk about that side of things. It's his back yard."

"Goddam right it is." Sal stood up and paced, clearly impatient and ready to talk.

Rho winced. *The English language is about to take a hit.*

"The bastards are here, and they're –"

Rho was used to Sal's jump shifts in what passed for ordinary conversation, but wanted to be sure to understand what Sal actually knew, so he interrupted immediately, "Sal? What bastards?"

"The fucking Turkish mafia, that's who."

Three sentences, three obscenities. Sal's speech had been described as "colorful" by local journalists. A local radio talk show had tried once to have him as a guest and almost lost their FCC license.

"Sal. Sit down. Please. What do you know about Reactra?"

"It's legit. Derek did most of the legwork on that. A day in Sacramento."

Riordan nodded. "A perfectly legal California corporation, all set to go. Papers filed, business taxes paid. Like an immaculate conception."

"Ha!" Sal exploded. "If someone gets fucked, it ain't immaculate!"

Rho looked at Sal, waiting for the rest. "Try to find out who owns it! The damn bureaucrats bury you in paper. And once you come to the surface, you still don't know diddly squat. Your raghead names don't even appear anywhere. "

"What business is it in?"

"I quote: 'Labor-related services for the construction industry.' That could mean anything at all."

"Is it a plausible business?"

"Plausible? You mean does it make any business sense? Would somebody pay them real money to help them actually do something?"

Rho nodded.

Sal thought for about ten seconds. "Yeah. It's not very original, but it can be a real service. There are thousands of small contractors around. They can't afford to maintain permanent staff in the hopes that some kind of work will come in over the transom. Or they get a job where they need special expertise; say, a decontamination job for a spill. So they use brokers who have access to big labor pools and a big Rolodex with lots of specialists."

Riordan added, "It's not just the small guys. The big ones use the brokers as well when they get an out-of-market job. And for the big companies like the Morrison Group who operate all over the globe, almost every job could be seen as out-of-market."

Sal exploded, "The cheap bastards use it against the unions. Why pay big hourly wages, plus overtime and fringes to some poor American slob when you can hire some hungry immigrant and throw him away when the job's over?"

"Sounds like our dog-eat-dog free enterprise system at work. Based on what you say, I'm going to guess that there are already lots of people already in the business."

Sal took on a positive sly look. He smiled and said, "There used to be, but my street sources tell me that someone is buying them up – they called it a 'rollup' – taking over their contracts and then shutting them down. Their methods aren't too nice. There are broken legs, strange fires, family members getting mugged, … ."

He smiled, a very faint smile. "Makes a person think about the good old days."

"Who's doing the buying? Where do the contracts wind up?"

"These are mom and pop businesses and they don't want to talk about it. But I have friends that have friends. Stuff leaks out."

He paused for dramatic effect. "I hear the name 'Reactra' mentioned a lot. And the buyer's reps? The fuckers with cash in briefcases, brass knuckles and what the arson squad calls 'accelerants'? They're from that part of the world.

A lot of Central European types, Armenians, more and more Turks."

"Back to the ownership issue one more time. I can help a little." Rho told them about Littleton's disclosure of the Morrison Group's minority investment in Reactra. "A wee bit of vertical integration, it would seem."

"Shit! That doesn't make any sense." Sal was vehement, "The Morrison Group is cutting its own throat. They use different brokers everywhere they operate. Why alienate a whole boatload of vendors by investing in one of their competitors, and for the sake of a very few bucks?"

The question hung in the room. Rho thought about what he had learned in the last half hour. *I know about rollups. Economies of scale and all that. Bigger but not necessarily better. But if it's a mafia operation …*

"Sal. And Derek. Bear with me for a moment. Assume two things for me. First, they roll up enough of these mom and pop operations to be the biggest game in town, whatever size that is. Second, assume it's run by the mafia – American, Turkish, Armenian, Russian, I don't care which. What will they do? As we say in the consulting business: What's their business model?"

Riordan and Sal looked at each other questioningly, clearly intrigued by the question. Sal spoke first. "I've seen it done. On the waterfront. In construction. Agriculture. It's a rotten, dirty business." He stopped, seemingly unaware of the others in the room. Rho imagined he was running through some old videos in his head.

When he resumed, he was subdued, even sad. A very different Sal. "They bring in laborers, mostly unskilled and foreign – Mexican, Chinese, Filipino, depends on the market – who pay them their life savings for a chance at a U.S. job.

Lots of promises made. Once they're here, they confiscate their passports and change the rules. They house them ten to a room, charge them a high rent, and drive them to and from the job. The poor fuckers don't have a chance."

Riordan nodded. "It's called human trafficking. Most of what you read about involves young women and prostitution. But it also includes a lot of unskilled labor."

Sal said, "Then – if you get big enough, and mean enough – there's another line of business."

"Extortion," said Riordan. "Imagine a big contractor, behind schedule and over-budget on a big job. How much would you pay on the side to somebody who could shut down the job site just by telling his captive labor force to stay home?"

Sal took up the argument. "Or you're a contractor bidding against bigger, better and more honest competitors. Some wise guy comes along and says he'll provide half your labor at half the going rate."

Riordan continued, "And all of this is so much easier to do in areas of the world where – shall we say – the rule of law is not quite so well established."

Rho was getting thoroughly depressed. *Where's Elliot Ness when we need him?*

As if reading his thoughts, Riordan said, "Sure, there are laws against all of these actions; and we have all kinds of 'task forces' that go after organized crime, but –"

"But" broke in Sal, "they're a bunch of wimps. They get to the game late and wring their hands. Too many rules. All this goddam 'due process' crap."

Rho spoke thoughtfully, "We need to know who the majority owner is. It can't be Sedat Beyh. His record in

Turkey would be like waving a red flag at the bureaucrats in Sacramento."

Riordan spoke up. "We're still trying to find out. So far, we've traced it back to a Netherlands shell company. Upstream from there, we run into a maze of shell companies in the Bahamas, the Isle of Wight, Dubai, Jerusalem and Brunei. Somebody's buried it real deep."

"Who's the Netherlands company?"

"Some acronym or other. Maybe TACA, or something close to that."

The word TACA hung in the air. Rho pulled the desk phone toward him and dialed Velma, using the speakerphone.

"Velma. I've got Riordan and Uncle Sal – "

"Velma!" Sal boomed out. "I thought that name died out when they shut down the goddam speakeasies and all the floozies went away! What a treat for old ears!'

Before Rho could say anything, Velma shot back, "Sal, huh? Isn't that a girl's name? Or a mule, maybe?"

Riordan and Rho looked at each other, and then at Sal, with growing alarm. But Sal was grinning quite broadly. He reached out and picked up the receiver, disabling the speakerphone as he did so.

"Velma? I'm seventy years old and have way too much money. How about having lunch with me?"

He listened for about twenty seconds, said "Great!" and reactivated the speakerphone feature.

Sal spoke first, to Velma. "We're live again, so be careful. These youngsters are easily shocked."

"Boss? You there?" Velma's voice was very tentative.

"Velma. Whatever just happened, it is my duty to warn you that you're on your own. But you may find it useful to know that he has a tricky knee and has trouble moving quickly to his left. You can outrun him, no matter what happens.

"As I was saying: I've got Riordan and my infamous Uncle Sal with me. They've been looking into a labor services company here in the Bay Area and came across a name of one of the owners – TACA."

"So, could we talk about TACA? And this AA, Ltd. company as well. I know it's too soon, but have you found out anything at all?"

Velma responded, "I'm about ninety percent sure on about ninety percent of what you wanted to know. And that may be the best I can do. But there are a few more tricks I can try."

"Tell me what you've got and then we'll see if we need more."

"OK. First, I know a lot more about TACA than I do AA, Ltd. But I can extrapolate, I think.

"Second, some of my search methods were, shall we say, unorthodox. I'm not sure I would want to testify in court as to how I got this information."

I wonder what I've unleashed? Rho merely said, "No need. This is purely internal."

"Right." She took a very audible deep breath. "TACA stands for Tel Aviv Consulting Associates, a very, very private company domiciled in Jerusalem. The office is on the top floor of a commercial office building and is apparently staffed by a single person who answers the telephone and collects the mail. The owners are eleven individuals. Each is an Israeli citizen with an Israeli home address."

"Do we know the names?"

"Yes. And I've done some checking on them. As far as I can tell, they are a representative "who's who" of the Israeli power structure. We've got generals, ex-ambassadors, ex-cabinet officers, entrepreneurs, even a couple of major rabbis. Put it this way, if you were throwing a party in Jerusalem, this is the A list."

"What do they have in common other than being on the A list?"

"That's part of the ten percent I'm not quite sure of. I can tell you what they're *not*, and that's ultra-orthodox fundamentalists. They're not even very politically conservative. I'd call them progressives with definite views about Middle Eastern policy. It's like what the Brits would call a 'shadow cabinet' or one of our American think tanks organized around a liberal theme, just a lot more secretive."

"How about our other mystery player – AA, Ltd.?"

"Still working my way through about the eightieth layer of Bermudan shells on that one. But one thing is clear: it's set up in the same Byzantine way that TACA was, probably by the same law firm but routed differently."

"How long to get to the end?"

"A couple of days. But I'll tell you now what I think we'll find."

"Go ahead. I can always fire you if you're wrong."

Sal shouted into the phone, "No, he can't, Velma. He doesn't have the balls to fire anyone! And if he does, I'll take care of you!"

Velma's voice took on a soothing tone. "Thank you, Sal. But you needn't worry. Rho and I have an understanding. We both know that he needs me. He even said so just two days ago!"

Rho said pleadingly, "Velma ..."

"OK. About AA ... I think it's going to turn out to be a Turkish equivalent of TACA. I'll bet the name will turn out to be Anatolian Advisors or Ankara Associates or something like that; and that the real owners will have characteristics very similar to our Israeli list."

"And Rho? One more side bet. Rob and I have continued diving down into that org chart and some interesting tidbits have turned up. I'm willing to bet that DaVinci Associates is owned by – drum roll, please – TACA and AA, Ltd., as equal partners."

The Hazards of Consulting

Kovacs did not often think about the past. But for some reason, probably the combination of weather and view from the Marina, he was thinking back to prior scenes and events. It was neither a linear nor a nostalgic form of recall, simply a series of inner videos, each one triggering a successor image. There was no accompanying cognitive sensation, no feelings of regret, nostalgia or guilt.

From here, if not for the two bridges that bracketed the view of the San Francisco Bay, it could be the Lake Michigan waterfront, as seen by a small boy from the North Shore on a fall day.

The whitecaps, stone buildings, a distant ship, and white sails all hung together for a brief moment, but then the absence of bare trees and the sight of the islands, bridges and a far shore made the comparison fail. The image shifted and a village in the Ia Drang valley came into focus, as seen from a nearby hillside.

Every day for seventeen days. We walked through the village twice, once in the morning going out and once more in the evening coming back. For sixteen and a half days, we didn't see a single villager. Then, on the evening of the seventeenth day, the little girls – three of them – were waiting in the middle of the street with flowers. When we stopped, the VC cut us and the little girls to pieces.

The image faded, to become a rooftop in Kosovo, overlooking the kind of village square that made the cover of the American tourist magazines. It afforded a clear view of the monastery on the other side of the square, a building that was ugly even before the shelling and machine gun fire had caved in one corner and pockmarked the entire front of the building.

He was an ugly little man too, in an ugly building – the priest, imam, or whatever his religious title was. Stupid too. Or impatient, which is often the same thing. If he had stayed inside one more day, he'd be alive. But it was worth ten thousand dollars to someone to make him dead. So I did. An easy head shot with the scope.

Now it's almost always an urban killing scene. Paved streets instead of jungle trails. And the victims behave differently too. In the war zones, furtiveness is automatic. In American cities, the targets feel irrationally secure in the midst of crowds, moving from triple-locked apartments to office buildings with key-coded entry systems and an overweight retiree manning the "security desk." *Funny, how much easier it is commit murder and remain anonymous in a city filled with people than in a war zone.*

His current target was cooperating nicely. His habit of going to the same bench in the Marina early in the morning, for instance, even on foul weather days. It was as if he had scheduled an appointment with his killer. The cold wind and hovering fog that was almost indistinguishable from rain insured that there were few witnesses, just the occasional jogger. Kovacs sat about fifty feet away, on the next bench toward Fort Mason, waiting for a pair of old Chinese men to pass by, walkers returning from their tai chi workout on the green. The only other pedestrian in sight was a lone woman cutting diagonally across the green, apparently headed for the yacht club. A three-minute walk on high heels that were clearly hobbling her on the rain soaked turf.

Kovacs figured he could wait until he had a clear field. But then he heard a faint ring tone and watched as the target reached in his pocket for his phone, listened for thirty seconds, and then stood up, drinking the last of his coffee. He was clearly preparing to leave. Kovacs scanned the scene once more. Not ideal, he needed to keep him in place for maybe another minute. He stood and closed the distance between them.

"Nothing fancy," the client had specified. "One of those mysterious celebrity murders, maybe gang related, that will remain unsolved and eventually become part of the San Francisco lore."

Rho threw the empty Starbucks cup into the waste can next to the bench and turned up his collar. *Not a nice morning. No sunlight. No spandexed joggers. Just as well that Celia wants me in the office.* He glanced at the man coming toward him; walking fast, wearing a dark pea jacket type of garment over a hooded sweatshirt, with a black stocking cap. He was clearly intent on talking to Rho. *Not your usual vagrant. Looks like a merchant seaman, probably with marginal English skills. At least he's not a homeless guy with an illegible cardboard sign.* Rho waited.

His English was impeccable. "I need you to sit back down for just a bit. I won't keep you very long."

Rho began, "I'm sorry – "

The man took his hand out of his coat pocket, showing him a black snub-nosed gun. He held it as though he was a clerk showing his wares in a gun store. Rho could clearly see the cross hatching on the handle.

"I only need a minute. Please." The polite phrasing and the unthreatening tone somehow offset the blankness of expression, almost making the gun seem accidental, an unnecessary adjunct to a civilized appeal.

Rho sat down, his mind racing. The man put his hand and the gun back in his pocket and sat down alongside Rho, but Rho could clearly see the outline of the muzzle directed approximately at his midsection. The elderly Chinese just passing them on the walkway paid no attention to either of them.

Fifty yards away and behind them, holding the paper bag with two latte's, Marcia stopped and considered her alternatives. She too had seen the gun, and it was abundantly clear from the postures of the two men that it was not a comfortable encounter. Rho was sitting rigidly, staring straight out at the Bay and leaning forward as if about to run. The smaller man's attention was fixed on Rho except for quick glances toward the pair of Chinese walking away from them. Neither of them seemed to speak.

Marie Lynne, Donnelly, and a runaway dump truck. Murder, suicide, staged accident. Man with a gun. Rho. She tried to form a plan, alternatives racing through her mind -- call 911 maybe, stand here and watch, scream. But the thoughts cycled. *Marie Lynne, Donnelly, and a runaway dump truck. Murder, suicide, staged accident. Man with a gun. Rho.*

Much later, she would remember nothing about her thoughts or any sense of crossing the fifty yards, even the difficulty of managing high heels on soft turf. Time and memory began again when she somehow found herself standing in front of the bench where Rho and his visitor sat, still unspeaking. Both men looked up at her -- Rho showing clear alarm; the other expressionless. No words came to her, so she reached into the white paper bag and held out one of the Styrofoam cups to Rho, an act so inane that she almost laughed. Both of the men stood up simultaneously and the hooded man moved quickly to put the bench between him and the two of them.

Kovacs recognized Littleton. He looked around quickly. The Chinese pair was two hundred yards away, clearly out of the scene. Otherwise, no one except a kayaker just offshore. He took the gun out of his pocket. *A twofer? The client wanted her dead last week. Could be done, right now.* But then he remembered Morrison's last admonition: "Leave her alone. We need her to stay alive." *I could shoot him, but then I've got a live witness. Best leave it.* As if to confirm his choice, a gaggle of middle-school boys in matching jerseys appeared in a straggling column to his left, running toward them at medium speed.

"Give me your cell phones." He realized how much control he had lost when they looked at each other, as if actually debating whether to comply. He raised the gun slightly, pointing it at Littleton. The gesture achieved the desired outcome; each of them promptly handed over their phone. He slipped them into his pocket and said, "Stay by this bench until I'm out of sight. Remember, I can still shoot you from a distance." And he added, waving his arm at the irregular line of boys running toward them, "I might even hit one of them." He left, walking quickly across Marina Boulevard and disappearing on Cervantes Boulevard.

Rho reached out and took the cup that Marcia was still holding out to him, as though a faithful participant in the child's game of "freeze."

"It's not very hot. You should have gotten it here sooner."

The words somehow released the incredible tension that had been holding her upright. The muscles that were braced against the impact of a bullet simply ceased to function. She collapsed onto the bench, taking in great gulps of air and shaking -- rippling, uncontrollable tremors that transmitted themselves through the slats of the bench.

Rho sat down very close to her and reached around her shoulders to enfold her. It was an awkward position and they made an odd-looking tableau as the stream of middle-schoolers passed them, slowing and staring in the sidelong way that preteens long ago perfected to deal with adults behaving in strange ways. He held on for what seemed like a long time, her shoulder pressed tightly into his chest and her chin digging into his arm, as the shaking slowly moderated and her breathing approached normal. Finally, she lifted her head and sat up straight. She reached up and gently pulled his arm down, moving a few inches down the bench and turning to face him.

"You're barefoot."

She looked with a sense of wonder at her feet, then back the way she had come. Her shoes – patent leather black heels – were lying neatly together about fifty yards away on the grass. *Did I run those fifty yards?* Then she realized that her feet were wet and quite cold. She pulled her feet under her on the bench, making her taller than Rho.

"What in the world were you thinking?"

"I genuinely do not know," she said wonderingly. "He was going to shoot you."

"Yes. I think so. But maybe not."

"I thought he was going to shoot me."

"He was clearly thinking about it."

Another shuddering wave went through her entire body.

"I'm freezing."

The fog had drifted in, lowering the temperature and bringing a fine but definite drizzle with it. Rho said, "Sit still" and went to pick up her shoes. She slipped them on, one hand on his shoulder for support, but then stood still, her arms hanging at her side as though she lacked both the ability to choose a direction for movement or the strength to start. She was still trembling, but now from the cold. He slipped his coat over her shoulders and guided her with his arm around her waist, heading for the street. She offered no resistance, stumbling slightly on the uneven ground.

He tried to steer her into the Starbucks, but she said "No. Not there." And bolted away from him toward the curb, alarming him. But she was waving down a cab. She came back, grabbed his sleeve and pulled him in, telling the driver "Millennium Towers." The ride took ten minutes, short enough that he could not think of anything to say that would recall her from wherever she had gone. The withdrawal was physical as well as emotional. She shrank back into a corner of the back seat, wrapping her arms around herself and burrowing into the coat still wrapped around her. At the front entrance, she left the cab without a word, leaving Rho scrambling to pay. He caught up just before the elevator doors closed.

She fumbled in her purse for the key to her condo, promptly dropped it and stood slumped by the door, staring at the key as though willing it to levitate to her. Rho picked the key up and opened the door, going before her, and stood waiting for her to follow. He was in a very large and modern living room with a floor to ceiling glass wall gray with fog. He heard the door close behind him and started to turn, but she enveloped him from behind, her arms slipping around him and binding them together with a force that surprised him. She pressed her head against the back of his neck and he heard a very faint voice say, "Thank you."

He raised his hands to hers, pried them apart and turned to face her, still within her encircling arms. He took her head between the palms of his hands and tilted her head back so that he could see her eyes. He watched with wonder as they expressed, first, fear and shock, then hunger, and finally ferocity, her breath quickening with each new emotional surge. Her need was so raw and elemental that it swept away, obliterated, all of Rho's churning doubts about responsibility and propriety. They became something primeval, one in their need to remind themselves that they were alive.

Later, they disagreed as to who moved first. They were joined together, their mouths locked, hands moving frantically either tearing at clothing or trying to touch everywhere at once, careening off the wall, stumbling together toward the gigantic U-shaped sofa that dominated the living room. There was sound, but no human speech; touching, but no gentleness; taking, but no giving. Violence took the place of passion, instinct displaced reason. There was only sensation and need. It was a savage, primordial encounter between a man and a woman in their most basic incarnations.

Rho felt as if he was surfacing from too long underwater. His breathing was rapid and his pulse racing. His bare shoulder was burning from scraping on the harsh fibers of the carpet. He was sprawled within the U formed by the couch. His shirt was half on, but most of the buttons were gone. The rest of his clothing was in a tangled knot near his feet. He tried to lift his other arm, but Marcia was lying on it, breathing even more rapidly. As far as he could tell from his position, she had on a single shoe, nothing else.

"Uh, Marcia?" His voice was raw, as though he'd been shouting.

"Um ..." She made an attempt to raise her head from the carpet but the effort seemed too much for her.

They were motionless for another five minutes. Breathing slowed and Rho was beginning to sort through phrases that might work to start a transition back to the world of civilized behavior.

She was the first to move, pulling herself into a sitting position, leaning back against the sofa and combing out her tangled hair with long fingers. The abrasions from the carpet contrasted with her white skin and the emerging bruises on her upper arm and – Rho was sure – definite teeth marks on one shoulder. She seemed utterly comfortable with her nakedness, which Rho appreciated because he was openly admiring her breasts.

He managed to arrange himself in a sitting position beside her, their flanks touching from shoulders to toes. They were facing the floor to ceiling glass wall and he was amazed that they were sitting in bright sunshine. The fog had disappeared. He looked at his watch, still on his wrist.

Survive an assassination attempt. Have wild sex with a beautiful woman. And it's only nine-thirty in the morning. Wonder what the rest of the day holds?

"What the hell just happened?" Marcia asked the question for both of them, and Rho realized that it was a genuine question.

"I don't know. I suspect that a shrink would be the most appropriate person to render an opinion. My guess is that it's a reaction to almost being killed, a need to verify that we're still alive."

There was a brief silence and then Rho began, "I have never – "

"No," she said. "Neither have I. It was the most utterly selfish act I have ever engaged in."

"Then it's quite a contrast with what happened at the Marina. You walked up to a killer and challenged him, armed with two cups of cold coffee. Pretty unselfish act." He paused, picturing the scene. "And you saved my life, I think."

"It wasn't mere coffee. Those were chai lattes, four-ninety-five apiece." She shivered, hugging herself. "That was stupid. I don't know why I did it."

"I'm glad you did." He had a sudden thought. "We need to call the police!"

She giggled. "And tell them what? That we were accosted by an assassin and really meant to call … we really did … but had to go have off-the-wall – literally – mind-blowing sex before we could get around to it?"

"Anyway, what would you tell them?" she continued. "That he stole our cell phones? All he did was show you the gun. No explicit threats, holdup demands or crazy behavior. You don't know him or have any idea why someone would be stalking you. I don't think the SFPD would get real excited."

She pushed herself to her feet, then extended her hand to pull him up alongside her. "I'm going to make some coffee. Why don't you go take a shower and then let's talk about next steps?" She pointed to a doorway into a bedroom and moved toward the kitchen on the other side of the room, still naked.

He found the master bathroom and a gigantic glassed-in shower with a window that looked down from its thirtieth floor perspective onto the Bay Bridge and its sluggish stream of cars. If he tried hard and had a telescope, he could probably see the bench on the Marina where his morning had begun....and where everything else almost ended.

He was standing motionless under the stream of hot water, enveloped in steam, when he heard the click of the shower door. He felt her nakedness against him before he could see her. He took the bar of soap and began to rub it gently wherever he could reach, wishing for longer arms. He kissed the bite mark on her shoulder. This time her mouth was soft, warm and gentle; her touch inquisitive rather than demanding. There was no hurry, until the very end. It was not about need, until the very end. It was about discovery rather than conquest, about the fine line between giving and taking, about the need to be close.

They slept in the king sized bed, using about one-third of the space. He woke when her bedside phone rang, to see her standing holding the receiver. She had a decidedly impish look on her face.

"It's Celia. She wants to know if I've seen you. What should I tell her?"

A Test Run

The message was delivered to the Turk verbally, by a courier that made regular trips between the poppy fields and Istanbul . Five words only. "Kiziltepe. Ulu Mosque. Tuesday Noon."

Kiziltepe was a small Turkish city in Eastern Turkey, near the borders with Syria and Iraq. *It looks exactly like Pakistan. But that damnable wind is gone. I think I have what the Americans call a 'home field advantage.'*

This time there was only one of the four men. The meeting was very brief.

"You said that you have access to – your words – 'new and terrible weapons.' We need to know more about these."

"We can arrange a demonstration of the technology, if you like."

"When? Where?"

"Between six and seven PM GMT on April first, in Israel, Finland, Egypt and Malaysia."

The man raised his eyebrows. "Four demonstrations simultaneously?"

The Turk smiled. "Any idiot can blow things up. But to arrange four simultaneous destructive events thousands of miles apart, without anyone knowing how it was done or who was responsible? That takes so-called terrorism to a new level!"

"And how are we supposed to verify these destructive events thousands of miles apart?"

"CNN, of course."

On a given day in the spring, four destructive events occurred. They were far apart and apparently completely independent of one another. Three of them were unremarkable in a world accustomed to car bombs exploding in crowded bazaars or mass shootings in schools.

The first would be construed as a 'terrorist attack' if it had come to the attention of the national press. But the damage was so ordinary, non-lethal and easily repaired that no one paid attention except for the local paper and the few dozen people that were temporarily inconvenienced; and even those cynical settlers viewed it as a more advanced form of vandalism rather than terrorism, a term reserved for Arabs with mortars and RPGs.

A new pipeline in the Negev Desert that provided irrigation for the fields surrounding one of the many little communities was damaged by explosives. The line was small, eighteen inches in diameter and no more than six miles long, running from an aquifer to the kibbutz. But it transformed the small valley where it ended, enabling a human community to form, as water does in a desert. The pipeline was a demonstration project by one of the many NGO's in Israel concerned with permaculture in arid regions. It was novel in that the pipeline was aboveground, supported by very modernistic stanchions at intervals, which were fashioned from a very lightweight concrete composite material.

The terrorists blew up three of the stanchions. The damaged pipes were easily replaced and temporary supports rigged. Water resumed flowing to the fields by late in the afternoon. The perpetrators were never seen nor apprehended. It is likely that the settlers did not try very hard and may even have felt some perverted sort of gratitude for being let off so lightly. No one questioned the absence of any sign of explosive material at the scene, except for a lone settler who had worked with explosives in oil fields. While working to clear debris and rebuild the pipeline, he became increasingly puzzled. But he shared his misgivings only with his wife.

"They say someone 'blew up' the concrete supports. That's misleading: I would say that the supports themselves blew up."

In fact, the explosions were detonated by a signal sent from twenty miles away by an Israeli engineer who left a dinner party to go outside for a cigarette. He was merely following orders, using the device he had been given the day before. He had no idea that he had participated in the world's first field demonstration of a new technology.

The second event might be termed an accident; or, if one is inclined to assign causality, an act of God. The cantilevered roof of a new soccer stadium in Helsinki collapsed during a heavy rainstorm. The lone fatality was a drunk who apparently was spray-painting obscenities on the section reserved for the fans of visiting teams. The stadium had won several architectural awards for its striking design and innovative construction techniques.

Authorities announced their intention to look into whether the architect and construction engineers had fully considered safety issues. The likelihood of success in their inquiries was infinitesimal, given that the "failure" was caused by a hundred pounds of precisely placed "special" concrete buried among the thousands of tons of ordinary concrete in the structure. The explosion was triggered by a special radio signal sent from several miles away.

The third destructive event was an act of deliberate public violence, carefully staged and designed to be viewed by as many people as possible. It would rank among the most viewed 'You Tube' videos for an entire week. An office building in Kuala Lumpur was imploded. A government official with a silly grin pushed the traditional "plunger" to set off explosive charges, transforming the solid-looking thirty-story cube into a neat pile of rubble while leaving the buildings on three sides unmarked. To those watching, the building seemed to fall of its own accord, folding inward on itself like a tethered balloon with a sudden leak. Even the dust cloud that formed seemed to hover directly over the site, as though it was not allowed to go beyond the boundaries of the original building.

The reality was that the "plunger" was not connected to any explosives. The destruction was caused by a shiny twelve-inch wide strip of metallic-looking tape that was affixed at the base of the weight-bearing outer walls of the building. When the politician smiled and pushed the plunger, one of the observers among the crowd of dignitaries watching the event, touched a single button on his cell phone, causing the metallic tape to vaporize, along with the concrete it was attached to.

These three destructive acts were non-malevolent; intended as covert field tests of an emerging technology.

The fourth event was also a field test, but one with another objective as well; somewhat like trying out a new drug cocktail for executing prisoners condemned to death row. In some ways, it was the most technologically impressive of the four events. A hotel ballroom in Cairo was utterly destroyed, leaving the surrounding rooms and adjacent floors unscathed. It was a masterpiece of contained destruction. However, the fact that thirty semi-prominent scientists were killed overshadowed the technological achievement.

There were about seven or eight individuals around the world who were aware of all four events. In fact, they were closely monitoring each of the incidents along two dimensions – effectiveness and publicity. At the end of the day, they were satisfied.

The tests led to two phone calls. The first was from Pakistan to Istanbul. The faint sound of wind could be heard in the background. It was in carefully coded language.

"The product tests were highly satisfactory and the executive team has agreed to your contract terms."

The second phone call was from Jerusalem to San Francisco. A single sentence.

"It's time for the real thing."

Federal Dollars at Work

Huggins poked his head in Rho's office. "It's been one of these interesting days. Care to hear about it?"

Rho waved him in. "Always available, that's me. It's a leadership style kind of thing."

They moved over to the corner seating area where there was a pair of well-worn leather chairs like those found in the reading rooms of stuffy men's clubs. Celia had been lobbying for replacing them with "something more executive-like," but Rho viewed them as the furniture equivalent of comfort food.

"Remember Velma's wall art -- that blue post-it note that she labeled 'Special Services'?

"I think so. Isn't that one of the Group subs that provides centralized services to the geographic units and individual contracts? A sister sub to GSI?"

"It is. And I spent most of the afternoon at their offices. As you know, our work-plan calls for us to interview key managers at each of the major subs. Carlton approved the concept, but" – a sly grin emerged – "I may not have been crystal clear about including GSI and SS."

"So what did you learn?"

Huggins settled into his chair. "First, some background. I know you know this, but it's important. You remember your remark about 'herding cats'? It turns out to be an understatement. The Morrison Group is the most decentralized large organization I've ever come across. 'Controlled anarchy' might be more descriptive. Until

Littleton came on the scene, there was a near absence of corporate level controls, reporting systems, or budgetary accountability. Morrison ran it like his personal fiefdom."

"Yet they've been very successful. Makes you wonder about the merits of getting an MBA, doesn't it?"

"They've been successful for two reasons, maybe three," Rob answered. "First, they have really good people in the field. Without exception, the operating core people that we've encountered are outstanding. Second, the loose control culture kind of matches the environment, especially in the developing markets. They need to respond quickly to rapidly changing situations. No time to bring headquarters up to speed and wait for them to diagnose the problem incorrectly and prescribe the wrong solution."

"You said, 'maybe three.' What's the possible third factor?"

"Morrison himself. He is connected to everyone that matters in the market. And he knows every aspect of the Group. Some analysts worry that the Group will suffer when he sells out."

"OK. So much for background. Tell me about your day."

"A scientist/engineer named Evan Donner is the General Manager at SS. We got along quite well. It seems we were in Afghanistan at the same time. He was installing a base for drone operations while I was slogging around in the provinces. We figured out there were at least a couple of times when his cute little flying robots were circling overhead while I was in a firefight below them."

"Sounds like a basis for a relationship."

"Let's just say that we agreed about the relative importance of a lot of things. Shortened all the foreplay considerably."

"Any real surprises?"

"How much autonomy he had. Basically, he could do more or less whatever he thought was best and tell Morrison and Carlton about it after the fact. Said that it was reciprocal. If Morrison wanted something, Donner would give it to him. No questions asked."

"You said 'an interesting day.'" Is that because of Donner?

"Did you know concrete is the most widely used material in the world? That we produce thirty-five *billion* tons of the stuff every year? That we're building concrete ships? That seventy percent of the world's population lives in concrete structures? That – "

Rho put out his hands. "Whoa! Stop! And no, I didn't know any of that. And I'm not sure knowing it now will help me get a date at a singles bar."

Huggins grinned at him. "You don't seem to be getting a lot of dates using your present pickup lines. Maybe you should learn more about concrete."

He turned serious. "Donner gave me a fifteen minute lecture. He's a fanatic about the stuff. Their business ... what SS does ... it's pretty exotic. Basically, they destroy things; mostly concrete structures, but they'll tackle anything that poses an engineering or environmental challenge. They are the only game in town for certain kinds of projects."

"You'd think that tearing things down would be easy. Should be lots of competitors."

"It turns out that there's lots of technology involved. Identifying stress points in a structure and then simulating implosion patterns, for example. SS has more proprietary knowledge than anyone in the industry. And that's their 'other' business, the one that doesn't make any money but enables them to stand out from their competitors. They run a major research operation, more basic than applied, in fact."

"I'll bet you're going to tell me that they have a DARPA contract."

Huggins looked slightly disappointed. "Shucks. I was trying to build up to the dramatic disclosure!"

"Yes, they do," He went on quickly. "In what the DARPA web site calls 'Materials Research.'"

"I assume it's highly classified. Did Donner say anything specific?"

"Not about the research itself. He did say that there are two main streams of research. The first has been going on for at least two thousand years – how to make the stuff stronger and lighter. The focus today is on what they call UHPC – ultra-high performance concrete. Obviously, if you're building defensive bunkers, you want them to withstand the other guy's biggest bombs."

Rho said, "That's the primary research focus of DaVinci Associates, isn't it?"

"Yeah, and that's one of the 'strategic fit' arguments for acquiring them. But there's another research direction, almost the exact opposite. It involves nanotechnology, molecular chemistry and all kinds of other hyphenated disciplines. It turns out that concrete has a number of dimensions other than strength and weight. And the military is quite interested in some of them."

"DARPA's own website provides some pretty good pointers as to what they are interested in. And it points to what Donner's group might be working on. I quote … "

Rob opened his laptop and read without any inflection. "The DARPA Reactive Material Structures program seeks to develop materials that can serve as high-strength structural materials *and* can be controllably stimulated to produce blast energy on demand. The technical objectives of the program are to develop and demonstrate the ability to tailor microstructure/architecture so that the material composite can be induced to undergo rapid and massive failure, so as to produce combustible ingredients with very large surface areas or to produce a high intensity blast."

Rho looked depressed. "Funny how the bureaucrats can make the horrific sound mundane…"

"Like saying 'collateral damage' instead of 'dead children'?"

Rho shook himself. "So if you're Donner and you're doing research on new and better forms of concrete … Surely concrete qualifies as a 'high strength structural material'?"

"Indeed it does. Donner threw out some lighthearted examples. A concrete structure that dissolves when it rains; or explodes if struck by lightning … or a laser beam; or acts like a giant batch of Semtex or C4 if it receives a radio signal from a highflying plane. He also emphatically disclaimed that his examples had anything to do with their particular research contract."

"But it's more than concrete. In its present form, concrete doesn't contain much in the way of "reactive materials," although the metal rebar apparently offers some interesting possibilities. So their main focus is on what they call "composites," new combinations of materials that are lighter, harder to detect and potentially much more violent."

"Any idea of their progress?"

"I tried, but he was quite emphatic that results were strictly classified. The only ones to get reports on progress other than Donner are the program manager at DARPA and Morrison. "

Rho said, "I'm starting to get a really bad feeling. You've got SS doing research on covert designer explosives and you've got GSI and maybe DaVinci doing research on building better detonators. And all of these efforts are imbedded in a firm that *builds* major infrastructure projects all over the globe. Put them all together and you've got some interesting possibilities."

"*Interesting* is one way to put it, I guess." Huggins leaned forward in the leather chair. "And there's something else."

Rho waited.

"I asked Donner about vendor relationships, specifically what AA Ltd. did for them. Remember one of Velma's blue magnets, the other being TACA?"

Rho nodded.

"The question made Donner nervous. He said that AA provided consulting services. When I asked him what kind of services, he hemmed and hawed and finally told me that Morrison arranged for the services and authorized the payments to be run through SS. Donner did meet with a couple of reps from AA about six months ago and gave them a tour of the place, but was not impressed. He described them as a couple of jetlagged civil servants with enough physics classes to be dangerous, maybe Middle Eastern or Central European."

"Donner gave you a lot, Rob. That shared time in Afghanistan must have been a real bonding experience."

"It changes a person," Rob said in a voice with so much sadness in it that Rho looked sharply at him.

"Him more than me. Donner is a double amputee. No legs. An IED the day before he was scheduled to rotate back."

A Job Offer

Could it be just a gigantic scam? Is Walter just an ordinary crook who happens to deal in larger amounts of money?

It was late, long after office hours, but Marcia sat at her desk. Its surface and some of the floor space around her was cluttered with numerous small stacks of paper. *Not clutter. It's quite organized. But what is it telling me?*

The numbers were clear enough, which was surprising, given how difficult it was to dig them out from the internal accounting records of the Group. Which is why her first reaction was to suspect a major fraud; a diversion of corporate cash into someone's personal bank account. It was quite clear that someone – probably Walter -- wanted these particular tracks covered.

Over the last four or five years, her clutter of papers indicated that the Morrison Group had routed approximately a billion dollars of cash to DaVinci, TACA and/or AA Ltd. All the payments originated in either GSI or SS and were accounted for as reimbursement for ordinary vendor services, although those services were always intangible in nature – royalties, licenses, advisory services and similar vague labels. The authorizations for payments came directly from Morrison's or Carlton's office rather than from the unit receiving the services; and those costs did not appear as a budgetary line item.

So far, her attempts to find out the exact nature of those services had been stymied. As CFO, she had access to the entire accounting system, but she still could not answer several key questions: What were the payments really for? Where did the cash wind up? Who owns DaVinci, TACA and AA Ltd? She had even approached the General Managers of GSI and SS to ask them, but was stonewalled politely.

In addition, the company had just paid a billion dollars to acquire DaVinci, a price that she thought was outrageously high. And it was providing startup money to a Turkish family to help obtain U.S. green cards. *I'll bet that Sedat Beyh turns out to be connected to AA Ltd. too!*

The reality was that Morrison was the sole owner. If he wanted to squander money on a pet project or for a favorite vendor, that was his prerogative. No public trust or fiduciary duty was being violated.

If the Chairman hires a consultant to provide advice and then authorizes the payment of the subsequent invoice, it's hard for even a very courageous green-eyeshade type to question the wisdom of that payment!

It was highly ironic, but one of her first reactions when she saw the totality of the numbers was admiration. *The audited financial statements required as part of the IPO process clearly portray an exceptionally profitable company. The company's profit margins are gold-standard, despite the large amounts of cash being siphoned off!* The single tallest stack of papers on the floor was the draft of the SEC prospectus to accompany the IPO.

She jumped about a foot when a voice said, "Working late, aren't you?" Walter stood in the door of her office. He was dressed in a dark three-piece suit and towing an overnighter case, looking like one of those first-class passengers that is being escorted from the airline lounge directly to the boarding gate.

Is this a random encounter? Or does he know what all this paper is about?

She said, "Normal hours, these days, what with IPO's and acquisitions. What about you? Coming or going?"

Morrison smiled and took two steps into her office, having to maneuver between the two stacks of invoices from TACA and AA Ltd on the floor. She realized that the distinctive TACA logo could easily be read from a standing position.

"Coming, actually. Just in from the last of the road shows. Three cities in three days. I know it's important, but I can't tell you how glad I am to be done with that."

"I know you don't like it. But trust me; you're quite good at it. I've watched a lot of them and I can tell you that you exude absolute integrity. It's a rare attribute in that kind of setting. The analysts love it."

He smiled quite broadly. "Ah! But is it genuine? Or merely a talent for dissembling?"

I wonder if he's trying to tell me something.

"In terms of getting the deal done," Marcia said, "I don't think it matters very much. Particularly when you are selling an outstanding company, as you are."

What the hell! Might as well push the envelope a bit …

She waved her arm to indicate the desk and papers scattered across the floor, "Actually, what I'm working on is the final, final pro forma… the financial statements that will show the new company after DaVinci is folded in and the ownership structure has changed from private to public."

"Not a problem, is it? The margins we've been reporting –"

She interrupted, "No problem at all. Our historical margins are top-of-the-charts. I am still slightly amazed when

I calculate them. But then I try to put myself in the new owner's shoes: What will the margins be after Walter Morrison is gone? So many of the key business decisions are controlled by you alone. Can that historical success be sustained?"

The question seemed to trigger something. He was silent and took on a brooding look.

She added quickly, "Walter, it's just a rhetorical question."

He smiled again, even more sadly. "Yes, I know."

After a few seconds pause, he surprised her with his next question. "How many people does the Group employ?"

"About thirty-thousand, half of those in the U.S."

Still another surprise. "And you, Marcia? What will you do after the IPO?"

"First, hold you to your promise of the company's Gulfstream to take me to a beach where the drinks have little umbrellas in them. After that, --" She paused, because she realized that she had not given any thought to life after the IPO.

"Would you like to be the new CEO of the Morrison Group?"

The question was posed in an ordinary conversational tone, as though a straightforward continuation of their so-far conventional discussion. She did not gasp out loud; nor did she gape open-mouthed. But the question floored her. It jarred her out of her need to be careful about what she said or to filter his comments through her own uncertainty as to his motives.

"But, Daniel is next in line –"

"Marcia, we both know that you can and do run managerial rings around Carlton. The only thing he's better at is sycophancy."

"But Morrison is an engineering company –"

"And you're a finance type, or think you are. But our operating heads are the best in the business. We don't need another engineer. We need someone who can make the parts work together. I've watched you. You pay attention; you take advice; you make people feel good about what they're bringing to the table; you make the tough decisions; you're a wickedly good negotiator ... And, please forgive the sexism, you look really good in a hard hat!"

"Walter, I'm flattered. You've just paid me a whole series of extraordinary compliments. You cannot begin to appreciate how many of my innermost fantasies have just been fanned into life. But I – "

"I know. It's a lot to think about." He paused to add emphasis to what he said next. "But I'm deadly serious. I will stay at the Group only long enough to fulfill my promises to the bankers and the Board. Then I am gone. Really gone. I would feel very happy to see you in the top job."

He turned to leave, slightly scattering the stack of TACA invoices with his foot. Standing in the doorway, with his back turned to her, he said, "And once you're in charge, you can run it like it deserves to be run; like a professional organization, rather than the personal piggybank of an eccentric old man."

He left without waiting for a response, leaving her still sitting at her desk.

Was that a bribe? A hint? A confession? To what?

The questions washed through her, pushing to the outer rim of her consciousness the awareness of the seduction that had just been practiced on her. *I'd be the youngest woman CEO of a Fortune 500 company. The only female CEO in a traditionally male industry. The head of a really good company that is capable of so much more!*

Her next set of emotions surprised her even more. *The company is Walter Morrison, and vice versa. What will he do?* She thought about that for a minute or two and came to a startling conclusion. *He's acting like he has no future after the IPO. No plans. As though life ends when the Group is sold.*

She stood up suddenly, as though the welter of questions and emotions required a greater physical expression. *What's going on at the Group? Who's behind TACA and AA Ltd.? What does Morrison want?*

The hell with Morrison: What do I want?"

And then yet another surprise. An emotion that was new to her experience. The desire to share these intensely personal questions and their possible answers with another person.

She sat down at her desk once more and dialed the number for Robert Harris Owens III.

Progress Reports

Jerusalem. Ahmed's hard-hat had a plastic rectangle with the name "Cheka" screwed onto the front. That name and his photo were also on the ID card on the lanyard around his neck. They made him wonder what nationality he was supposed to be. But the job didn't require deep cover, so he didn't worry about it.

This was his fourth visit to the site. His first was fourteen months ago when it was an empty field on the edge of the city. Then he came as a simple tourist, driving by and stopping as if the field was of little interest, just a good place to stretch and take a photo of the distant skyline. The domes and ancient walls in the center of the city were just barely visible if one walked to the small rise that ran along the northern edge of the field.

Now the structure filled and dominated the field, concrete stretching from one end to the other and soaring into the sky. But concrete without angles, only curves. Not gray, but bands of muted colors. Seemingly not heavy or bound to the earth, but poised to fly.

Ahmed thought of himself as pragmatic, not susceptible to aesthetics. He was surprised by his reaction. *It is truly beautiful.* Briefly, another surprising thought flashed into his consciousness. *It is too bad that it cannot last.*

The last of the construction cranes was being disassembled and loaded onto trucks. Most of the activity was now concerned with interior finishing, landscaping and installing equipment.

Ahmed threw his hardhat and the sheaf of blueprints that he was carrying into the rear compartment of his SUV. He was done with his last checks. Everything was in place and ready. His last view of the structure was through his mirror as he drove away. His final thought was both pragmatic and aesthetic: *After all, many tombs are beautiful structures. Those buried here will have that to console them.*

Istanbul. Omar's hardhat and ID placard displayed his real name. And his title, which he was inordinately proud of – "Construction Manager." He recognized this vanity in himself, and had memorized the Koran's admonition: *And when they hear vanity they withdraw from it and say: Unto us our works and unto you your works. Peace be unto you! We desire not the ignorant.* But in his heart, he knew that he had achieved his position by hard work and study, not by bribery or inheritance as so many of the incompetent and often corrupt government officials that he encountered.

His pride in what he had accomplished was sharpened when he came to work every day in the last three months. He liked to think of the buildings that he worked on as his "clients," and this client was the most magnificent of all. The marble palace was originally built on the edge of the continent almost one-hundred-and-fifty years ago, part of a city that dated its origins in the Neolithic age and had presided over a succession of empires. At one time, the palace had been the seat of government of one of those empires. Today it was a hotel, although its grandeur and history, together with world-class service, combined to make it one of the most luxurious hotels in the world.

Omar's job was to help insure that the palace would continue. His company was engaged in what the American contractor called an "earthquake retrofit," using new composite materials to reinforce the foundation and to add flexibility during a quake. Omar's job was to prepare sixty subterranean forms into which the new materials would be poured and, once hardened, provide "smart piers" that could adapt to tectonic shifts.

To Omar, the material looked like ordinary concrete as it flowed from the line of specialty trucks into his forms. But he was assured that it was different, the latest and best ultra-high-performance-concrete. And it had special instruments imbedded within it to monitor minute stress movements and to adapt to them, things the Americans called 'nano-sensors.'

Afghanistan. Abdul walked by the construction site every day. For the last several months, it had not changed; remaining a collection of semi-finished concrete columns and slabs with rebar projecting out in all directions. Then the Americans announced that they were leaving, making the announcement credible by ceasing field operations in the province. The announcement made the project come alive. Workers swarmed over the rising structure; lines of trucks queued up; and senior military officers started to appear, carrying blueprints and clipboards.

Abdul and several other male members of his sprawling family obtained jobs on the site. Nothing fancy, manual labor; but the Americans paid well and he enjoyed building something, even something as ugly and functional as this building. He kept expecting the local Taliban commander – who happened to be his uncle -- to enlist him in a sabotage operation, but no approach was made. When he asked, he was told, "Let the Americans build it. Once it is filled with their stooges, we shall see about destroying it. Or perhaps we shall be able to use it once we are back in full control."

Abdul was a poor farmer, so he could not appreciate the sophistication of the new materials that were being employed in the foundation of the building. To the extent he thought about it, he marveled at how American's would spend so much money and effort on a project that they were about to abandon.

Washington D.C. In another capital city on another continent at about the same time, another structure was nearing completion as well, but it had taken two days rather than two years to complete and it would never stimulate any aesthetic thoughts. It was a flat, rectangular concrete slab, gray and featureless other than the narrow grooves running inside the perimeter and forming different patterns across the sixty-foot width of the slab.

The foreman of the finishing crew watched his workers closely as they poured the neon orange specialty concrete into the grooves. The garish color somehow emphasized the symmetry of the otherwise drab rectangle. To an observer unfamiliar with sports, it could be a piece of pagan art. The foreman was amused that the designated observer followed the pourers foot-by-foot as they worked filling in the two-inch strips. *It's just colored concrete, for god's sake!*

The extraordinary level of attention was beginning to get on the foreman's nerves. *I've been interviewed on Good Morning America, for chrissake! About how he felt about pouring a concrete slab!* The work was being done at half-price using donated materials and even that was being paid by a private donor who wished to remain anonymous. The press secretary had issued an official statement to assure the press that "no taxpayer funds were used on the project."

He'd overheard one of the security guards talking on his cell about "a christening." *What? They're going to break a bottle of champagne on a slab of concrete? Good luck with that!* From what he knew about the properties of the surface, the bottle would probably bounce rather than break.

A Tragedy Revisited

Rho stopped by Velma's cubicle.

"Velma, when you and Rob were briefing me on DaVinci ... their business, why they were for sale now, that sort of thing ... one of you said something about their founder being murdered. Do you remember?"

"Yeah. His name was Rahm Izak. You can call it murder, I guess, but he was killed by a bomb that also wiped out thirty or forty other people."

"Could he have been the target? The rest of them were just in the wrong place at the wrong time?

"I wouldn't think so. An offshoot sect of al Qaeda claimed responsibility and their manifesto – shown on Al Jazeera, by the way – was aimed at – their words, not mine – 'the infidel Western scientists designing weapons for the extinction of Muslims.' They were a bunch of geophysicists, not munitions types!"

She went on. "As for Izak being the target? Not likely. There were at least half-a-dozen more eminent figures there, and two or three of them were very unpopular with the radical imams for their close ties to Western oil companies."

"You said 'a bomb.' Was it a suicide bomber? A planted device? What?"

"I don't know, but I know how to find out." She pivoted around in her chair and began typing on the keyboard on her desk. Rho watched the characters fly across the gigantic computer screen. He couldn't follow the details, but she was clearly sorting through a series of web sites using links generated by a search algorithm.

"This one looks like the best bet," she said, and expanded the page view to full screen. "It's taken from the major English language newspaper in Cairo, dated three days after the explosion."

They both read through the article quickly. And then once more, slowly.

Rho spoke as if to himself. "Very tight security. Metal detectors & body searches. Only the delegates permitted in the conference room itself."

Velma indicated a paragraph near the end of the article. "They don't actually know how the bomb got in there or how it was detonated. But they do know that the blast originated at the perimeter of the room, at the base of the wall. And here," she pointed to a sentence in the middle, "a senior police official speculated that there may have been more than one bomb and they were probably directional."

"Directional?"

"Picture a conventional bomb. There's a crater, a kill radius with equal blast effects at all points around the circumference. Contrast that with a bomb where the blast impact and/or shrapnel follows a distinct path, leaving other areas untouched."

"Could the bomb, or bombs, have been put in place a few days in advance?"

"Both the hotel staff and the government anti-terrorist group did a sweep just before the meeting. Nothing."

"Wait a minute," Velma said. She turned back to the keyboard.

"There's another link, showing a picture of the Cairo hotel at the grand opening of its spanking new conference center. It's dated two weeks before the bombing. The geophysics group was its first major conference."

She paged down in the article on screen. It was taken from an English language architectural magazine. The entire issue seemed to be devoted to innovative and commercial construction projects in Europe and the Middle East.

"Here's some detail," Velma said, and started reading. "The conference center contains side-by-side ballroom-sized rooms. The walls separating them are 99% soundproof because they used a very lightweight composite material for interior wall shielding, supported by floor to ceiling pillars no more than six inches wide."

She paused, and then read very deliberately, "The design engineering was led by The Morrison Group and featured recent research on new uses of composite materials for construction."

The Chronology of Disaster

Rho stopped by Velma's cubicle again on his way home. Typically, she was gazing at a computer screen that was filled with numbers. As he came in, she pressed a single key and the numbers went away, replaced by a colorful bar graph with flying icons.

Rho said, "If I get to choose, I prefer the graph to the numbers."

"It's a pretty picture ... and a complete lie, of course. The numbers are better."

Rho knew better than to debate the point with Velma. Instead, he changed the subject. "Did Rob tell you about his visit with Donner at Morrison's Special Services subsidiary?"

"Yeah. Did you know that more concrete is consumed every year than any other substance except water?"

He affected a tone of horror, "Not you too!"

"Don't worry. I'll leave the construction business to the boys. What can I do for you?"

"Suppose I asked for a list of all non-military explosions or catastrophic structural failures that took place from a month before the bombing of that Cairo hotel where Izak died through today?"

"Assuming you're talking worldwide, it would take some advanced search techniques in Google and what you'd get would be those events that would have received some form of media coverage. Maybe an hour at most."

I feel like Captain Kirk querying his computer on the Star Ship Enterprise. No wonder there are no more encyclopedia salesmen going door-to-door. "Now, once I have that list, suppose I wanted to narrow it down to those events where concrete was present."

Velma frowned. "You'd probably have to do it by hand. And from Rob told me about concrete, I'm not sure you'd eliminate many events from your list."

Rho nodded. "Two more sorts. Suppose I eliminated those where the cause was evident, no chance for any alternative explanation?"

"That would knock the number way down, I think." She began jotting notes. "What's your last criterion?"

"Suppose I wanted to know which of those locations had at some point in the past been a project of any part of the Morrison Group?"

Velma's frown deepened and she turned back to her keyboard. "Well, we have a list of –." She stopped and snapped back to face Rho. "You're suggesting that --," but did not finish.

He said. "It's just a hypothesis for testing. View it as an interesting challenge to your data grubbing talents."

Three hours later, Velma walked into Rho's office with her laptop and a very determined expression.

It must be the data grubbing comment I made. I think I'm about to be put in my place.

She put the computer on the corner of his desk and hooked on a device about the size of a deck of cards. It projected a light beam onto the opposite wall and the lighted square was instantly filled with a worksheet.

"Here's your first list. Fifty-seven media-reported cases of non-military explosions or catastrophic structural failures where there was concrete present, from one month before the Cairo bombing through yesterday."

"I'm impressed Velma. That was fast."

She shrugged off the compliment. "That's what computers are good at. Speed. What they're not so good at is the judgment part."

She pressed a key and more than two-thirds of the list faded from the screen. "Assuming that you're only interested in those with a sinister force at work, I've eliminated those where a definitive cause was identified. That included earthquakes, natural gas explosions, and – with one exception – deliberate demolition projects. If in doubt, I left it in."

"I count four explosions and five structural failures, including our Egyptian hotel. Do you see any of your beloved patterns in that list."

Rather than answering, she pressed a key and Rho watched as the nine items crawled across the screen and lined themselves up on a time line over the four months that Velma had researched. Four events were tightly packed together, the other five spread out more or less uniformly along the time line.

"Four unexplained catastrophes within twenty-four hours, including Cairo?"

"Curious, isn't it? Actually, they happened within a one hour time period."

"Why did you leave in that Kuala Lumpur demolition? Surely that's a known and non-sinister cause?"

"But you're forgetting the last criterion you asked me to apply..."

"Ah, yes. The Morrison Group involvement."

"All of these have DaVinci, GSI or Special Services contracts at some level of construction."

"And this Israeli pipeline?"

"Was installed by an NGO sponsored by an advisory firm named TACA."

Protocol as Fate

Almost every governing executive has a person or even an entire department that controls access to the seat of power and the perks that are associated with it. The titles vary, ranging from "social secretary," "chief of protocol" or even a "chief of staff." Their duties are stressful, whether it's deciding who gets to sit next to the first lady or the guest list to the inauguration.

Jerusalem. The fact that it is was a cultural event – an opera – had very little influence on the choice of guests. The event would showcase everything that Israel offered to the world. The new Performing Arts center was the embodiment of the belief that Jerusalem could become a center for creativity on a global scale. The new center already was the single most talked about architectural event of the year. The twelve hundred seats in the performing arts auditorium in the center of the structure would be occupied by government officials, luminati from the arts, and wealthy patrons whose money had brought the center into existence.

Istanbul. In Turkey, invitations were sent to universities, foreign embassies, media organizations and corporate leaders. Given the program title – "Turkey's Role in the New Middle East" – and the assured attendance of the Minister of Foreign Affairs, the mid-ranking officer in the World Bank who was preparing the list assumed that all seats would be taken by prominent individuals. It helped to have the rumor circulating that Prime Minister Erdogan would provide the keynote talk. She had many years of experience organizing such affairs and she knew that venue was critical. Offering three nights of lodging in one of the world's greatest luxury hotels would not hurt attendance!

Afghanistan. Strict protocols dating back hundreds of years dictated the guest list for the opening of the new barracks and police station. Tribal elders headed the list, followed by high-ranking members of the military and defense ministry.

The event began to assume extraordinary importance when the American departure was announced. President Karzai intended to attend the opening ceremonies and make a speech to mark the transition from dependence to independence, with a strong vote of confidence for Afghanistan's ability to manage its own affairs.

Washington D.C. Every national holiday offers photo ops for politicians and their Press Secretaries. In the American White House, the annual Easter Egg Hunt, lighting of the Christmas tree, and visiting the Tomb of the Unknown Soldier on Veteran's Day are such events. The guest list must and does reflect a carefully selected cross section of the American ethnic kaleidoscope. The guests are props, albeit willing ones.

This one was different. The nation had never had a chief executive who played pickup basketball. Golf, tennis, boating, or even bowling, was the norm. So the White House tennis court was gone, replaced by a basketball court. The President had challenged Congress to field a team to play against him and his Executive Office staffers to properly inaugurate the court. Younger justices of the Supreme Court would referee. It would be a sporting analog to the American constitutional system with its three branches of government and the famous 'checks and balances.' Guests would be primarily family members and the closest staff members to the players. And the press, of course.

A Celebration of Capitalism

The "initial public offering" or "IPO" is perhaps the single most important ritual within the capitalist creed; a rite of passage that is celebrated not unlike a bar mitzvah. And so it was for the Morrison Group launch.

Historians generally agree that the creation of the corporation was one of the four or five breakthroughs that enabled society to emerge from a feudal existence where life was 'nasty, brutish and short' into a new age; one marked by industrial and technological revolutions that vastly improved the quality of life. The limited liability of the new firm created access to capital, enabling entrepreneurs to invent and market on a grand scale. The concept of "progress" became woven into the new economic order.

The alternative means of organizing economic activity – socialism or its extreme form, communism – competed against capitalism for a bitter seventy years, failing spectacularly when Gorbychev dissolved the Soviet Union and Russia and its satellite states joined the capitalists. For Morrison, a patriot and a capitalist, the fall of the Berlin Wall and the collapse of the Soviet Union were the most reaffirming moments of his lifetime.

For Walter, the IPO made for a long and very dull day, and he was eager to be done with the endless photo ops and congratulatory meetings. It was always difficult for the founder to sell off his creation, knowing that henceforth it would be subject to the whims of distant shareholders and hostile regulators. But Morrison was indifferent to that prospect. He suspected that the Morrison Group would cease to exist in its present form once he was gone.

Late in the day, his bankers told him that the sale of his shares had netted him over five billion dollars. It would be transferred into his account within forty-eight hours. From that point on, the money would disappear, weaving its way through the equivalent of a monetary pachinko machine and coming out the other end in the hands of a dozen different covert organizations. Morrison neither knew nor cared how the process worked, but Avi had assured him that the recipients would be invisible. Banking officials and tax authorities would be distraught with Morrison, but that too was of little concern. *Given Dr. Weber's timeline, they'll have to exhume me to ask where the money went. And they'll have other things on their mind than the whereabouts of a few billion dollars by then anyway.*

The organizations receiving the money had two things in common. They were unofficial, secretive, underground groups and they were dedicated to bringing about radical change in the Middle East by a variety of extralegal means. Money was their scarce resource, and they used the phrase "real leverage" when he pressed them about their agenda. He was amused by their ingratitude and annoying air of entitlement, but supposed that was one of the irritating character traits of fanatics. Avi had vetted them very carefully over the past year and was confident that the money would be well spent.

Now the clock starts.

Almost eight thousand miles away, four bearded young men in Mogadishu, Somalia groomed themselves carefully and then each of them separately recorded a five-minute video. The scripts varied in phraseology, citations from the Koran and degree of emotion; but their message was the same. *America is the Great Satan and those who ally with America will suffer with her. Allahu Akbar.* Three of the men spoke in Arabic. The other spoke in English and had a much longer trip to his assignment.

On the outskirts of Jerusalem, an international cast of opera personalities was preparing for its final and full dress rehearsal of Tosca. To a person, they raved about the architecture and acoustics of the magnificent new performing arts center. The Israeli security personnel were setting up their screening devices at the entrances and reviewing how they would handle the queue of arriving dignitaries.

On the banks of the Bosphorus in Istanbul, the delegates to the International Conference had just finished applauding politely as the opening speaker finished her remarks on "Turkey's Role in the New Middle East." It was an unremarkable start to the three-day conference. Security was especially rigorous due to the presence of several finance ministers from the OPEC nations and the European Union.

In Washington D.C., it was business as usual. Congress was in session and the President was in town. An unusual number of tourists seemed to be on the streets, but locals chalked that up to the cherry blossoms and the unusually mild weather for this time of year.

Most of the world simply slept, worked, traveled, dined and engaged in all those mundane acts that made up their ordinary lives, secure in the belief that a certain level of recurring tragedy was normal and survivable. Some – a very few – knew better, but they were so encrusted in cynicism that even they could not foresee that the course of history could be altered.

Synchronicity

Marcia seemed increasingly distracted. "I feel like I'm missing something really important."

"Your clothing, perhaps?" Rho suggested, noting that it was – this time – neatly folded on the dresser on the opposite side of her bedroom. His, on the other hand, was strewn along a relatively straight line from the front door to the very rumpled bed they were currently sharing, sitting up resting against the cushioned headboard and looking out over the Bay. From this angle, about all that was visible were the lights on the tops of the Bay Bridge towers and the Berkeley Hills.

The depth of her distraction was made clear to him when she only smiled faintly and squirmed slightly closer, saying "No, definitely not that."

Rho was well aware of the source of her uneasiness, and shared the same misgivings. He had been trying to convince himself that it was why he had suggested this meeting away from the Morrison Group offices.

Sure it was. Absolutely no thought of anything except a purely professional exchange. Right! Well, it was certain that their exchange was neither pure nor professional. At least not yet.

He had called her several hours ago and she agreed that they needed to talk as soon as possible. He remembered clearly standing outside her door, his finger on the bell, but the subsequent images were blurred considerably, starting from the instant she opened the door. She was naked except for a long green scarf and an exceptionally wicked smile. The impact was considerable; he was literally stunned. Finally, she simply reached out, hooked her finger into his shirtfront, and pulled him through the door. The blurring continued, up until she said, "I feel like I'm missing something."

Rho sat up straighter. "OK, let's review what we know, or at least strongly suspect."

"We've had three deaths – Izak, Donnelly and Broder; two probable attempted murders – you and me; and at least two subtle attempts to coopt you. All of which we believe are to prevent – or delay – the discovery of something going on at the Morrison Group."

Marcia broke in. "And we have a money trail that runs from the Group to very private Israeli and Turkish cartels of very connected and important individuals, all of them with a strong point of view about the reshaping of the Middle East along democratic, stable lines."

He continued, "And aforesaid money trail seems quite legal, although its apparent connection with obscure technology transfers and classified research is troublesome."

"Especially because some of that research and technology is aimed at applications that lend themselves to terrorist activities."

"Aforesaid applications having been tested via four apparently disconnected and highly explosive 'incidents' on three different continents …the destruction of four different concrete structures … all at the same time."

The rapid-fire back-and-forth stopped abruptly. They looked at one another.

Marcia said, "That's it … what you just said … 'All at the same time' … I think I know what we're missing."

Then she breathed, "Synchronicity. "

Rho recited, "The coincidence of events that seem related." And then, "What about it?"

"It's what we're missing. We've been focused on figuring out who's who, and what's going on. But I think *timing* – the *when* – is at least as important."

"Why is timing so important to Walter? He's has been pushing very hard to make certain things happen in the same time frame. Things that have a natural life cycle have been warped to fit the timetable. The DaVinci acquisition and the IPO have been rushed to completion for no apparently good reason. On the operating side, he's pushed three of our biggest contracts to finish at the same time, either by speeding up or slowing down. *Why?*"

Her question hung in the air.

He said it for them. "Something extremely bad is about to happen,"

She nodded. "And there is nothing in any of this reasoning that we can take to the police, the FBI, the CIA, DOD, Homeland Security, or Mothers Against Drunk Driving. It's all innuendo, shadows and hypotheticals. Good for movie rights, maybe."

Marcia kissed him on the cheek and scrambled off her side of the bed. "I need to make a call."

She went into her closet and reemerged within ten seconds in jeans and a sweatshirt. Then to the desk phone, where she dialed a number, spoke for thirty seconds or so, and then made some notes. Rho used the time to get himself dressed and followed her to the kitchen counter where she was booting up her laptop.

"I'll bet I know what you were inquiring about on the phone."

She smiled quite primly.

"You were asking about the location and nature of those three major projects that Walter was pushing so hard to finish at the same time."

She smiled in a dismissive way. "Pretty obvious deduction." She looked at the notes she had just made and began reciting.

"The first ever stand-alone performing arts center in Jerusalem… an architectural masterpiece according to the world press. An earthquake retrofit of the Ciragan Palace in Istanbul, using the latest and best technology, mostly from the U.S. And a state-of-the-art police station and military barracks in the Kandahar Province of Afghanistan."

She shook her head. "What is it about these three structures that makes it so important that they all come on line at the same time? What do they share?"

Rho said, "Well, for one thing, they're all in the Middle East, more or less."

They were both silent, then Rho spoke as though to himself. "Maybe it's about who or what's going to be in those structures at the same point in time … It's my turn to make a call."

He sat at the desk and dialed. He spoke without interruption for a minute. The call lasted ten minutes, with frequent stretches where Rho sat idle, obviously waiting for the person on the other end to respond.

He hung up. "That was Velma … and her computer."

Marcia waited for more, but Rho seemed stuck in some dreamlike rut.

"Rho?"

He roused himself. "Did you know that four heads-of-state will all be attending ceremonial events in their home countries at precisely the same time on the same day in the near future? Erdogan is speaking at a conference at the Ciragan Palace in Istanbul, Karzai is cutting the tape for the new military barracks in Kandahar, and Netanyahu is attending the inaugural opera – Tosca, apparently -- for the widely-acclaimed Jerusalem Center for the Performing Arts. How's that for synchronicity?"

She stared, her expression slowly becoming one of disbelief. Then she said, "You said four; that's only three."

"That's the best – or worst – of all. At that same time, our very own President is hosting a basketball game at the White House for selected members of the Executive, Congressional and Supreme Court branches of government... breaking in a brand-new basketball court made out of new composite materials."

Marcia tried to ask a simple question, but her voice didn't work. It took three tries.

"Why ... Why would Walter ...? Why would anyone ....?"

He continued in the same questioning voice. "What would happen if the democratically-elected leaders of the U.S., Israel, Turkey and Afghanistan were assassinated simultaneously, along with thousands of their fellow politicians and elite citizens?"

"The reaction would be horrendous. The world would never be the same again."

Both were silent, thinking. Then she said, "And if it was traced to Islamic fundamentalists, it would trigger a backlash that would make the last ten years of killing look like a mere skirmish!"

Rho paced, unable to sit. "I think that's what Walter wants. And he wants to shape it. That's why he's routing money to obscure movements in Israel and Turkey. Remember his views on American exceptionalism."

Marcia had slumped into a posture of severe resignation. A sudden thought snapped her upright. "Rho. You said these happened at the same time on the same day. And in the near future. When? When does everything coincide?"

Rho looked at his watch. "About three hours from now."

A Search for Solutions

Rho and Marcia took turns playing devil's advocate, seeking weak spots in their narrative. Instead, they kept turning up new and confirming evidence – always circumstantial and, even to them, fanciful in the telling.

They role-played hypothetical conversations with different law enforcement agencies, trying to allow for the fact that they were cold-calling at six in the morning. They tried to recall college friends or professional contacts that would give them access to someone that would listen and had some authority to act.

Rho actually got through to Ben Appleby in Turkey.

Rho could hear traffic noises in the background when Appleby answered his cell. "Rho. It's the early morning hours in California. I gather this isn't one of those 'just keep in touch kind' of calls."

"As far as you could be from that," answered Rho. "And I promise you that I haven't gone insane. Just don't hang up on me, no matter what you think!"

Rho looked at Marcia, took a deep breath, and just blurted it all out in single run-on sentence. "I think I've stumbled onto an international terrorist plot and that it may involve an attack on the Ciragan Palace in Istanbul when Erdogan is speaking."

I sound like a paranoid schizophrenic who's gone off of his lithium!

There was a very long silence from Appleby's end.

"Rho. That's … That's … Are you sure? Do you – "

"No. I'm not sure. And I can't prove it. But I think it's real."

"I'm on my way there right now. Ten minutes at most."

"To the Ciragan?"

"Of course. I'm the ambassador. He's the head of state. Ambassadors do that sort of thing … Attend speeches."

His tone changed from sarcastic to concerned. "What Turkish authorities have you notified? Anybody in Washington? Who else knows about this?"

"You're the first person I could think of to call. Can you get the event moved or postponed?"

"Not based on what you've told me. I'd sound just as loony as you. We get dozens of threat notices every week. Somebody at NSA picks up some weird cell phone chatter from Africa or some Interpol analyst has an informant with hot information. One time, we evacuated the embassy because the Turks lost contact with a known al Qaeda operative. We've looked stupid too many times."

From his increasingly impatient tone, Rho knew that he was losing him. *I sound paranoid even to myself.*

"Ben, it's got something to do with an earthquake retrofit at the Palace. It may be that some kind of explosive has been planted; something that isn't detectable by normal means."

He heard sounds from the other end of the call. Appleby was giving instructions to someone else on another phone. It sounded more like an argument than a polite discussion of possibilities.

"I've just put my head of embassy security onto it. He's there – at the Palace -- and, by the way, he says security is tighter than he's ever seen it. And if you think I'm skeptical about your paranoia, you should hear him! He'll check out what he can. And for the record, I'm referring to you as an anonymous informant!"

Appleby said abruptly, "I'll call you back. Keep your phone free."

Appleby called thirty minutes later. "I'm in the basement. We've got Geiger counters, bomb-sniffing dogs, and half of the Turkish security forces and we've been all over this place, with special attention to the retrofit work. The local cops have grilled the construction supervisor who oversaw the work – Omar somebody or other – and he was here for every bit of the installation. Which was mostly pouring cement! There's nothing! "

"It's concrete, not cement," Rho said.

"Whatever! Erdogan's security guru made the call: the speech will go as planned. You'll be glad to know they're confiscating anything that has an on-off switch or that can send a signal from everyone in the building. That includes the cell phone that I'm talking on, so I won't be in touch for a while. Rho, you owe me big time for this one!"

Rho thought, but did not say, *I hope that you'll still be around so that I'm able to repay you.* The line went dead. He looked at Marcia and shook his head.

She said, "The time window where the four are all in place at the same time begins about now and will last for maybe another hour after that. If we're right, they must have it timed so that the incidents will be simultaneous. Otherwise, once the news of any single assassination attempt at this level is on the air, the other three individuals will cancel whatever they're doing and head for their command centers and press rooms."

He said, "More calls?"

"No. I think we've seen the futility of that."

She began pulling on a pair of sneakers. "I think it's time that we dropped in on Walter. He's our last, best and only chance!"

A Series of Lesser Events

San Francisco. It was a sunny Saturday morning. Walter Morrison sat alone in his office. His desk was bare except for a telephone, his few personal possessions in the two sealed boxes near his door. The starkness of his office was relieved only by the flashing colors of the flat screen TV on the far wall. It was tuned to CNN.

Jerusalem. In Jerusalem, one of the bearded young men from Somalia stood on the precise spot he had been directed to, standing with his back to the massive steel sculpture in the center of the Crowne Plaza of the Israel Museum. From here, he could see the blaze of light that was the new Performing Arts Center approximately two miles away. He knew that the opera hall was filled with thousands of Jews and had been assured that his sacrifice would be the beginning of the end of the hated Israeli occupation of their lands. He held an instrument designed to look like a cell phone, watching the digital counter approach zero.

When the time was up, the young man held his breath, fixed his gaze on the blaze of light on the horizon, entered the five numbers and pushed "send."

If he had listened very carefully, he might have heard the "click" behind him.

A lone camera that had been carefully shielded to survive the blast recorded the event. When slowed down as much as technology would allow, it showed three distinct phases. First, the concrete base immediately beneath the metal sculpture heaved upward as if pushed by a giant underground hand; then the sculpture itself seemed to semi-vaporize, forming a perceptible cloud around the object. Finally, the viewfinder went blank as a massive explosion radiated outward on all sides.

The young man was gone.

The blaze of light on the horizon did not change. Tosca's lyrical rendition of murder, suicide and torture continued to delight its audience of Israeli dignitaries.

Istanbul. The Ortikoy ferry was precisely on schedule, close to the European side of the Bosphorus. From near the stern of the boat, the bearded young man was just coming in line with the brightly lit Ciragan Palace grounds that set off so well the magnificent building. From his vantage point, it was easy to see the security forces, their members placed every ten yards along the bank, on the rooftop and at the entrances into the Palace.

The young man was ignorant of many things, but the one thing he did know was that he was on a glorious mission. He neither knew nor cared about the details of that mission, only what was essential for him to perform.

He nudged the overnight case at his feet and – for the hundredth time in the last hour – checked to make sure that the lock was exposed, the circular tumblers showing "zero - zero." One of the details he did not know nor care about was the contents of the case, although he supposed he should be proud to be carrying what the imam had referred to as "the infidel's own tools," something electronic that the imam promised would turn the Palace into a charnel house. He also did not know that he had been chosen over two other candidates to be the bearer. The two others had expressed puzzlement, even reluctance, about slaughtering other Muslims, even though they were Turks. He did not know, although he would have approved if he had, that those two were now buried in sand dunes north of Mogadishu.

He watched the timer on his cell phone closely, and when it was precisely at "zero," he reached down and turned the first tumbler to "1." Then, standing and holding the case tightly, he murmured to himself "Allahu Akbar!" and turned the second tumbler to "1."

He was looking forward to watching the Palace disintegrate in what he had been told would be a "fountain of fire." But the final thing he did not know was of his own disintegration as the case in his arms exploded, the blast shearing off the final fifty feet of the ferry's stern and alighting the rest. The fire was brief, as the waters of the Bosphorus closed over the remains of the ferry. Perhaps a dozen swimmers were left flailing in the water.

The Turkish security forces arrayed along the waterfront of the Ciragan Palace Hotel had the best view of the catastrophe and watched open-mouthed until their commander screamed at them, shouting about a possible diversion.

The President's speech was not interrupted. And the attending dignitaries were not aware of the tragedy until they left the conference room.

Kandahar, Afghanistan. The third of the bearded young men from Somalia was the youngest and the most fanatical. He was eighteen years old and had lived his entire life in the care of an imam who dedicated all of his preaching to jihad. Not the force for good that comes from the Koran, but the bastard variety that condones killing in support of ignorance and darkness. The promised virgins in paradise loomed large in his mind as he approached the entrance road in his overloaded truck. That road led to his target, which was ablaze with light in the distance.

His instructions were simple, so much so that they would have made a more experienced jihadist wonder about the qualifications of his superiors.

"Once you turn onto the entrance road, drive straight at the building, as fast as you can. Do not stop, no matter what. Security will be light and you should be able to get quite close."

When he asked with genuine concern, "What if I fail to get close?" he was told, "It doesn't matter. The explosion you will detonate is so powerful that it will set off a bomb inside the building ... a bomb the infidels know nothing about."

The truck had some modest and homemade armor plating to protect the driver and the engine. It was packed with explosives that would detonate when he released the "dead man grip" that he maintained with his left hand. He was not told, but a secondary detonator would activate if the truck came to a stop once on the entrance road.

He turned into the road and – to his horror -- was immediately confronted with a temporary striped barrier, a simple horizontal pole across the road. However, a row of Afghani soldiers with assault rifles stood behind the pole. The building itself – his target – was at least a thousand yards away. He slowed to a crawl and watched with horror as the NCO in charge approached him. He knew he could not survive even the most cursory inspection. He crouched as low as he could, gripped the steering wheel and the built-in detonator as tightly as he could, and pressed the accelerator to the floor.

The roar of the engine was quickly drowned by the sound of a dozen automatic weapons firing as he crashed through the barrier and accelerated. The bullets found gaps in the armor plating and the young man was struck repeatedly within the first ten seconds, but his grip on the wheel and the weight of his foot kept the truck unexploded and moving for a hundred yards. When it stopped, the truck simply disappeared in a gigantic fireball.

The angular and ugly concrete building at the end of the road was untouched. It had been built to withstand rockets and bombs at close range. The state ceremony inside was briefly interrupted while security forces rechecked both the interior and exterior for other intruders. President Karzai's comments resumed without any reference to the incident.

Washington D.C. The last of the young men from Somalia had been dead for the last two hours. His killer was wearing the uniform of a Staff Sergeant in the U.S. Army. He was sitting in the driver's seat of an army staff car at the Pentagon. His nametag read "Katalo," a name that seemed to allow for his dark complexion and hard-to-label ethnicity. It had been good enough to fool the original driver of the car – a Sergeant Sutherland – who was now in the trunk of the car, also quite dead and wedged in with the Somali.

The driver's instructions were simple. He did not have to blow anything up. His assignment was to detain and kill a high-ranking military officer. It did not require any stalking or subterfuge; the victim would come to him. They did not tell him any details, but it was easy for him to find out that his intended victim was the Chief of Staff for the U.S. Army. The young man was pleased to learn from his internet searches that the man had commanded significant U.S. forces in both Afghanistan and Iraq. *Allah is good. I am blessed today.*

The placard in his windshield with the three stars on it made the car easy to find for his passenger. Three-star general Farley Purcell returned the salute from his driver without thinking. He sat back in the seat and instructed, "The White House."

General Purcell was not naturally a reflective man; the phrase "mission-focused" appeared frequently in his military records. But today was different. He thought of all the times he had started off on a killing mission. From the first time as a raw lieutenant in Vietnam jumping from a Huey under fire to leading the first combat unit into Kuwait in 1991. It was all so straightforward. The enemy was identifiable and would kill him if he could. "Winning" was measureable, and valued by the public that you served. Being a soldier was a good thing and he wore his uniform and medals proudly.

How did it come to this? His last mission – to kill his Commander-in-Chief and an entire swathe of his country's leadership because they had lost their stomach for drawn-out war with a hard-to-see enemy, especially when the beneficiaries of that war seemed so unworthy. And the means! Not with a soldier's weapons and skills, but with a bomb designed as a basketball court and a modified cell phone for a detonator.

His reverie was interrupted by the deceleration of the car. He was startled to see that his driver had taken the old 14th Street Bridge and was exiting into the parking lot of the National Park Service, deserted on this Saturday morning. His military instincts, honed over thirty-seven years of military discipline and protocol, took over and he barked "Sergeant! What are you --"

The driver turned in his seat, smiling. He pointed a large handgun at the general and fired once. General Purcell died as he had lived most of his life, in a state of indignation.

The driver took the General's modified cell phone and placed it in a preaddressed and reinforced envelope addressed to a man named Ahmed near San Francisco. He drove back over the bridge, detouring briefly to drop the envelope in a curbside mailbox and then parked the car in a far corner of an outdoor lot at the Pentagon, amid a hundred or so other government sedans. The placard was removed from the window so that the vehicle seemed merely one of many awaiting Monday morning. The driver placed his Koran atop his carefully printed 'manifesto' and makeshift fatwa proclaiming the General to be evil and under a death sentence. He said his final prayers, breathed *Allahu Akbar!* and then fired his pistol once more.

Somewhere Over Montana. Daniel Carlton knew that he was going to miss the Gulfstream III. The jet was one of the luxuries that would not survive the scrutiny of return-minded shareholders now that the Morrison Group was a public company. In fact, Carlton was the most frequent user of the jet and viewed it as his personal vehicle. He was reconciled to the fact that this would probably be his last trip on the GIII.

At the moment, the jet was at thirty thousand feet over the middle of Montana, headed for Mitchell, South Dakota. The "official" purpose of the trip was listed as "visiting remote customers," but its real goal was to deliver Carlton and General Mervin Cannell to their annual pheasant hunt with a group of Washington lobbyists. Even that was a sham; Carlton simply wanted to be as far away as possible when

Morrison's crazy scheme was put in play. He looked at his watch. *Should be happening right around now.*

The horizontal stabilizer on the tail fin controls what pilots refer to as the "pitch" of the aircraft, nudging the nose up or down depending on movements of the control surfaces. When the timer reached "zero," the device that it was attached to did precisely as its designer intended. It simultaneously locked the ailerons at maximum to induce a near-vertical dive and ejected itself from the surface of the stabilizer, self-destructing five seconds later.

To the few observers on the ground, the plane's speed, attitude and trajectory remained unchanged until it arrowed into the side of a hill and became a fireball. As one witness put it, "It looked like he was aiming at that particular hill and got there as fast as he could." She could not hear the screaming from inside the plane.

A Pair of Anti-Climaxes

They parked in the underground lot at the Morrison offices. She pointed out Walter's car in the far corner, one of only a half-dozen vehicles this early on a Saturday.

The lighted elevator panel indicated that the elevator was on the tenth floor, the executive office suites. They waited without speaking as it descended to their level. When the doors slid open, they moved to enter and found themselves face-to-face with Kovacs.

Rho and Marcia stood side-by-side blocking the opening, frozen in place staring at Kovacs. The automatic door kept trying to close, repeatedly bumping Rho's left shoulder. Kovacs reached out and pushed the "door open" button. He did not seem surprised to see them; nor did he seem disturbed by them blocking his exit. He stood with his finger on the button and a patient expression, as though dealing with a slightly retarded child or an elderly person with disabilities.

Marcia moved first, very carefully and slowly sliding her feet and moving closer to Rho. The increased pressure caused him to turn slightly and move against the door. Neither of them could unlock their gaze from Kovacs' eyes. Seconds passed. Then Kovacs smiled, not at them, but as if amused by some novel and private thought. He nodded and said, "Mr. Owens, Ms. Littleton. Nice to see you again. Mr. Morrison is in his office." He walked past them, out of the elevator, without looking back.

The door resumed thumping his shoulder as though reminding Rho to breathe again. He pulled Marcia into the elevator and the door slid closed behind them.

She breathed, "That was – "

"Yes. It was."

Close encounters of another kind. I wonder how many chances we get?

And then another thought: *What's he doing here?*

Marcia was clearly beginning to think along the same lines. She said, "Walter … He said Walter was in his office. I wonder what condition he's in?"

They both jumped when the door slid open again, still at the garage level. The foyer was empty. They reached simultaneously to push the "10" button. She kept jabbing it until the door closed and the elevator started up. She did not stop pressing against him during the ascent and he could feel her trembling.

They found Walter at his desk. He was tipped far back in his high-backed leather chair with his feet on his desk, seemingly watching the TV screen and the CNN logo. The volume was turned low enough that it was barely intelligible. He waved at them to come in when he saw them in the doorway, but did not change his position. They stood, one at either corner on his desk, staring at him until he seemed to become aware of them.

"Marcia. And Mr. Owens. Why am I not surprised to see you here?" He took his feet from his desk, but maintained his laid back posture in his chair.

Marcia and Rho looked at one another. He shrugged, so she began. "We just met a man coming from this office, one that has been trying to kill us, we think."

"That's very melodramatic of you, Marcia. Mr. ... ,″ Walter began, but then stopped as if trying to recall a name. "Mr. -- Never mind the name. It's not important – has been doing some work for me, but his present duties will not lead to any harm to either of you."

Rho spoke in the same conversational tone that Morrison had adopted. "If we accused you of masterminding a terrorist plot to assassinate several heads-of-state this morning, would that be melodramatic as well?"

Morrison smiled. "I'd say that you were vastly overestimating my abilities. Have you seen the recent news?"

He pressed the volume control on the remote TV controller that was on his desk. They turned to the CNN broadcast. The announcer was speaking in that breathless voice reserved for genuine news events while sorting through a steady inflow of new bulletins being handed to her from off-screen. The continuous scroll at the bottom of the screen read, "Breaking News – Coordinated Terrorist Attacks!" about every ten seconds.

They watched for about three minutes; long enough to learn of simultaneous bomb blasts in Istanbul, Jerusalem and Kandahar, each of them in close proximity to the head of state of the respective countries. The total death toll was thought to be in the hundreds, mostly from a ferry sinking on the Bosphorus. While they watched, the CNN anchor announced another flash. The body of the Army Chief of Staff had just been discovered, apparently murdered in Washington D.C. by an apparent al Qaeda operative disguised as a military driver. CNN then shifted to their Atlanta studio, where they had convened a panel of three Middle Eastern experts on terrorism, the classic talking heads.

Walter lowered the volume once again, saying, "Terrible, isn't it? They've killed hundreds of innocent people without achieving anything except making themselves more hated and exposing their incompetence. What a terrible waste!"

Marcia spoke. "Oh, I'm not at all sure about their incompetence. The synchronicity is very impressive."

Walter looked directly at her and spoke with an enormous weariness. "But they failed! Think of how much outrage it would have generated if those blasts had taken out the political leaders that were so close by at the time."

"It would have changed the world," Rho said. "And destroyed four of the Group's recently-completed engineering/construction projects."

"Anybody can build things. But to change the world, that's --"

"Megalomania," interrupted Marcia harshly. "Psychopathic, delusional, twisted thinking." She pronounced each word slowly and distinctly, with a clear tone of disgust in her voice.

Each word seemed to drive him deeper into his chair and somehow increase his sadness.

He said abstractedly, "Yes, I suspect you're right." The words seemed to trigger some inner resolution. He stood up and looked around his office as if seeing it for the first time.

Rho said, "Walter. We know what you've been trying to do, all of it. It's time for you to -- "

"Yes, of course. You're absolutely right. I completely agree. Now, I've got things to do and places to go. If you'll excuse me ..."

And he simply turned and walked out of the open door, leaving Rho and Marcia standing at the corners of his desk looking at his chair and hearing the contending voices from the CNN panel of experts.

Friends and Traitors

Walter's cell phone rang, the special one that only two callers knew about. The phone was deep in the pocket of his rain jacket and he barely heard the ring over the noise made by the wind in the steel cables. He almost didn't answer it.

"Avi. I wasn't sure if I'd hear from you."

"I wanted to tell you that it was nothing personal. That it's a dirty, filthy business and I feel unclean."

Walter's reply was soft, almost wistful. "I was hoping that it was the Turk ... that you were as blindsided as I was." After a pause, he added, "... that you were as idealistic ... no, not idealistic ... as gullible and naïve as me."

"No. It was me. Completely aware, no illusions. It's what I do for my masters."

"You're very good at it." Walter laughed. "It's funny. We planned and almost executed the most sophisticated and audacious terrorist attack in the history of the world. And then pulled our punches at the last minute. We'd be famous if they knew who we were."

"You got a piece of what you wanted, Walter. The U.S. and its allies are reenergized about the need for a comprehensive and coordinated increase in anti-terrorism. The Middle East is first on their list. And your money is at work." *Although some of it has been diverted into more suitable channels than we had discussed.*

"I wanted massive and sustainable moral outrage. You gave me a temper tantrum. al Qaeda views it as a victory, not us."

Avi tried again, but the absence of conviction in his voice was apparent. "We still have the option. The technology is still in place, and the Turk has the devices to activate them."

"Any madman can reduce a building to rubble. But to remove *those four men* -- Obama, Netanyahu, Karzai and Erdogan ... all at once ... It's a once-in-a-lifetime scenario."

There was a long silence. The wind was stronger and the fog was beginning to thread itself across the roadway and through the cables. The lights from Sausalito were blurry and the San Francisco waterfront was fast disappearing in the shroud of fog. Walter felt cold.

"Goodbye Avi."

"Goodbye Walter. I'm sorry."

Avi shut his cell phone and sat staring at the wall opposite him. The two men in the room with him watched him closely. The American -- an ex-Director of the CIA, fired for his public defense of waterboarding in Iraq -- sat at the table across from Avi. His counterpart – recently resigned from the Israeli Mossad as a gesture against his government's policy on the settlements --stood leaning against the door. *I wonder what their emotion is at the moment for me? Do they feel anything? Disgust? Admiration ... or perhaps sympathy?* He felt like putting his head down on his arms and going to sleep.

The Israeli spoke. "I thought we'd agreed that you would tell him that Dr. Weber's 'twelve months to live' was a lie? That the tests were faked on our orders. That we needed him to speed things up ..."

"I couldn't do that." And Avi knew that they thought less of him because of that inability. He also knew that they were worried about Walter as the proverbial loose cannon, a particularly dangerous one if he believed he was condemned to die anyway.

That was evident when the American asked "And what about the four initiation devices. They're one-of-a-kind. Until we have those, we have no control over the explosives in place."

"The Turk has them. I have arranged to get them back," Avi said. He did not tell them that it was his intention to destroy the devices; that his betrayal of Walter had somehow lessened his ardor for mass destruction.

And they need not worry about Walter. Walter's cell phone contained a locator. Avi knew precisely where Walter was when they said "Goodbye" two minutes ago. He was standing at the precise midway point of the Golden Gate Bridge, on the pedestrian walkway two-hundred and forty-five feet above San Francisco Bay.

He opened his phone and pressed the button to call Walter once more. The screen readout flashed "Device Not Found."

Retirement Day

Kovacs was amused. That was unusual in itself. He was not a person that found humor in either people or situations. What others experienced as curious he found to be a confirmation of imperfection, an unattractive naivete. It was even more unusual because the amusement was at his own expense. It was not self-doubt, rather the opposite. For the first time in his life, he was acting against his own self-interest, for reasons he did not understand.

He had taken the job. For a million non-refundable dollars, in advance. It topped off his retirement fund nicely, sufficient to his needs. However, the client was gone, irretrievably; so he could default with impunity. Pocket the cash and walk away from the risk.

Worse, the job was a particularly difficult one. Kovacs had no illusions about the risk. His target was another professional; a dangerous one with good reason to be extra-cautious. And he was an important figure, with friends in high places who would remember, and might even seek some form of vengeance.

So why am I doing this? Take the money and disappear. The only one who would either know or care is off the table.

He suspected Morrison knew that Kovacs would be bothered by the choice and that he had deliberately structured it that way because of ... what? Irony? Affection? Kovacs had never analyzed it, but he was aware that their initial encounter in Moscow, when Morrison calmly offered him a hundred-thousand dollars to shoot Townsend rather than him, had formed some kind of bond between them; a recognition that they had the same view of the world and its people. It was the best explanation Kovacs could construe for his present ambivalence.

That last morning in Morrison's office, with CNN in the background, Morrison made the deal with him. A million dollars in whatever bank account he named, in return for his promise to do one last job. In his own time and in whatever manner he thought best. Only one condition: If possible, the man should know why he was chosen.

Two weeks had gone by. Kovacs had followed the man, studied his habits and chosen the ground. He was ready. *Ironic. I've come full circle.* Once more, he was on a rooftop, crouched behind a wall with a sniper rifle, waiting for a particular man to come out of a building on the opposite side of a city square in a remote city.

When the man emerged, he stopped on the top step to shield his eyes from the bright sun that was so omnipresent in this climate. He slipped on sunglasses and checked the scene around him. When he started down the marble stairs into the plaza, Kovacs waited until he was midway and then pressed the "call" button on the cell phone that he had taped to the wooden stock of his rifle so that he could talk while keeping the rifle aimed very precisely.

The man in the middle of the marble stairs stopped and pulled his phone from his pocket. He took off his sunglasses and glanced at the screen, clearly puzzled by the number that was displayed. He turned completely around twice, as if he could see where the call originated. Very tentatively, he raised the phone.

"Yes?"

Kovacs repeated the words exactly as Morrison had recited them. "Walter wanted you to know that moral outrage requires an outlet... that it's nothing personal."

He watched through the scope as Avi processed what he heard, his expression changing from puzzlement to surprise and, finally, fear. He looked around wildly and then, as if Kovacs had willed it, looked up at the rooftop and directly at him, his face filling the scope. Kovacs chose to believe that his last expression signified a form of acceptance.

He fired once and then simply walked away from the rifle without a backward glance.

It was his last job.

The CFO and the Consultant

A month had elapsed.

Enough time for the tired old cycle to complete itself: the initial outpouring of outrage, indignation and horror; followed by a frantic need to find someone to blame and punish; that in turn succeeded by the sober evaluation of real alternatives; and finally settling for what one of the sarcastic pundits labeled "an enhanced status quo."

The analysts pointed out that, after all, the terrorists had selected "soft targets" in the U.S., Turkey and Israel and had demonstrated serious incompetence and bad planning in the execution of the actual attacks. The official view was the attacks were more of a dying spasm of a decaying movement than they were a harbinger of things to come.

Certain facts were not disclosed to the public. Unofficially and among the anti-terror specialists, the greatest single concern was about the terrorist's apparent acquisition of a new bomb-making capability. The film of the phased explosion at the Israel Museum was being analyzed intensively, particularly by DARPA and its Reactive Materials Program scientists.

Marcia was named Chief Executive Officer of the Morrison Group. The simultaneous disappearance of Walter Morrison and the death of Daniel Carlton most likely would have led to that result in any case, but she learned that Morrison had been lobbying the Board persistently in the two weeks prior to the IPO to name her as CEO when he stepped down.

Her first acts as CEO were to seek a completely new slate for the Board and to expand the scope and accelerate the schedule on the consulting contract with the Owens Consulting Group. This latter move was greatly helped by hiring Velma away from Rho and making her the new Chief Risk Officer for the Group.

She also initiated an internal investigation into the Group's relationship with two vendors – TACA and AA Ltd. – but was stymied by a nearly-total absence of internal documentation and the legal dissolution of the two entities in their home countries. To backstop that effort, she requested that DOD immediately conduct rigorous audits of all defense contracts where the Group was involved.

"The business press loves it," she said in a faint tone of wonderment. "They view it as an expression of my total confidence in my company rather than as a red flag suggesting that I smell a rat."

She and Rho were having dinner with Uncle Sal and Velma at Scoma's, on the deck in the shelter of Lucite wind barriers. It created the sensation of privacy, with the darkness of the Bay waters separating them from the luminous San Francisco skyline as viewed from Sausalito. The setting seemed right for what Rho could only think of as 'the new Velma.' Her hair was still unruly, but seemed artfully arranged to highlight her remarkable eyes. And she had dressed herself as though she cared. The impact was visible not only on Velma, but also on Sal.

Velma said, "I can't believe that neither of you has been contacted by any of our famous agencies with all those letters – FBI, CIA, NSA, ... You're smack dab in the middle of one of the biggest conspiracies ..."

"Stupid bastards! All of them! So busy trying to outsmart each other that they forget there's another side out there!"

As usual, Sal had strong opinions. And Rho knew what was coming next.

"And we pay taxes so that they can screw us in –"

Rho was about to break in even though he knew it would not stop the invective. But before he could say anything, Velma simply reached across the table and put her hand on Sal's forearm. The touch seemed magical. Sal stopped talking and actually looked slightly embarrassed.

Marcia smiled at Rho.

She then said, "Think about it. We'd sound like serious paranoids. We don't even have the proverbial smoking gun. The only suspicious occurrence is the disappearance of Walter's sizeable cash balance. And that's a tax issue, not a homeland security concern."

"Ben Appleby did call me," Rho said. "Given that a serious bomb did go off about five hundred yards away from Erdogan, he's convinced that I did in fact know something about what was going on, but that I drew the wrong conclusions. I let it ride."

Velma asked, "What happened to Ebenezer Scrooge's dead partner? Donnelly's killer."

"Jacob Marley? He's clear of murder charges and living in an SRO south of Market. The SFPD found a camera on the front of the convenience store across the street. It's fixed on their parking lot, but picks up things from there to the parking structure where Donnelly was shot. It clearly shows a man coming out of the structure carrying objects that he puts near Marley, including an overcoat that he takes off. That's the same guy that phoned in the 911 call."

"Did they ID him? Arrest him?"

Rho and Marcia looked at one another before he answered. "No. The video's not good enough."

Velma asked in a tone that implied a purely rhetorical question, "I wonder who he is?"

Sal said, "A hired killer, I'd guess. A lousy psychopath who likes to kill people."

"I don't think so," said Marcia in a carefully neutral tone. "Somehow, I'd like to believe he's a soldier-of-fortune with a troubled past but with traces of conscience. A darker version of Lew Archer, maybe ..." And she smiled at Rho in a private way.

"Wow!" said Rho. "And here I thought he was just a killer!"

Marcia smiled ruefully. "Between the four of us, that's what worries me about this whole affair. We took a boatload of coincidences and made up a narrative that fit. But that narrative was only one of an infinite number of possibilities. We liked it and bought it because it was such a good story. It had elaborate conspiracies, doomsday machines, super-villains and – let's face it, Rho – we cast you and me as the hero and heroine. But maybe it was just that – nothing more than a boatload of coincidences."

Sal said, "To quote a famous philosopher: 'Sometimes a cigar is just a cigar'!"

Rho followed up. "So we're just over-imaginative, borderline-bored people trying to make our lives seem more interesting than they really are? Conspiracy theorists?"

She shook her head vigorously. "I refuse to think so. But that's the story I intend to tell if anybody comes calling."

Sal spoke in a tone that Rho had never heard him use. "I think you're right, Marcia. It's not just a bunch of coincidences. There is a narrative that makes it all hang together, but it's not of the mystery/thriller genre."

They all turned to look at Sal.

He reached over and took Rho's hand and placed it on top of Marcia's hand that was resting on the table. And held it there.

"It's a goddam love story."

The Dark Man in San Francisco

Ahmed had chosen well. From here, looking west, the view was quite like overlooking the Black Sea from the hills bordering the Bosphorus. San Francisco could never become Istanbul, but it's still one of the world's great cities. Here, my daughters can overcome my reputation and marry Americans. And me? I can finally simplify my life. Play with my grandchildren. Reactra can be a real company. They say that geographic cures don't work. But why not? "Insha'Allah!"

The dark, very stocky man watched as his son Ahmed approached him as he stood watching the sun sink into the Pacific fog bank. As they embraced, he felt the intensity in the young man and recognized the simultaneous and now-familiar fatalism that it triggered within him. *This is why there are no geographic cures. Our children carry expectations of us. And we are foolish enough to try to live up to them.*

They spoke English. It was as though the green cards not only made them fluent, but required them to forego their first language.

"I'd like to show you some of the things that I've been working on." Ahmed lifted his arm to indicate the garage – really almost a barnlike structure – fifty yards down the hill from the house. "It is truly amazing what is possible by just making small adjustments to existing technologies."

So innocent looking. The sturdy, bright-white structure with its red trim standing out against the green hills. So untrue to the character of the devices that are inside it.

As they walked together, he thought of the American – Walter -- and the Israeli that he trusted, Avraham. He had wished them no harm, even admired them. Yet they were both dead. He had been amazed at the audacity of the American, finally coming to admire his vision as much as he did the incredible managerial skill he brought to bear. He almost did the impossible! And would have if the Israeli had not enlisted him, the Turk, to sabotage the grand strategy. *No, 'sabotage' is the wrong word. We 'diluted' it; made the outcomes 'acceptable' instead of 'cataclysmic.'*

He thought back to his meetings in Northern Pakistan and how the two currencies he carried with him – promises of infidel deaths and U.S. dollars – were so persuasive, even when they knew that the mission would make them pariahs, even more than they were. *I taught them the American phrase, 'a package deal.' They liked that. Easier to explain than the Arabic version. They even introduced me to the four boys. How I despised them for their willingness to die! I wonder what they will do ... those unforgiving men who expected so much and were disappointed. They expected shock and awe, four simultaneous world-shifting assassinations. And they destroyed a museum, a ferry boat, a truck and a single American general!*

Ahmed held open the door of the garage for him to enter, eagerness and pride apparent in his expression and in every line of his body.

Despite himself and his desire for simplicity, he began to conceive of how these new devices might be employed. Or sold. From there, it was easy to remember that the magnificent Ciragan Palace in Istanbul, the new Center for Performing Arts in Jerusalem, and an ugly concrete barracks and police station in Afghanistan were his to destroy, thanks to Ahmed's new toys.

And in Washington D.C., there was a new basketball court for the young, athletic president; marked with neon striping with enough explosive power to vaporize anyone on its surface.

"Let's see what you've done for yourself," he said to his son; and went into the garage filled with curiosity and a renewed sense of possibility.

www.ingramcontent.com/pod-product-compliance
Lightning Source LLC
Chambersburg PA
CBHW071302170626
46809CB00001B/326